A SEALED FATE

A SEALED FATE

Lisa Gordon

JANUS PUBLISHING COMPANY
London, England

First published in Great Britain 2009
by Janus Publishing Company Ltd,
105–107 Gloucester Place,
London W1U 6BY

www.januspublishing.co.uk

British Library Cataloguing-in-Publication Data
A catalogue record for this book is available from the British Library

ISBN 978-1-85756-654-3

Cover Design: Janus Publishing

Printed and bound in Great Britain

The question of whether fate or free will is the dominant factor in life's journey has fascinated many philosophers and authors over time. In Macbeth, Shakespeare examines the idea as the conflict of choice over chance. So which is it? When our conscious will is at odds with our spiritual will, which one prevails?

If we, indeed, have a destiny, can we change it? Or is our fate sealed from the moment we take our first breath?

Whatever the answer to these questions, Valda and Larissa were about to embark on a journey, where they would unwittingly test the assumptions about fate, free will and destiny.

Chapter One

At three o'clock in the morning, the streets of Jumeirah were alive with music and a carnival atmosphere, which would rally even the most morose character into a party mood. The smell of exotic food lingered in the humid night air and bright lights advertised a very global selection of cuisines in the side-street cafes. It was apparent that one could become an expert in international cuisine without having to venture further than Jumeirah's main street, providing one's digestive system could stand up to the punishment. Not that health seemed uppermost on the minds of the late-night revellers, none of whom seemed averse to a cigarette or two. Valda enjoyed a fag herself and was tired of being almost criminalised for it back home. In Cape Town, as in the rest of South Africa, a "Smoking Apartheid" had developed: in restaurants and other public places, no smoking was allowed and hefty fines were gleefully handed down to anyone still audacious or stupid enough to smoke in a shopping centre – God forbid. Some restaurants had glass sections, perhaps better described as cages, where smokers, the new lepers of society apparently, could sit. There were separate areas for smokers everywhere, as if smokers were in themselves a new underclass.

Valda was amazed at the hive of activity that was Dubai, even at this late hour. At 3.00 a.m. in Cape Town, only the burglars and the cockroaches were still roaming the streets. She was a night-time girl and this was a late-night city. Valda watched the scenes whizz by from her air-conditioned cream coloured taxi as she sped towards her hotel. After an eight-hour flight from Johannesburg, she was ready to shower and hit the pillow ASAP. Sleeping on the plane had been impossible: an elderly techno-befuddled man sitting next to her had spent most of the night poking away relentlessly and with increasing ferocity at the touch-operated TV screen. It had been a relief when he had finally "buggered" the thing up totally and the screen had gone blank, although that merely gave him an excuse to complain to the Emirates air hostess for the remainder of the flight – in Arabic, thankfully.

As the taxi headed towards a quieter residential area of Dubai, Valda allowed her mind to wander back to the life she had left behind in Cape Town: her old flat in Clifton; her 1995 Lotus Esprit S4; Ritz Rasputin; her old friends, or "acquaintances" rather – though she doubted they would ever email, despite their promises to the contrary: true friendship was not something she had experienced thus far. And, of course, she could not stop herself thinking of Richard and his new fiancée – the thought immediately brought on a twinge of anger, mixed with hollowness and a large dose of hurt, which was apparent in her stomach and became so severe that she almost felt nauseous. Yes, the feelings were still very raw. She wondered if he ever thought of her, or if any memories he had of their seven years together had been dumped in some mental dustbin. Enough already, she thought! She had promised herself to make a conscious effort to remove any thoughts or memories of Richard from her mind. Although her psychologist had said that thinking things over and "grieving" for the relationship was an essential part of getting over it, Valda had decided that there was a fine line between mentally working things through and wallowing in self-pity and moroseness. The Prozac helped a bit, but it only took the edge off her feelings, never totally eliminating them. Getting away from Cape Town and breaking away from her old scene was to be her "new" Prozac. Memory Lane is not always a great place – it can be dark, scary and unpleasant.

The taxi stopped abruptly, wrenching Valda from her thoughts. Apparently, they had arrived at the hotel, which was hardly of any note architecturally; in fact, it reminded her of a sandwich loaf with windows. Valda jumped out of the taxi and after the air-conditioning of the cab, the humid air felt somewhat like having a balaclava pulled over one's face. Her black leather jacket was hardly the best choice in the Gulf climate. The driver had removed her belongings from the boot and had unceremoniously dumped her large selection of cases and duffel bags on the pavement. His general muttering and unwillingness to drive off reminded Valda that a tip was in order. She rummaged through her Camps Bay Travel Co. pouch, found a ten dirham note and handed it over, clueless as to its value. The driver seemed vaguely satisfied, not that Valda cared, for she was too tired. She managed to pick up her extensive baggage in one go and carted it into the lobby. Valda was used to doing things for herself: she never expected help or favours, which was just as well, as they were not often forthcoming.

It always amazed Valda that despite the high-tech, cyber-speed world she lived in, checking in to a hotel was as tedious and as long-winded as it had been twenty years earlier. Though at least the wait was worth it, as the room was large and had all the facilities one would expect from a four-star hotel anywhere in the West, if not more; but at that stage, who cared about facilities, all Valda wanted was a shower and bed. She was asleep before any troubling thoughts from the past could enter her mind.

Valda had no idea of the time when she eventually woke up. The heavy blackout lining at the windows blocked out the light completely and the air-conditioning was so powerful that she was clueless as to the blazing heat outside. She looked at her watch; it was ten o'clock. It slowly occurred to her that that was South African time – Dubai was two hours ahead of SA and so it must have been noon. Whatever, she thought!

After ten minutes, she was ready to make the brave step of venturing out of bed. Valda staggered to her feet and walked over to the kettle, carefully avoiding the mirror. 'No need to depress myself this early!' she muttered to herself. Even though there were mugs and tea bags, etc., Valda decided that making tea looked too much like hard work and she settled for a chocolate from the basket of confectionery in the room. Nothing like chocolate to pick you up! she thought. Valda thanked God it was something she didn't need a prescription for, or the risk of incarceration to get hold of. After a shower and a makeover courtesy of Estée Lauder, she was almost back in the land of the living and ready to brave the mirror.

Valda looked younger than her thirty years, despite her lifestyle of late nights, excesses of all sorts and general disrespect for her health. She had always been thin, but had shed pounds after her split from Richard. It had been a bombshell, which had come out of nowhere, and one which had totally shaken her usual "I don't care" attitude to life. She was way too light for her 5 foot 6 frame and her face looked gaunt. Her big, dark-brown, deep-set eyes and black eyebrows were quite distinctive and her high cheekbones and pouty pink lips made an attractive combination. Her hair was a rich chocolate brown, long and wavy and her skin was olive, yet untanned.

She inevitably chose to wear jeans, a white top and her black leather jacket. That black leather jacket was her favourite, it helped her to pull off that "ultra cool cat – couldn't-give-a-shit image", which was her trademark. It was an effective mask, hiding the vulnerable Valda underneath, who so much needed to be cared for and loved. To most, Valda was brittle and facetious, not forgetting that temper that one chose not to mention; she didn't just lose it, she blew the mother of all fuses.

Although her meeting with Jo at Flanagan's was scheduled for the next day at two, she had decided to rock up a day early. That way, she could set the tone of the meeting and take the upper hand from the outset of the relationship. Control, was another way of putting it.

Soon, she was in a taxi heading for the Burg Emir, which the taxi driver was delighted to inform her was one of Dubai's tallest buildings. Holding on to the title of the tallest or most innovative building in Dubai was akin to staying at number one in the charts for any length of time. She was soon to discover that Dubai's taxi drivers were all frustrated tour guides and every taxi ride involved an obligatory information blitz on all of Dubai's attractions: "Here is Wafi Centre ... there is the Royal Dubai, that is where they just held the Dubai Desert Classic ... there is the police station (not a place Valda intended to see the inside of, at least not if she had anything to do with it) ... there is the Ministry of Information, etc., etc., *ad nauseam.*"

The taxi swerved in and out of the traffic, while the effervescent driver thrust his hands around, gesticulating in all directions, with his eyes everywhere except on the road. Valda enjoyed driving; however, her journey to the Burg Emir was enough to put her off driving in Dubai for ever.

Valda did her best to diplomatically discourage any more conversation and once again turned her thoughts to her life, which had been parked on the corner of Shit Street and Crap Avenue for some time now. She hoped her new position as lead singer with a band, who performed regularly at a string of salubrious nightclubs in Dubai, would bring back her glory days. Valda had been singing and playing the piano ever since she was young and at sixteen, she had formed her own covers band and had gone on to delight and dazzle the great and good of the Western Cape with her sensational performances. She had graced the Cape's best stages, venues and concert halls in a glittering career. However, despite her remarkable voice, rhythm and powerful stage presence, the recording contract and international fame she had thought was her birthright never actually came her way.

Valda had begun to believe that success and fame were a function of luck, rather than talent. Over the years, things had wound down, until she had been forced to survive as a wedding singer, where the perks included cheap Argentinian champagne and the "downs" included taking the can when the wedding didn't turn out quite like the darling, blushing bride had envisaged. Valda managed a wry smile as she remembered one such occasion, when a mollycoddled young bride had tried to shift the blame for the shambolic flop of a ludicrously expensive wedding onto Valda.

Valda's retort had gone something like this: 'The divorce rate in South Africa is 70 per cent, so the odds are you'll rue this day and not remember it anyway, hun!' Well, they say crime doesn't pay and in this case, honesty didn't, either – Valda's diary was soon very clear for weeks on end.

When they had met at university, Richard had been a struggling student, while Valda was already riding the waves of success and acclaim. However, as the years went by, Richard's career as an aeronautical engineer had gone from strength to strength, while Valda's had gone from realistic hopes of international stardom, to dreams, to just, well, wild fantasies. The shift in power in the relationship had heightened her insecurity and her confidence levels had fallen further and further.

At one point after the split, Valda was so desperate that she even considered hauling out her Economics degree to see what kind of job that could procure. She doubted her ability to hold down a normal job, especially one in business – after all, the only thing she had ever been economical with was the truth; except where the wedding was concerned. Her future had seemed so black that she would have needed to borrow a floodlight off the new Wembley Stadium to brighten it up. But a little voice inside her kept telling her that something would pan out and despite her deep pessimism, she was inclined to believe it.

Just three months beforehand, an old school mate, Bella, had emailed Valda an ad she had found when on holiday in Dubai. Jo Keane, the manager of a string of Dubai nightclubs, was looking for a versatile singer, who was able to play an instrument and who had a huge repertoire of popular songs up their sleeve. The way things had been going in her life, Valda was sceptical rather than excited at the chance, but she nevertheless got in touch with Jo immediately. She went through the whole application rigmarole and was flabbergasted when she nailed the position. Cape Town to Dubai was exactly the kind of distance she wanted to put between her and Richard, not to mention his fiancée.

As they drove along the highway, Valda could see Dubai's twin towers looming ahead as a misty heat haze rolled in from the Gulf. Soon, they were cruising along Sheikh Zayed Road. Things were eerily quiet and despite being surrounded by plush, modern skyscrapers, Dubai had the feeling of a ghost town. The ever-informative driver told Valda that it was "siesta" time in Dubai; owing to the heat, not much went on between two and six in the afternoon, but the town would erupt with life again at six o'clock. Valda handed the driver forty dirhams and a ten-dirham tip and stepped out onto the pavement. Standing there in the shadow of the 125-floor tower, an ominous feeling came over her and she shivered, despite the scorching heat. Valda dismissed the feelings and marched off into the lobby with a look of determination about her.

On the other side of Dubai Creek, in her Deira City flat, Larissa stared at her laptop screen. She had that sinking feeling again. She pushed the laptop aside and went to stand by the window with her cup of strong, sweet black tea. As she looked out onto the quiet street, she asked the question she had been asking since she was sixteen, "Will my life ever change?" Having asked that question for the last fourteen years, the answer was probably no, or so she thought.

Larissa was the subject of much envy amongst her peers, owing to her bubbly, confident and carefree demeanour – indeed, she appeared to breeze through life, which provoked much jealousy in others. Larissa had to chuckle at how misleading appearances could be.

At school, Larissa was not only popular, but had excelled academically and artistically and although not athletic, she had made a fist of things on the sports field as well. She had gone on to read a university degree, which had not inspired her, and she had since found huge frustration at not being able to find a career in which she could use her full potential and find fulfilment.

Ever since she was about 3 years old, Larissa had had this burning feeling of destiny! It was as if she had a special purpose or mission in life. However, despite nearly exhausting every New Age, religious and spiritual technique, she was as much in the dark as before over what this "thing" that she was destined for was, although the feeling was as strong as ever.

Business had been slow and although her motivation was pretty low as well, Larissa decided to take the plunge and book a series of ads in *The Gulf News.* She could no longer rely on word of mouth alone to generate enough income to survive on. She made the call, booked the ad and then decided that a dose of retail therapy was in order. The Deira City Shopping Centre was a stone's throw away and she would use any excuse to get down there. That sinking feeling was ebbing away fast as she pulled on a denim skirt and grabbed her pink Ralph Lauren jacket and raced out of the door.

Chapter Two

Jo had wavy, bleached hair, a smiley face and a Bondi Beach body. He greeted Valda flamboyantly.

'Hey! Val, Doll, great to finally meet you. Hotel OK?'

Jo was obviously gay an occupational hazard thought Valda. 90 per cent of men in the entertainment industry are gay.

'Terrific and likewise! I couldn't wait to see Flanagan's; you made it sound pretty damned good and so far, I'm not disappointed,' said Valda enthusiastically.

'Flanagan's and our sister clubs are the hottest places in town and I'm counting on you to keep it that way!'

'No worries there, Jo! When do I get to meet my other band members and start rehearsals?'

'You like to dive right in, don't you; you only touched down, what, twelve hours ago?' Jo was surprised yet pleased.

'Yeah, I've always liked the deep end!'

'That's why I hired you; you are so direct, not like your typical flaky, hysterical performer!'

Valda had to smile; Richard had insisted that she was "the" epitome of a flaky, hysterical performer. So what did he know?

Jo continued, 'The rest of the guys will be here 'round six, so I'll do the intros and then and leave it up to you to make the rehearsal arrangements. If you can get a set together for a week Wednesday, that'd be super. Oh, yeah, you probably already know, but I'll just mention it anyway, the working week here is Saturday through Wednesday; Thursday and Friday are like the weekend! Been here three years and it still mixes me up,' he laughed out loud. 'Have you done lunch yet? If not, we'll have a whizz around the hotel and grab a snack downstairs. OK?'

'Absolutely.' Valda had forgotten all about food, but the mention of lunch had brought on hunger pangs. While the Burg Emir was an impressive place, Valda had high standards and was not easily impressed, but so far, Flanagan's, the Burg Emir and Jo had lived up to her expectations.

Much to her relief, Jo volunteered to do most of the talking. Valda was disinclined to share too much about herself; her past was in the past and was damn well going to stay there. Jo had been born in Liverpool, brought up in LA and had lived in about a dozen other countries since. His personality seemed to be a patchwork of different cultural influences and his accent was such a mixture of all sorts that it would have been impossible to place. The menu demonstrated the dominance of the Anglo–American culture; even in the Gulf, the choice ranged from burgers and fish and chips to roast beef and Yorkshire pudding. Valda settled for a club sandwich and a beer; she hardly noticed what Jo had had, as it had disappeared off his plate so fast – he obviously ate as fast as he talked.

Jo gave Val (as she allowed him to call her) the low-down on etiquette in Dubai. Normal Western clothes were fine; however, it was polite to avoid tops that were too revealing, especially in the city centre, streets and hotels. A female Italian friend of Jo's had been spat on and called a *sharmuta* for wearing clothes considered to be too risqué, although this was the exception rather than the rule. It was not acceptable to take photographs of Muslim women or government buildings and one should ask before taking a snap of a local man. Alcohol was available in hotel bars, clubs and restaurants, but not in other restaurants outside of hotels. Jo also gave advice on where to get groceries and where she could start looking for a flat, etc. The shopping centres of Dubai got a five-star rating from Jo, who was evidently a believer in retail therapy. Valda listened and tried to take it all in – it had suddenly dawned on her that she was a novice in a completely alien environment. She had not even grasped the value of the currency yet and she was required to negotiate a lease on a flat. What were rates like in Dubai? Was food cheap? What about transport? Walking in the heat was insane, so should she fork out for a car? So many questions raced through her mind – this really was the deep end.

After lunch, Jo showed Valda to his office and left her there with a property guide, a selection of maps and a phone directory, while he disappeared to do whatever it is that nightclub managers do! She soon discovered that there was a large English and Irish, not to mention South African, expat community in Dubai and English was widely spoken. Apparently, 75 per cent of people living in Dubai came from elsewhere: most were from Pakistan and the subcontinent and many were from Lebanon and Jordan; nearly all spoke English. By the end of the afternoon, Valda was feeling far more au fait with things!

That evening, she asked the taxi driver to drop her off on Jumeirah's main boulevard, so that she could walk the rest of the way to the hotel. It was a sultry night, yet quite bearable compared to the searing heat of the day. It was only March, so Valda dreaded to think how hot it would become in August. People tend to think that cold weather is more confining and restrictive and Valda was sure that in Siberia and in the Yukon this was the case, but she was now coming to realise that hot weather was just as restricting. Being outside during daylight hours in the summer months in Dubai was impossible, unless you were a camel. It was a case of running between air-conditioned homes, cars and offices in order to survive.

Valda craved a cigarette for the first time since arriving in Dubai; perhaps the change of environment had confused her cravings or maybe she had just been too busy. Luckily, cigarettes were readily available and she purchased a pack of twenty JPS. Valda drew deeply on her cigarette as she strolled along, quietly taking in the sights and sounds of Jumeirah. There was an impromptu concert taking place on a makeshift stage on the pavement in amongst the general hustle and bustle, where people would stop briefly to listen and then resume their walking or conversations.

Years of living in South Africa had made Valda slightly nervous about wandering the streets alone at night, as even though Cape Town was nowhere near as violent as Joburg, the Crime Capital of the World, neither men nor women walked alone in the street at night, unless they had nothing to live for. Crime was no problem in Dubai though; justice in Dubai was of the "eye for an eye, tooth for a tooth", variety. Liberal judges did not spare murderers just because they had been badly potty-trained.

Valda had been very impressed with the pedigree of the rest of her band. Together, they had more than fifty years' experience. Shoib Al Huq and Inzie Akhram, the drummer and keyboard player, were from Pakistan. They were both lively, easy-going sorts. Danny Sinclair, who played rhythm and electric guitar, was from London – real streetwise, hard-boiled type, but most down to earth. There was also Julian Brun from Canada, a typical, shy bass player, and Giuseppe Pelletti from Italy (no kidding) who played the sax and the piano. Although socialising and meeting new people was not usually her bag, Valda had surprised herself at the way she had established an immediate rapport with her fellow musicians when they had dined together and drawn up a demanding rehearsal schedule.

By the end of the week (the Monday to Friday type of week, that is), Valda had found a modest yet new, and more essentially air-conditioned, flat in Jumeirah to rent. She had decided to stick to taxis for the time being. Owning nothing but four suitcases of belongings gave her a sense of freedom; she was free to pick up and go anywhere, at anytime – she was totally unencumbered. Buying a car seemed like too much hassle and responsibility: possessions had a way of being a noose around one's neck and Valda was enjoying her new-found freedom and uncomplicated existence too much for that.

Visiting the Gold Souk was one of the first touristy things she did. She had seen a programme on Abu Dhabi years beforehand and had never forgotten the sight of all that gold. It was something that had to be seen to be believed. Gold jewellery as plentiful as aluminium foil. In the Emirates, all that glitters is most definitely gold. Valda was intrigued by the viciously strong coffee that was so popular with the locals; it gave new meaning to "so strong, the spoon stands up". Valda wondered if that was how Uri Geller prepared his spoons – by soaking them in Dubai coffee. Dubai's shopping centres were very similar to those back home and were thus a great place to hang out when homesick. Fatal for finances though, and at the end of her first week, Valda had three new leather jackets; one red, one black and one yellow – she convinced herself they were all for performance purposes, of course!

It's funny how the small details about a new town or country are often the ones which make the biggest impression. For Valda, it was the Arab men dressed in their white – she was absolutely certain this was not the technical word for it, but for lack of a better one – frocks. No matter what the time of day, their attire was snow white, beautifully pressed and immaculate in every way. Personal appearance was obviously something in which Dubai nationals took great pride.

Over the next few weeks, Valda was flat out; rehearsals intensified and once the Wednesday performance had gone off with a bang, Jo lost no time in filling up their calendar. Rehearse, perform, sleep and rehearse again basically summed up life for Dubai's hottest new singing talent. Valda put an immense amount of energy into her singing; she was not just a broad who stood behind a mike, she was a performer in every sense of the word. At times, she felt totally exhausted and could have done with an ice pack, a glucose drip and a week in bed, but she never complained. This was what she loved and for the first time in many years, that heavy, empty feeling in her gut began to lift.

Chapter Three

'Hey, Val!' Jo had the expression of someone about to play an April fool's joke. 'Guess who just loved your show last night!'

'You'd better tell me, I'm only in first gear mentally right now.' Valda was sitting on the stage with a mug of black coffee, leaning against the piano and feeling pretty lousy.

'Sheikh Abdullah bin Rashid Al Khaimah!' exclaimed Jo, with excitement.

'Hey, you didn't tell me I was doing a royal command performance!' quipped Valda sarcastically; the coffee had obviously hit the spot.

'Well, you're doing another one tomorrow and he wants to meet you afterwards, so don't let it go to your head!' Jo was obviously not kidding.

'So he's the one with the tablecloth round his head, right?' Shoib and Guiseppi could not help but giggle at Valda, although Jo immediately tensed up,

'He owns this hotel, six others and the Flanagan's chain, Valda, and since we're all rather attached to our jobs, we'd be grateful if you kept your jokes about his clothing to yourself!'

Valda took the point; the PC revolution had not quite reached her planet yet. She wondered what Sheikh Abdullah had liked about the previous night's music mix. Valda had sung a lot of Queen, her personal favourite and lucky for her, a great favourite in Dubai, as well. But she was curious as to why he wanted to meet her, it seemed unusual. Valda was not sure what to make of it, but there seemed no need to read anything into it at that stage.

Flanagan's was packed as usual on a Wednesday night – it must have been the TGIW feeling! Valda and her band, which Danny had decided to name "Wotzamazoos" (only he knew why), had performed a diverse selection from Barry Manilow to Bon Jovi and from Cher to The Corrs and by one o'clock, they were all shattered.

Flanagan's was a huge club: at one end was the impressive stage, in front of which was the dance floor, and the bar was opposite the stage at the other end. To the sides were tables and the sides were tiered with three different levels, thereby increasing seating capacity. It was on the third tier near the back that the Sheikh sat in a secluded lounge area, with an excellent view over the entire club. The club was comprehensively decked out in its theme colours of midnight blue and silver, which extended from the silver coasters to the midnight blue baby grand.

It took a real effort to get up those stairs to the Sheikh's lounge and Valda felt faint by the time she reached the top. Her eyes took time to adjust to the gloom. Not only was it gloomy, but very smoky up there, which created an unreal, spooky atmosphere. As her eyes adjusted, she saw the Sheikh rise to greet her. The Sheikh was a member of the extended royal family of Dubai and Jo had not briefed Valda on any relevant protocol, other than avoiding the tablecloth analogies, of course. He held out his hand and for a moment, Valda wondered if she was supposed to shake it or kiss it. She chose the former. The Sheikh was not very tall, perhaps around 5 foot 10, but he had a commanding presence, almost omnipotent, in a way. Valda was not easily intimidated though. He was immaculately dressed, his skin was flawless and his beard was so perfectly shaped and shaved, it almost looked as if it was painted on. Valda was rather mesmerised by him and for once, was at a loss for words.

'A pleasure to make your acquaintance!' The Sheikh had a deep, rich voice and an accent which sounded like a cultured mix of a French and Mumbai. 'May I offer you a cigar?' the Sheikh gestured towards his pack of Cubans.

'No thank you, but I will join you with one of my own.' With that, Valda took a seat on the couch and reached inside her jacket for a JPS.

The Sheikh was quick to offer her a light and he went on to describe how much he had enjoyed and appreciated her performances. He had a very deliberate and formal way of speaking which, combined with the murky atmosphere, was almost melodramatic in effect. Valda thanked God for cigarettes, for the meeting was a tense affair and at least taking a puff every minute helped to ease the tension of the moment. Valda tried to chat light-heartedly about her experiences as a singer, although she was not sure whether her anecdotes amused or bemused him. The Sheikh's Lalique ashtray was full and Valda felt almost ill when she thought of how many cigars he must have been through that night already. The Sheikh had a very defined face, with high cheekbones and piercing brown eyes, which were locked on to Valda. She met his gaze many times with one of her own "so what the hell do you want from me?" looks.

'Do you remember Claire?' the Sheikh asked.

'Er, no. Should I?' Valda was genuinely disinterested.

'She used to work here as a hostess.'

'She must have left before I started,' said Valda, still less than interested.

'Claire used to stay in an apartment of mine, just near here. A very large apartment, with panoramic views over Dubai and towards the Gulf. She was immensely happy there, but now she has returned home to England, I feel that it is a pity for such a beautiful apartment to go to waste ... if you were at all interested, I would be delighted to offer you the use of the apartment.'

Valda drew deeply on her JPS again; she didn't like his tone of voice. If this Claire had been so happy, then why had she gone home? Valda mused as she exhaled very slowly. 'With all due respect and apologies if I have misunderstood you, but I am not the kind of girl you set up in a fancy flat for your rich mates to visit.'

If Valda's words had been strong, her stare was stronger. It was clear from the absence of any reply that Valda had not been far off base. But what had just happened had neither bothered nor made any great impression on Valda. A throwaway conversation of no lasting relevance – an offer and a rejection. Simple as that – and she made her way home to Jumeirah to her little flat and after a shower, she fell fast asleep. Totally cancelled.

"Vanessa" was the name that popped into her in-box. Vanessa was an old uni friend, who had gone on, like most of Valda's peers, to have sensible careers and lives. Vanessa was a successful lawyer, who happened to be dealing with the sale of Valda's car and flat in Cape Town and the general tying up of that side of things. Valda was delighted to read in the email that Vanessa had found a buyer for both her car and her flat. She was sentimental about her Lotus and sad to have to let it go, but as for "that" flat, she would toast the fact that she would never have to set foot in it again. She could not wait to sign the papers and close that chapter of her life for good.

She allowed herself to briefly contrast the happiness and optimism she had felt when she had first moved into that Clifton flat with Richard and the desperate depths of despair she had endured alone there when he had left her. A few weeks ago, the surge of extremely painful emotions stirred up by these thoughts would have been too much for her and she would have been inclined to take a paracetamol and wash it down with a stiff vodka to quell the agony. But she must have come a long way since then, as now, as those feelings were less severe and although it was still painful, she was able to shrug it off and continue reading the email.

Vanessa was humorously describing the woes of turning thirty, apparently a major crisis for her. So far, turning thirty had been a change for the better in Valda's life and besides her grey hair count that was increasing by the day, things were looking up.

Vanessa was urging Valda to return to Cape Town as soon as she could to sign the papers, so that she could finalise the various sales. Valda cursed Vanessa's efficiency. Valda had hoped the sale would drag on, like such things normally did, as she was not quite ready to return to Cape Town yet. She was virtually certain she would bump into some tactless moron, who would insist on giving her an update on the "happy couple". Valda was astounded at how insensitive people could be. A few months after the split, Valda had been in hospital suffering from "exhaustion", when one of her visitors who had seen Richard and Sonja at a function the night before had given her a detailed description of how well they both looked and how "stunning" Sonja was. Not one to hold her feelings in, Valda let rip – Ward 16 had been treated to some choice language that day. Valda resolved to speak to Jo and see if some time off was possible. She was determined to literally fly in, sign those papers and get the hell out again.

'It's highly inconvenient. This is one of our busiest times of year, what with the Shopping Festival on. And now you lay this on me. If I get any more stress today, my brain will explode out of my head!'

Jo was just slightly tense at Valda's request for a few days off and she explained that she was as irritated at the prospect of having to take time off for this trip as he was, but despite Jo's rant, she got the feeling he'd swing something.

Valda had seen the Sheikh watching her from his lounge up there on quite a few occasions during evening performances. She had been meaning to ask Jo about him. What was his case? But Jo had been so stressed out and edgy that Val had decided the matter could wait. Shoib, Inzie and Giuseppi seemed far more interested in the endless stream of talent that poured through the doors of Flanagan's on a nightly basis to care about the Sheikh; Danny was going through a messy divorce (as if there was such a thing as a tidy one) and Julian was miles away on his own planet, so any questions Valda had about the Sheikh were bound to remain unanswered. When their eyes did meet though, he would smile and for a few seconds, she would feel guilty for the way in which she had cold-shouldered him. There were obviously loads of things she had yet to understand as far as Dubai culture went.

Jo must have had a great night's sleep or something, as the next day he was full of the joys. Valda was pleased to hear that her time off had been sorted – she had four days to handle things back in Cape Town, plenty enough for what she wanted!

Larissa, Jamie and Ellen were whipping up a storm conversation-wise and anyone sitting at a nearby table or even in the same coffee shop for that matter would have been forgiven for thinking they were on the set of *Sex and the City*. Larissa was animated as she dramatically related a story from her vast repertoire. She was one of those people who went through life collecting bizarre and often hilarious experiences – if ever there was a crackpot within a 5-mile radius, they would be sure to make a beeline for her. Although many of these experiences had been patently unfunny at the time, she was always able to convert them into highly entertaining and amusing stories. Larissa saw the funny side in everything; she had long ago stopped taking life too seriously.

There was a pause in the conversation as the waitress brought over three chocolate cheesecakes. All three girls were genuine "foodies" and would meet every Thursday to try out a new cake shop. Keeping the taste buds satisfied was just as essential as quenching their appetite for gossip. Ellen and Jamie were also from England and so any conversation always involved a segment on affairs back home.

An Arab man was sitting not far from them, legs crossed, with his espresso in hand, reading his broadsheet, which was held out in front of him. A headline on his newspaper jogged Ellen's memory.

'Did you hear about that British girl whose body was found on the beach?'

'Yes, that was terrible!' said Jamie as she paused for a sip of latte. 'They say she must have been struck by a motor boat or something while swimming. I heard she was very pretty. Have they named her yet?'

'Yes, I forget what it was though.'

Larissa was surprised that she had not heard this particular story and enquired, 'Where was she swimming that she managed to get hit by a motor boat?'-

Neither Jamie nor Ellen knew the details, except that the unfortunate young girl had worked at a Dubai nightclub and foul play had been ruled out.

Chapter Four

Valda's flight was booked; she would leave for Dubai International after her Tuesday performance, at the Maharani Club at a seafront hotel in Jumeirah. From there, she would catch the 3.00 a.m. flight to Johannesburg, arriving at 9.00 a.m. South African time, leaving plenty of time to catch the 10.30 a.m. connection to Cape Town. She would be in Cape Town by lunchtime, where she would meet Vanessa, sign the papers, visit Ted and hopefully make it back to Johannesburg in time for the 8.30 p.m. flight back to Dubai. Or at least that was the general idea.

The Burg Emir was an ultra-modern, enormous skyscraper, the top of which was shaped like a spiral, giving it a very elegant, distinctive finish. Flanagan's was on the one hundred and twentieth floor and at the very top was a pool deck, with sauna rooms, jacuzzis and a poolside restaurant. There were a total of eighteen restaurants in all, scattered amongst the many floors. There was a second pool deck on the twentieth floor, overlooked by a buffet restaurant called Henley's, where a traditional British roast dinner was on offer on Sundays – something which was strongly supported by the expat community and visitors to Dubai. There was a piano there, too, and Valda often used to play it on Sunday afternoons and maybe sing a little. Henley's had huge windows facing onto the pool deck, overlooking the Dubai skyline. It was a bright place with white tiled floors and every table was covered in a crisp white linen tablecloth.

The Sunday before Valda left for South Africa, she was playing at Henley's. It was packed as usual and had a great laid-back, lazy Sunday afternoon atmosphere. She welcomed requests and it had become "a thing" for diners to write their requests on serviettes and drop them on the glass table next to the piano. Someone had requested the Curtis Stigers' song, *I Wonder Why*, but Valda knew there was no way she'd make it through that one without cracking up: she had come along way, but that would be pushing it. The entire afternoon, she'd had the uneasy feeling that she was being watched, closely!

At four, things were beginning to wind down and as Valda was starving, she decided to pack in the piano playing and go over to the buffet to see if there was anything left over. Much to her delight and relief, there was some roast beef and a decent helping of cauliflower cheese waiting for her. She found a plate and was busy dishing up the roast beef, with generous amounts of horseradish, when she heard a voice behind her. 'Valda!'

Even though he had only said the one word, the accent was unmistakable. Valda turned to see the Sheikh; it was the first time she had seen him in the daylight. He looked as well turned out as ever, but his eyes were red and his distinguished appearance had a jaded edge to it. Valda greeted him politely, but did not intend to let him stand in the way of her and the cauliflower cheese.

'You will join me at my table?'

It sounded like a question, but Valda was sure it was more like an instruction. She followed the Sheikh with her now full plate to a large table. She could tell immediately where the Sheikh had been sitting by the overflowing ashtray. Whoever he had been dining with had now departed and all that was left were a dozen soiled napkins and empty bottles of mineral water.

'Would you like a drink?' asked the Sheikh.

'No thanks, I'm on the wagon these days.' The words were out her mouth, before she realised that the Sheikh was probably not offering her that kind of drink anyway. He gave her a confused look, obviously not acquainted with the expression "falling off the wagon". Valda had had nothing stronger than a beer since coming to Dubai and that was nothing to do with lack of availability or opportunity. At one stage a year ago, friends had joked that she should start looking for a new flat in the vicinity of the Betty Ford alcoholism and drug rehabilitation clinic. Nowadays, the sight and smell of hard liquor filled her with a sickening and morbid feeling.

Valda sat next to the Sheikh and started tucking in. He watched her with an amused look on his face. She realised that her table manners left plenty to be desired, but hey, she was starving. Even away from the surreal atmosphere of Flanagan's, the Sheikh still had something enchanting about him. Valda was flattered by the apparent interest he took in her. Perhaps it was a symptom of growing up in foster care, but Valda craved attention, any attention, even the worst kind of attention would do.

'So you are going to Cape Town on Tuesday,' said the Sheikh between puffs.

'Yes, Jo tell you?' It was a rhetorical question; who else would it be but Jo.

'It is very pleasing to us that you are so impressed with Dubai that you are willing to relinquish your home in beautiful Cape Town!'

'Dubai has been good to me. I am amazed at what a change in geography has done for my fortunes!'

While she ate, the Sheikh chatted away. Valda listened with surprise; she hadn't had him pegged as a master of small talk. He even touched on the weather – that universally renowned safe subject – although there was a limit on how long any conversation about weather could go on in Dubai; Valda had been there for five weeks now and every day had been identical.

Valda was wearing white jeans and a turquoise T-shirt and as she finished her food, she slipped off her shoes under the table, leaned back and pulled her left leg up, so that her foot was on the chair, with her shin squashed against the table. They were the last diners left at Henley's.

'I have a cousin in Stellenbosch,' ventured the Sheikh.

Valda was rather sceptical; she doubted Stellenbosch, a quaint university town in the heart of the wine lands, was a likely home for any cousin of the Sheikh. However, these days, one could never tell and according to a rumour Richard had relayed to Valda, bin Laden owned property in Durban.

The Sheikh continued, 'He has an important package for me, which I am anxious to receive!'

Valda realised what he was hinting at. 'Had any quotes from DHL or UPS?' she said in her most sarcastic tone.

The Sheikh's eyes widened and he sat back, roaring with a raucous burst of laughter, which was just as sarcastic in itself. 'As if I would trust a courier with such a precious cargo; all couriers are imbeciles!'

Couriers may be imbeciles, Valda thought to herself, but they also have strict policies on what they will and will not accept and all parcels are subject to scrutiny!

'I would be much obliged if you would collect this parcel and bring it back for me!' The Sheikh stared right into her eyes, as if he was trying to impress upon her how serious he was.

'What is it?' asked Valda in the flattest voice.

'I cannot say!'

'Then I cannot do!'

'That is your prerogative!' The Sheikh leaned back, sighed and looked away as if he was greatly disappointed in Valda.

Valda felt very awkward and started to reach for her jacket which, of course, was not there – she had not worn it that day. Her JPS were in the pocket and if she ever needed one it was now.

The Sheikh sucked the last puff out of his cigar, looked at his diamond-encrusted Rolex, rose from the table and then turned to Valda. 'You have until Tuesday to decide. If the answer is yes, 200,000 dirhams in cash and a note of the address will be delivered to you before your flight.'

Valda was, indeed, shocked at the offer, but she gave no indication of any surprise. Luckily, no response was necessary: Ahmed, the Sheikh's trusted companion-bodyguard, was approaching. Ahmed was tall and surly and was not only thickset, but plain thick as well, in Valda's opinion. He never spoke much, but he shadowed the Sheikh like a trusty Labrador.

'Thank you for your company. A pleasure as always!' The Sheikh spoke in one of his most unctious tones of voice. He turned without waiting for any response and left Henley's.

If anything, Valda wanted to get away from the Sheikh's territory. The discussion over lunch had thrown her into a quandary, so she made her way out of the hotel and sped away in a taxi with relief.

Everyone has their price! A cliché is a cliché for a reason and Valda was not sure what her "price" was, but 200,000 dirhams pretty much topped it. She did not even have the money yet and it was already burning a hole in her pocket – another apt cliché!

Valda did, for one moment, attempt to convince herself that the parcel may well be innocent: why bother with a courier, when someone you know would be visiting Cape Town anyway and could bring it back for you. It happens all the time. The level of naivety required to maintain that line of thought was monumental though. Valda knew that the parcel was dodgy – the 200,000 dirham "reward" the Sheikh had offered was a measure of just how dodgy.

She spent the whole night agonising over the decision. Valda knew there really was nothing to agonise over, any sensible person would just walk right away. Every line of thought reached the same logical conclusion: no way! It was not even a case of weighing up the pros and cons; the cons were so enormous, they practically knocked the proverbial scale over. Just when she was enjoying an uncomplicated life, things had to get messy again. Her mind had already formulated a clever excuse for the Sheikh and a way of discouraging him in future; however, her heart knew that no excuses would be needed! Valda had always loved risk and a challenge both motivated and excited her. She was a smooth customer and she always backed herself – she was 99 per cent confident that she could pull this off. It was like betting on a certainty and the reward was 200,000 dirhams; the equivalent of £40,000.

Valda woke as she had gone to sleep, with the Sheikh and his mysterious parcel on her mind. She had a shrewd idea of what it was and she had a day and a bit to make up her mind. The question was whether in that time her sensible head would win over her impulsive, daring heart. The Chinese have a saying that a decision made in haste is always a bad one – yet a hasty decision was exactly what was required.

The money was only one aspect of the decision matrix; Valda had a strange need to impress the Sheikh – her ego had been boosted by his apparent trust and confidence in her ability to bring his parcel back safely. In a strange and twisted sense she would feel like a bit of a drip to walk away from his proposal. And although the emotional momentum towards a "Yes" was building, she was tormented by the fears, the morality and the potential consequences of failure. What was she letting herself in for? Was the money worth the risk? One thing which haunted her was what would her dad, Ted, think of her? He would be very disappointed in her if she took the bait of money to do something dubious. Needless to say, Monday was a very long and arduous day.

Chapter Five

Valda arrived at Cape Town International Airport at 12.30, just as planned. She hired a car and headed straight for the offices of De Jong and Clarence on Adderley Street.

'Vanessa Da Silva, please; I have an appointment!' she said as she approached the receptionist.

It was not long before Vanessa appeared. 'Valda, hi! You look so well!'

'Are you trying to say I look fat?' joked Valda.

'Yes! And you needed fattening up, you were like a stick. How are things?' asked Vanessa smiling. Her sunkissed cheeks and bronze, toned limbs indicated that she was in training for another triathlon.

'Looking up, touch wood. Be even better once I get those papers signed!'

'I've arranged for us to meet the buyers down there, we can use my car,' said Vanessa as she reached in her handbag for her car keys.

'Whoa! Meet who? Down where? I am not going near that flat! You know how I feel!' There was tension and apprehension in Valda's voice.

'The wife is rather superstitious, she believes in karma or something, don't ask me! She wants to meet you before they finalise the sale. She really takes these things seriously.' Vanessa was pleading; she knew Valda could be stubborn and was regretting not having warned her beforehand.

'Fine, let's meet, but why can't it be at a coffee shop, rather than there,' protested Valda.

Vanessa could see her friend was getting tense and it was time to plead a little more. Vanessa had a day full of appointments and the slightest change in arrangements was bound to extend her working hours beyond seven o'clock again. She was sure that someone who had never worked a nine-to-five day in their entire life would not understand this though, so she put on one of her most anguished looks and said, 'Please, Valda! I promise it won't take long.'

Valda decided that Vanessa looked pretty tired and desperate, so she swallowed her own feelings and braced herself for a painful ride down memory lane.

They were at the flat within fifteen minutes. Vanessa had the keys and she opened the door to let Valda in. It was a warm, sunny, autumn day and the sun was streaming through the French doors and picture windows of Flat 11 De Kaap. All the furniture was gone, of course, and the flat had a bright, airy and cheerful feel to it. Valda was astonished that she felt absolutely nothing: for eight years, she had eaten, slept, fought and made love there and yet that day, she felt as though it was the very first time she was seeing it. It could have been any of a thousand Clifton flats. There were no vibes at all, no personal stamp. All the angst connected with the place seemed to have dissipated. Valda remained silent, looking around, waiting to lay eyes on something that would bring back that searing pain again. But nothing came. Vanessa was rattling off the prices she had obtained for the various bits of furniture she had sold at auction, but Valda heard nothing.

'Are you OK?' Vanessa eventually noticed how quiet Valda was.

'Yes, actually! I'm glad we came down here, it gave me a chance to make peace with this place that was a part of my life for so long.'

There was no way Vanessa could ever understand and she didn't need to.

Meg and Norman arrived at the flat about twenty minutes after they had. They were from Wales, but were retiring to Cape Town. They had a light-hearted chat, after which Meg appeared quite content and ready to proceed with the sale. She obviously did not pick up on any negative vibes, either.

On the way back to Vanessa's office, Valda thought again of the empty yet welcoming flat. She was sure Meg and Norman would be very happy there and she sincerely wished them well. Valda had been living in her first flat for six months, when a blabbermouth neighbour had revealed that the previous owner had shot himself in the shower. Valda had been aghast and had moved back home immediately and sold the flat. On thinking back though, she realised that there had never been any bad vibes there, even in the shower – it was a great flat and she had been happy there. Maybe the guy who had shot himself was at peace, so all the vibes and emotions tied up there had dissolved; Meg probably knew about that kind of thing, she thought to herself. Valda thought how ironic it was that eight years later, she had tried the same thing; in fact, she had almost achieved it! Had it not been for Ted's reading glasses ... Valda had never wanted to know the details of the state in which they had found her. Exhaustion was the polite way her doctor had described her condition.

The car drew into the office car park. 'Signing the papers will only take about five minutes, if that's OK?' said Vanessa, breaking the silence. Valda had been very quiet on the drive back and Vanessa was questioning the wisdom of forcing her into going back to the flat.

'Fine. How about lunch afterwards?' asked Valda.

'Can't, appointments all day; see what I mean about getting to regret my career choice daily?' They both laughed.

The papers were history within five minutes as predicted and Valda climbed into her hired Citi Golf, wondering where it would take her next. She had missed driving herself around and it gave her a huge sense of freedom to be behind the wheel again. Perhaps a car would have to be her first purchase when she got back to Dubai.

There were two scraps of paper in her jacket pocket. She took them out and looked at one of them:

Brett Morgan
158 Igwababa Rd
Kloof
Durban
Mobile: 083 789 2162

She did not plan on a trip to Durban this time, even though it was one of her favourite places, and what's more, she was afraid of going down the romance route again – it was too soon. She had met Brett in the departure lounge. Cheeky guy, very good looking though, and extremely tall and slender, she remembered with a smile. Valda was sure that if he went anywhere near Hollywood, they would snap him up – however, she mused, the best-looking guys are often unassuming and tend to shun the limelight.

Valda had been in her own world, obsessively checking her passport and boarding tickets – there was something about travel that brought out a neurotic side to her. She had not even noticed the thin, long-legged dude sitting opposite. He had noticed her though.

'Woman are so disorganised,' he'd laughed.

Valda had looked up in surprise, but equally sure that he was talking to her. 'I'm even disorganised along the lines of female standards!' Valda had retorted, before pretending to continue faffing with her hand luggage; she was not going to be the one to make conversation.

'Just look at all your kit! Me, I've just got my passport in my pocket, that's it, so much easier!'

With that, he'd removed a ropy-looking passport from his faded jeans and waved it at her. To Valda, the sight of that tatty passport had been no demonstration of organisational ability; indeed, it had looked as if it had been round in the washing machine in his jeans' pocket. What was obvious though, was that this fellow traveller had wanted to talk! Valda had put it down to pure airport-lounge boredom. She was wrong though.

'Been on holiday in Dubai?' asked Mr Harry Cool.

'I work here.' Valda hadn't elaborated any further, she knew that people tended to stereotype other people on the basis of their job and she was very much aware of a certain "Bimbo" tag that came with being a singer.

The stranger had no such reservations; he was free to tell her that he was a geologist who worked all over the Far and Middle East on oil rigs and what a fantastic income it was. Apparently, he was going home to Durban for a three-month holiday. He'd seemed intent on drawing more information out of the coy Valda though, saying, 'What exactly do you do in Dubai?'

'I'm a singer, entertainer if you like,' she'd said offhandedly.

She realised that this was almost handing him an opportunity to suggest a future meeting and she had been right.

'OK, you'll have to give me your details. If I'm ever at a loose end in Dubai, I'll come and check you out!'

What a player! she thought. 'Yeah, you do that!' said Valda, making no attempt to hand over any details. 'What is your name by the way?'

'Brett Morgan,' he'd said, extending a hand. 'And you are?'

'Valda Kramer.'

Any more conversation had been haltered by the gates opening; Brett was travelling business class and Valda was doing the cattle wagon routine again. During the flight, one of the air hostesses had delivered Brett's note with his address on it to Valda and she, in turn, had sent one of her own back, with her address and number in Dubai being written on the back of one of Flanagan's midnight-blue-and-silver business cards. Valda realised that she may well be opening up another Pandora's Box of relationship nightmares, but she had just thought, what the hell!

Valda had been able to collect her luggage quickly; she had only brought a duffel bag for the short trip and luckily it was one of the first on the conveyor belt. A couple of other eager passengers had tried to grab it, thinking it was theirs – Valda couldn't understand why luggage always tended to come in navy and black; if anything cried out for bright, distinctive colouring it was luggage! As she had walked away to the "nothing to declare" door, she had looked back to see Brett waiting by the conveyor belt staring after her. She'd fought the urge to go over and chat and instead had given him a friendly wave and on impulse, she had blown him a kiss.

'What an idiot!' said Valda to herself as she thought back to her airport encounter. She'd never expected to hear from Brett again, guessing that between now and the end of his three-month stay in Durban, he would be inundated with gorgeous Durban dolls.

Valda's attention now turned to the other note:

Joanna's Herbal Health Store
19 The Avenue
Milnerton, C.T.

This was not focused on for long though, for she safely tucked it back in her half-empty JPS packet and wiped it from her mind.

Valda rang Ted next and was delighted that he at least had time for the important things of the day – like lunch. They were meeting at a swanky restaurant in Kloofnek Street, one of Cape Town's trendy restaurant streets. Valda would be staying with her adoptive dad Ted for three days, so she would have plenty of time to see him in the evenings; there was no harm in getting a head start on the catching-up though. Like Vanessa, Ted was surprised and relieved to see that his daughter looked so much healthier. He was also pleased to tell her that Richard was in Joburg for a conference with the "unmentionable" fiancée, so there would be no chance of an uncomfortable run in. Although Valda divulged every detail of her life in Dubai, she only touched briefly on the Sheikh – she was almost sure Ted would issue some kind of sensible parental warning and she did not want to hear it.

Valda was constantly amazed that nothing had changed back home. She had to remind herself that of course nothing had changed; she had only been away for five weeks. Yet so much had changed for Valda that to her, it felt as if she had been away for years and she was shocked that everyone else still seemed to be doing the same old boring things.

It was 3.30 p.m. when they finished lunch and Ted was needed back in the office – he ran his own ad agency and was testament to the fact that you can be a real down-to-earth, honest person and yet survive and succeed in a bitchy, superficial and back-stabbing environment.

Valda felt at a loose end, so she jumped in the hired VW and started driving, almost hoping the car would decide upon the destination. After purposelessly driving past some old haunts, Valda took the turn off for Milnerton. She had decided it was time to see what Joanna's Health and Herbal or whatever it was looked like. Valda did not know Milnerton that well and The Avenue was harder to find than the G spot. She had to stop twice to ask directions: a cyclist had tried to be helpful, but his detailed directions had made no sense whatsoever. She had also made the mistake of asking a pedestrian for directions; he had turned out to be motherless and had sworn at her, something about *Foetseck julle wit bliksem*! She got his gist and had to laugh out loud, it was funny. In South Africa, it's a case of: AK47s can blow your brains out, but words can never harm you – they should translate it into Latin and make it the national motto.

At last, and partly by accident, she arrived in The Avenue. At first, all she could see were modest houses with the obligatory walls, barbed wire and Armed Response warning signs. After driving for half a mile, she could see a parade of grotty little shops on her right. No Lalique ashtrays and golden bidets in this locality.

Then there it was – big green lettering advertised: Joanna's Herbal Health Store. The shop was sandwiched in between a video rental store and a popular steakhouse chain. Valda made a U-turn, backtracked and double parked, while she briefly tried to get a better look at Joanna's from the safety of her car. Various boards advertised herbal remedies and special discounts in the windows, but that was about all she could see without getting any closer. An old woman was coming out with a green plastic bag and there were a few people still inside. Motorists were getting a little aggravated with the fact that she was blocking the flow of traffic and the last thing she wanted was to aggravate anyone in that vicinity unnecessarily. Besides which, it was nearly knock-off time and Valda did not want to catch the traffic on the way back to Camps Bay.

No such luck! She had chosen just the right time to snag the peak-hour jam, which was made all the worse by the heat in the car – a basic model without air conditioning. A twinkling sound coming from her pocket indicated she was receiving a text. Not an everyday occurrence for Valda. She flipped open her mobile, curious as to who it could be from.

"Whatz up? B." was the message that popped onto the screen.

Valda decided against playing it cool and ignoring the message, so she typed back, "Don't be jealous, but I'm stuck in traffic!"

"I'm sitting with an ice-cold Castle Lager at Joe Cools," was his response.

Chapter Six

'Vali!'

'Sox!'

Bella and Valda greeted each other with the bizarre nicknames they had been using ever since they had first met at tennis club twenty-three years earlier. Their enthusiastic greeting drew some attention – mainly negative – from the other patrons of Harper's restaurant in Cape Town's massive Century City Shopping Centre.

'My God, you look great! We were all so worried about you. You're a survivor!' Bella looked genuinely pleased.

'We're all survivors – I don't think we have a choice!' laughed Valda, adding, 'So, how's married life?'

'Complicated!' moaned Bella. 'I've got him in training though, and he's catching on slowly.'

'Should I be planning any baby showers?'

'Absolutely not! I had enough sleep deprivation when I was morning news anchor; I'm not going in for that again any time soon.'

It was ten thirty in the morning – the perfect time to sample waffles with maple syrup and ice cream. After they had ordered, Valda slipped a little wooden chest-shaped box out of her jacket and handed it to Bella.

Bella's eyes widened. 'What's this?' Always impatient, she wasted no time opening the box and finding the gold Gemini pendant and chain. 'This is beautiful!' She was obviously surprised and delighted. 'What did I do to deserve this?'

Valda grinned and laughingly replied, 'Oh, nothing much, just rescuing me from my old life! And, rescuing me from the clutches of my psychologist. If I hadn't left the country when I did, I'd have been sitting in his chair every Monday afternoon till one of us dropped dead!'

Their raucous laughter once again drew attention and irritated stares. Their conversation focused on Dubai and its attractions, as well as the low down on her brief romantic encounter in the departure lounge.

The delicious-looking golden waffles swimming in maple syrup and fast-melting vanilla ice cream arrived, putting a temporary end to their conversation. Between mouthfuls, Bella summoned up the courage and said, 'I saw Richard last week ... he came up to me at the supermarket ... wanted to know how you were.'

The first thing Valda was inclined to blurt out was "So what did you tell the SOAB?", but she decided not to show her irritation at hearing "Richard-news" and shoved in another mouthful, to avoid having to comment. She was sure Bella would go on to elaborate.

She did. 'He seemed really concerned.' Bella paused to see Valda's reaction, which was simply to roll her eyes and take a long sip of milkshake. Then she continued, 'I told him you were doing great and very happy, working hard, having lots of fun ... that kind of thing! He looked very tired, stressed out like.'

'Doesn't sound like him, he's usually on top of everything!' smirked Valda.

'He asked me to tell you that he is really pleased for you,' Bella said with some trepidation, as if it may provoke an outburst of some kind from her friend; she remembered the volatile Valda very well.

Valda just shrugged and said nothing and Bella appeared to relax now that she had gotten the "news" off her chest: she had felt obliged to tell Valda she had seen the SOAB, but she had feared her reaction. Valda had decided to make no further comment on the subject; she was well into the recovery phase and did not want any setbacks.

'So what do they think of the volcanic Valda temper in Dubai?' teased Bella.

'They haven't heard of it yet! I've been far more placid – hard to imagine, I know. I found out that losing my temper was upsetting me more than it was upsetting everyone else!'

'That bad?' Bella raised an eyebrow and then giggled. 'So, what are you doing this afternoon?'

'Errands to run, nothing wildly exciting. You?'

'Packing. I leave for Vancouver on Friday ...' Bella rambled on.

Valda was not listening though, she was thinking of her trip to Joanna's and it gave her an uncomfortable feeling; what was she letting herself in for?

* * *

There was little traffic on the N1 at one o'clock and Valda travelled with speed in her green Citi Golf towards the Milnerton turn off. It was a cooler day, the sun was shining, music was playing on the scratchy car radio and the glorious sight of Table Mountain was in the rear view mirror. It should have been idyllic, yet that dark, foreboding feeling was creeping all over her. This time, the feelings were nothing to do with any memories conjured up by Cape Town either.

Valda groaned to herself as she wondered whether The Avenue would be as hard to find second time around. This time, however, she arrived outside Joanna's within minutes, almost too soon, for there was not enough time to psyche herself up. Finding a parking space was more of a challenge though; being lunch hour, patrons of the steakhouse had bagged most of the places nearby. After some illegal traffic manoeuvres, she found a spot and squeezed in. 'Bless these hired cars,' mumbled Valda. 'No need to get concerned about parking next to some idiot who'll scratch your car!'

Valda had some cash in her pocket, sunglasses and nothing else. She had dressed plainly, so as not to attract any attention to herself. Some burger-eating kids were congregated on the pavement outside Joanna's, but they took no notice of her. Valda wanted to be sure that no one else took any notice of her either. She pushed open the glass door and stepped into the health shop. It was warm and rather musty inside. The walls were cluttered with shelves accommodating a multitude of herbal potions and remedies and there were also wooden gondolas of organic goods, vitamins and supplements. Valda made her way towards the Evening Primrose Oil as advertised in the window and pretended to take great note of the various brands and differing IUs. There were two other customers; one was paying for something that looked like herbal tea and another was hanging around waiting for assistance. The only member of staff was a short, stocky woman, with a bright green floral dress, black hair and very weather-beaten skin. It was impossible to tell her age. Joanna? wondered Valda. There was an acrid smell in the shop which caused Valda to look around, half expecting to see a budgie cage – it sickened her and she could not wait to get the hell out.

"Ask for the sciatica relief," the note had said. Valda had no intention of doing that right away; she was only there to suss things out. The South African police were no fools and if they suspected that there was something fishy about Joanna, they would be watching both her and her patrons. She remained focused on the vitamins; she could now hear the woman giving the other customer some advice on soya products. She picked up some EPO and went over to wait at the counter. The customer appeared to be uninspired with the soya "stuff" on offer, or maybe it was the price that was not to her taste, but she soon vanished.

'Canna help you?' asked "Joanna" in a real Cape Flats' accent.

'I'd like to take these and some Devil's Claw, if you have any?' Valda knew Devil's claw would cost at least 150 rand.

'Devil's claw we got, but it cos' you hunnerd and fifty rand. Plus the Primrose Oil is over two hunnerd rand!' Joanna said with emphasis.

Valda pretended to look pained at the price. She took out a batch of twenty-rand notes, flipped through them, put on a dismayed look and then said, 'I'll just take the EPO for now and I'll come back for the Devil's Claw tomorrow.'

She paid and headed out with her green bag, none the wiser really. Before returning to her car, Valda ambled along, looking with apparent interest at the other shops and even the steakhouse menu: a catalogue of "what not to eat" would better describe it. Valda wanted to look to anyone watching like the average Milnerton shopper, without going as far as actually sampling the local food on offer – a pudding of Pepto Bismol would be required for sure. After ten minutes of aimless window shopping, she headed calmly back to the car.

Valda drove back to join the N1, half regretting not having just asked for the "parcel" and been done with it. She knew that being impatient never paid off though, and besides, there was no hurry.

This time, there were no texts from Mr Morgan to distract Valda from her tormented thoughts. It was still not too late to turn back, throw the 200,000 dirhams in the Sheikh's face and say hello to her carefree life again. Every traffic light was red and Valda could feel her irritability and frustration levels rising. Those familiar old volcanic lavas were beginning to simmer and hiss again. Valda had done everything she had wanted to do in Cape Town – besides the obvious – and she was anxious to return to Dubai. Cape Town held no nostalgia for her; in fact, she almost felt like a stranger there. Although the weather was mild, Table Mountain looked cold and the whole city felt quiet and lonely.

In an attempt to while away the long afternoon, Valda headed towards one of Cape Town's many shopping centres. She found herself an outdoor table at a restaurant, ordered a cheese burger and Coke and was just enjoying her first drag, when she saw a familiar figure approaching St Elmo's. It was Charles, one of Richard's work colleagues – as she had feared, there was not a square inch of Cape Town that was free from torturous encounters of her past. The unfortunate thing for Valda was that the ever-observant Charles had spotted her and was on his way over. Goodbye peaceful lunch. Valda's hostile look did not deter Charles from attempting to make conversation with her.

'Hi, Valda, thought you had debunked Cape Town?' said the tall, willowy and strawberry-haired Charles.

'I am only back to tie things up.' Valda's voice was icy and left no doubt that she was in no mood for small talk.

'By the way, smoking is not allowed here!'

Now Charles had really touched a nerve. 'For Christ's sake, I'm sitting outside. What? Are they legislating for the great outdoors as well now?'

Valda was wide-eyed and ferocious, yet Charles was unsurprised and continued, 'It's still on shopping centre property ... I'm just telling you, because I have heard they are slapping hefty fines on anyone who lights up here, even in the damned car park. I agree with you, it's like the Gestapo!'

'Well, I've got no ID on me, only 100 rand and a one-way ticket outta here, so I challenge them to try and slap a fine on me.' Valda was arrogant and defiant as she spoke.

Charles pulled up a chair, sat down and then asked belatedly, 'Mind if I join you?' To which Valda shrugged, sighed and then tossed a menu in his direction. The only thing that made Charles sufferable was the fact that he had never liked Richard. 'It's nice to see you again anyway!' said Charles smiling. 'I hear life in Dubai is good!' Valda was not sure if he was referring to her life or to Dubai life in general, but she nodded, adding nothing. 'I don't know if you heard, but Debra and I broke off our engagement.'

Valda was not sure if she had heard or not and was hardly fussed either way, all relationships were potential disaster areas as far as she was concerned, but she offered a sympathetic, 'I'm sorry to hear that, Charles.' Then, changing the subject, she added, 'I've ordered a burger, are you going to join me?'

Charles jumped at the apparent invite and waved over a waitress, so he could place his order. Valda could not remember if Charles smoked, but she offered him a JPS anyway.

'No thanks, I've given up. You should, too; it's bad for you!'

'It's only bad for you if you want to live forever!' replied Valda, while lighting her second.

Charles was diplomatic enough to avoid sensitive subjects. Instead, he stuck to stories about his parents' vineyard; including an amusing one about the time they had taken their staff, who had never seen the sea before, for a day-trip to the beach. All sorts of alcohol and excitement-induced shenanigans had ensued and he painted the picture so well, that Valda burst out laughing on more than one occasion.

'... so that's the last time my parents will be attempting that! Although they have been hearing rumblings amongst the staff that they are quite keen on another excursion,' Charles concluded.

'No, no. I think they had better leave that out!' laughed Valda. 'Isn't it always the way though, you try to do something nice and it blows up in your face.'

'Yes, I agree! I have this dentist friend, who says: whenever you do a good deed, start checking for the knife in your back. Sad, but true, huh?'

The delicious burgers dripping with melted Cheddar arrived and Valda and Charles tucked in. Valda had been surprised that she had enjoyed Charles' company. There had been a relaxed, easy-going atmosphere between them and the laugh had eased the tension she had felt over "Joanna's" health store. Between mouthfuls, Valda offered some of her Dubai news: culture, food, etc. which, since Charles had never been to the Middle East, was all new to him.

Charles was looking at his Longines watch, obviously worried about returning to the office in time. 'I'm gonna have to dash off in ten minutes, Valda, but what would you say about drinks tonight? Sevenish? At the Waterfront.'

Valda was clearly surprised at the proposal and pleased that she could momentarily delay answering as she swallowed her mouthful. 'OK, why not? Leave me your card though, in case I'm held up and have to take a rain check!' Always helpful to build in an escape clause, she thought to herself.

Charles reached into his jacket for his business card and six twenty-rand notes and then dashed off, leaving Valda to devour the last of her chips.

A few minutes after Charles had left, Valda heard that familiar jingle. She reached into her jeans pocket for her mobile phone. The envelope icon was flashing: one message. Valda knew immediately who it was. Brett!

"B in CT 4 surfing on Sunday. MayB C U then! Brett."

Valda was due to fly out on Saturday night, so there would be no rendezvous with Brett this time at least! Valda had to smile to herself – it was the old bus analogy again! You wait ages for one to come along …

After lunch, Valda returned home to Ted's. The sight of the peach toned villa with wrap round terrace set against the back drop of the Twelve Apostles was one place in Cape Town which did inspsire warm memories. She was tired and there was just too much going on in her head. She decided that the best course of action was to hit the bed and go to sleep. In Valda's book, there was a lot to be said for an ostrich mentality: when the going gets tough, bury your head in the sand, or in her case, in the pillow and fall asleep.

Ted had kept her room just the same as when she had lived there. It was filled with all the clothes and memorabilia that Valda had not been able to take to Dubai with her. She felt secure and warm inside surrounded by all her things, and in the knowledge that she was safe, she fell asleep almost instantly.

It was almost six o'clock when she woke up. Just an hour to get ready and meet Charles – if, indeed, she still wanted to keep the date. She wondered if there was any reason behind his asking her for a drink; she could not help but be a little puzzled if not suspicious. She had never imagined that Charles had ever seen her in a romantic light and until that afternoon, she had always seen him as a bit of a pain.

Meeting him seemed preferable to a long night on the couch watching some reality TV drivel or worse and Ted was working late as per usual. After a shower, Valda rummaged through her wardrobe to find something appropriate that did not need ironing. She settled for a dress in her favourite halter-neck-style – it was long, in a burgundy paisley pattern, with gypsy-style asymmetric frills at the bottom and was very sleek-fitting around the waist. After touching up her make-up and grabbing some cash, she was ready to go.

Charles had suggested a trendy wine bar at the Waterfront. He was not typical of the kind of guy Valda would usually go for, but she had decided that she should give people more of a chance – her old criteria had led her up too many dead-end streets for her not to consider changing tactics. Charles was already there, as Valda was fifteen minutes late after trying to find a parking space. He was dressed in some stone-coloured chinos and a casual white linen shirt.

'I'm so sorry I'm late. It's not like me!' Valda began, with a genuine smile.

Charles waved his hand dismissively and said, 'I've only just arrived myself. You look gorgeous! Can I get you a drink?'

'Yes, Coke for the moment. Thanks.'

Charles and Valda found a table in a quiet area and began perusing the menus. Being brought up on a vineyard, Charles was a wine connoisseur and so Valda left the choice of wine to him. They were both ravenous, despite their heavy lunch, and Valda chose lemon veal, while Charles went for the King Clip. Once the orders were taken care of, conversation became sticky, unlike that afternoon, when it had flowed so well. Perhaps it was because there was more tension and expectation this time. Valda was reluctant to enquire about Charles' work – there may be unwanted references to Richard – so she decided that South Africa's test match in the West Indies was a safe bet. Sport was clearly not a subject that wildly inspired Charles though, and so it was lucky that the meals arrived fairly quickly.

Alcohol has very different effects on different people and while it made Valda volatile, it made others sleepy, some philosophical and some melancholy. Charles fell into the latter category. He began talking about Debra and it was soon clear that he was still hung up on her, despite his repeated insistence that he was "so glad it was over". Valda did not relish the idea of spending the whole evening lamenting on past relationships, so she tried her best to steer the conversation onto something more positive. Charles briefly dropped the Debra droning and began talking about a mate, who was opening a restaurant in Sea Point: apparently the local orang-utan population was out of control and many hairy invaders were plaguing Sea Point residents. Horrified home owners had walked into their kitchens to find unwelcome orang-utans helping themselves to bananas and shiny ornaments. They laughed and Valda was relieved that Charles once again appeared to be back on form.

It did not last for long though, and although Charles had not quite finished his wine, Valda felt inclined to order him an espresso.

'I have to admit, I was too hasty in calling off the relationship,' continued Charles, 'you don't know what you've got until it's gone. I guess you and Richard know all about that!'

The hairs on the back of her neck rose at the mention of Richard. 'I have no regrets, Charles, it was Richard's decision and I've moved on,' said Valda sincerely.

'I was talking about Richard,' said Charles. 'He hasn't been the same ... he was never in love with Sonja anyway ... and now that that's on the rocks ... I can sympathise with him ...'

Charles was speaking in an incoherent and disjointed way that was typical of someone after a few glasses of wine, yet what he was saying sent shock waves through Valda. On the one hand, she had secretly dreamt of the day when Richard would ditch Sonja, yet at this point, just when she was moving on, it was not what she wanted to hear. Anyway, could she trust what Charles was saying? Perhaps it was a minor relationship hitch and nothing more. Either way, there was no point in analysing it; she was not the same "hung up on Richard" person she had been, she had a new life and there was no way she was going down that road again.

Valda decided to make her excuses, the evening was really dragging and Charles' company was becoming more unappealing by the minute. Richard was on her mind all the way back to Camps Bay: was it really over between him and Sonja? Divine justice, thought Valda. If it was over though, then what were they doing in Joburg together? They are probably back on track. Valda chastised herself for even entertaining such thoughts, it was pointless and negative – whatever Richard did with his life was no longer any concern of hers and she longed to be back in Dubai, where such issues could not reach her.

Once at Ted's, Valda wasted no time getting to bed. Her body was craving sleep after weeks of overdrive.

Chapter Seven

It was 10.30 a.m. and Valda was heading along the now familiar route to Milnerton's The Avenue. It was far quieter that day and parking was easy to come by. Valda parked some distance from Joanna's and she stopped off at a small pharmacy first to buy some Ibuprofen – just in case the herbal sciatica relief didn't work, of course. Holding her white-and-green Western Cape Pharmacy paper packet, she once again entered Joanna's. The shop smelt no better than the day before, but the floor looked freshly wiped. There were no other customers. Valda took her time looking at the aromatherapy oils, while Joanna was in the back room behind a grubby curtain talking on the phone. Valda wondered for a second if that was where the budgie was kept. She appeared within a few minutes, once again flamboyantly dressed in an orangy-coloured shirt, hanging over red trousers. She immediately recognised Valda and said, 'The Devil's Claw, ya?'

Joanna reached for a box of Devil's Claw and placed it on the counter.

Valda took a deep breath and asked, 'I also want some sciatica relief.'

Joanna looked up and gazed with interest at her new customer. 'But of course. You wait while I look inna back, ja!'

Valda smiled and braced herself for whatever would happen next. Joanna returned within two minutes with a brown paper parcel about the size and shape of a packet of sugar. She placed it on the counter alongside the Devil's Claw and tapped away at the old cash register. Computerised tills had yet to reach this corner of the world.

'Two fifty, pleess!'

Valda was happy to oblige and passed the correct amount of cash over the counter. Within seconds, Valda was on the pavement with her two parcels, heading towards the car. Instead of driving straight home, she took a minor detour to check if she was being followed. Nothing out of the ordinary appeared to transpire and she was sure that the first hurdle had been negotiated successfully.

* * *

Valda was sifting through the kitchen drawers looking for a suitable knife. Things were chaotic in Ted's kitchen since she had left and nothing was in its logical place. Despite having been told specifically not to open the mystery package, it was the first thing Valda was going to do with it. Eventually, she found a pairing knife, which would have to do. She slit the brown paper, to find an inner lining of plastic. In her eagerness to see the contents and cut the brown paper, she had already managed to pierce the plastic and fine white powder was now pouring out.

'Just what I thought,' she muttered to herself.

Valda hastily grabbed a new plastic bag and put the whole package in it, along with an amount of powder she had brushed off the kitchen work surface. She weighed it on the kitchen scales: 300 grams. Those scales had been one of Richard's highly romantic birthday presents and this was the first time it had come in handy. She then took the package and thrust it under her bed, which was at that moment the best place she could think of. It was then time to plan the repackaging of it, for which she had an idea in mind, so Valda headed off to Century City.

The department store was busy, owing to a Thursday late-night shopping discount day. People were buzzing around as frenzied and hysterical as bees trying to land on something sweet. They were mainly women – the fairer sex become far less so when placed in a shop full of bargains, just watch the aggression show. The number of staff was nowhere near in proportion to the number of customers and tempers were becoming frayed. Valda was wandering in and out of the cosmetics counters everything had changed since her last trip there and she was constantly on the lookout for an assistant to point out what she was after. She could see a young member of staff walking towards the cosmetics, so Valda dashed over to collar her.

'Excuse me I'm looking for –'

'I'm sorry, I am with another customer, but I'll be with you as soon as I can, ma'am,' interrupted the girl.

'Yes, if you would, please; it's just a quick question,' said Valda with urgency.

There was no real hurry, but at the same time she was eager to get away from the shopping mayhem ensuing all around her.

It was not too long before the assistant returned. 'What I am looking for is the Dead Sea mineral salts, you used to stock them?' she asked.

'We have various sizes, does it matter which?'

'Yes, I'd like the salts in the 500 gram or 300 gram plastic container ... bottle thing, not the sachets. And I don't want the fragranced ones. Just the pure, natural type, please.'

The required bath salts were pointed out. The old, clear plastic bottle containers had been changed and they were now sold in colourfully-decorated plastic containers with fancy lids. Valda chose two 250g and one 500g bottle and then made her way to the long queue at the till, before hurrying into Cardies, where she purchased two sheets of tissue paper in different shades of pink, some bright pink glossy ribbon, some heart-shaped pink tags and a pink gel pen. She also bought herself a birthday card; it was, after all, her birthday next week. Feeling satisfied with her purchases, she nabbed the last table at Shelly's coffee shop and ordered some crumpets and tea.

Rather full and sleepy after her decadent meal, Valda headed home. Things were very quiet at Ted's and there was no chance of her being disturbed; however, just in case Ted decided to pop home during his lunch break, Valda took the precaution of ringing his office.

'Hi, Sheila, it's Val here, can you put me through to Dad?'

'Sure thing, nice to hear your voice by the way. How are things?' asked Sheila perkily.

'Great, thanks, much better, and you?'

'Fine, other than morning sickness. Brian and I are doing it all again!'

'Congratulations. When are you due?' asked Valda politely, while inwardly feeling totally indifferent.

'Oh, long time still to go – seven months, thank goodness; enough time to get organised. Listen; let me put you through to Ted.'

'Hi, Val.'

'Hi, Dad, just wanted the check what time you'll be home tonight, so I know when to put dinner on,' said Valda.

'Six, for a change – or at least that's the plan.'

Great, just what Valda wanted to hear. The house all to herself for the whole afternoon. She had her plan all worked out and if the practical outcome was as good as the theory, she was assured of success.

She went to her room to retrieve the parcel from under her bed. More of the fine white powder had seeped out, but that was no problem. Once in the kitchen, Valda emptied the contents of the brown paper bag into a big cake-mixing bowl, having weighed the bowl first. She then fetched the Dead Sea mineral salts, which were also white, but far larger and crystalline. "Don't hide a needle in a haystack; hide it amongst other needles", she had heard said once. She went ahead and without reservation, she placed the bowl on the scales and emptied the Dead Sea minerals into the bowl, until the combined weight of the "white mixture" was 500g. At first, Valda was unsure whether to fill the two 250g containers or just the one. The 500g container being larger and heavier would attract more attention, yet having two containers of the same thing seemed suspicious. Valda decided to go for the 500g container. She grabbed a spoon from the drawer and diligently mixed the two ingredients – she was sure that the fine white power would be easy to sift out at a later date and if not, she would worry about that when it came to it. Once thoroughly mixed, she placed a funnel in the mouth of the 500g container and poured the new substance into the container. A perfect fit. Valda congratulated herself on her ingenuity – the sea salts and the white power had blended together very well and in the childishly decorated bottle, it looked very "bath time-ish".

Then it was time to get artistic. Valda lay the two sheets of rose and candy pink tissue paper out on the dining-room table on top of each other. She then placed the Dead Sea salt's bottle in the middle and drew the tissue up around it in a Christmas cracker style, tightly tying the pink ribbon around the tissue at the neck of the bottle. She finished it off by decoratively trimming and shaping the edges of the tissue paper. The overall effect was very professional. She grabbed the pink gel pen and wrote on the card:

Dear Valda,
Happy birthday! Take time to relax!
Love Sarah
xxxxx

Valda laughed, it was rather tongue-in-cheek. Sarah was a common name; she knew at least six of them. She attached the card to the pretty parcel to complete the effect. The beauty of the whole idea was that anyone who wanted to could see the name and brand of the Dead Sea Salts through the tissue paper if they looked carefully enough. The lid was also exposed. A package wrapped in opaque wrapping looked so much more sus. Valda would later write herself the birthday card and put it in her case near to the parcel.

Still pleased and somewhat relieved, Valda jumped in her car and headed to the supermarket for some food. Spaghetti Bolognese and a Greek salad seemed like a good idea; it was high time Ted had a home-cooked meal, too. When she was growing up, Valda had cooked every night, as Ted's idea of home cooking was toast and jam.

On the way home, something caught her eye. It was nothing out of the ordinary, but it made her heart skip a beat. How could she have been so stupid? There, on the pavement, was a man walking his two dogs!

Valda had gone from feeling self-congratulatory to feeling panicked and she was so distracted that she cut herself twice whilst slicing the onion a few minutes later. Why had she not thought of this before? This was a major hitch.

Suddenly, out of the blue, an idea popped into her head and she raced for the phone, without even bothering to wash her hands. She flipped through the address book and dialled.

'Hello, I'm not in right now, but if you leave a message, I'll ring you back!' was the recorded message she heard on the other end of the line.

'Hi, Frances, it's Valda. I'm back in town. Ring me tonight!' Valda knew that Frances would be in touch, she was excellent at returning messages.

Feeling calmer, Valda headed back to the kitchen, not caring that the phone would smell of onion and garlic for weeks now.

It was eight thirty when Frances rang. Conversation with Frances was always easy: if the other person didn't feel very verbal, she would be delighted to do all the talking and yet when someone did want to share, she was always ready to listen. What's more, she was adept at looking at the funny side of life. They chatted for an hour about nothing in particular and then agreed to meet the next day at Frances' place.

Valda hated mornings and preferred to lie in as late as possible; however, Frances liked to start motivating herself early, so Valda had to force herself out of bed the next day. After some strong tea and a shower, she headed off to Frances', who lived only about five minutes away.

If Valda's life was parked on the corner of Shit and Crap Street, then Frances permanently resided there. Her life was a yo-yo event between the frying pan and the fire, with little in between. Frances was thirty-nine and had never been married, although it was not for want of trying: over the past few years, she had become addicted to "Net dating" and had travelled as far afield as Townsville, Queensland and Zagreb in an attempt to meet Mr Right, Mr Nearly Right or even Mr Half Right. All she had managed to do though, was to collect a bunch of forgettable memories, a stalker and some off-the-wall pen pals. Luckily for Frances, her sense of humour was healthy and she was always able to turn every experience into a joke. Valda and Frances had often discussed writing all those stories down and creating a book – the Internet was fertile ground for literature, if nothing else. Frances ran her own business, The Pampered Pooch, which sold an extensive range of pet products, food and accessories, and she had recently introduced her own aromatherapy range for pets. This was the main reason behind Valda's visit.

Valda rang the doorbell and was immediately greeted by excited barks and frenzied scraping at the door. She could hear Frances shouting inside. Valda giggled at the way Frances scolded the dogs like a bunch of rowdy toddlers. After a few minutes more hysteria at the door, Frances appeared to have succeeded in herding the dogs into the garden and was able to let Valda in.

'Hi!' Frances looked exasperated. 'Now you can come in; Beccy is being such a cow today!' It was the first time Valda had heard a pet dog referred to as a cow and she laughed out loud. 'Excuse the mess; I had seven members of my aikido class here last night for dinner!'

'Last night?' said Valda with surprise. 'You should have told me, I wouldn't have kept you on the phone for so long!'

'Oh, don't worry about that, they are all Japanese, only the instructor speaks English anyway.'

'Must have been a night of scintillating conversation then?' Valda smiled.

Frances went on to rattle off a list of the gastronomic delights she had prepared for her guests. The amount of dishes and pans in the kitchen bore testament to the extent of her efforts. Somehow, she managed to find some clean mugs and it wasn't long before a cup of coffee was sitting in front of Valda.

'You know what?' Frances began. 'You never even told me you were going to Dubai! Ted had to tell me when we met in the supermarket. That was naughty, you know!'

'I told as few people as possible – you know what it's like, you tell everyone you are going to do something and then it all goes west and you have to return with your tail between your legs ...' Valda tailed off, realising that she had been slightly tactless – she had just described exactly what Frances did at the outset of every doomed relationship.

'Tell me about it!' sighed Frances and without waiting for a reply, she launched into, 'I'll have to tell you my next bit of news touching wood and crossing fingers then. I'm not putting the mockers on this time!' Frances looked at Valda with wide eyes and a huge smile. 'I'm engaged.'

Valda was shocked. 'OK, don't just leave it there, details!'

'We met five weeks ago, he's 6 foot 2 (height was Frances' number one criterion in a man) and he's the funniest guy. Name's Ben and we met at the bank – he's the bank manager.'

'Not the one who wrote you all those nasty letters, surely?' Valda was becoming more and more aghast.

'Yes, him. We met when I had to see him about my mortgage arrears. Isn't life strange? He's divorced and he is going to move in with me next month.'

Valda offered her hearty congratulations and then sipped some coffee, while Frances left the room to dispose of another hairy gatecrasher; this time, it was her ginger cat. Valda wondered what was destined for her as far as love went: do the best things pitch up when and where one least expects? In Frances' case, searching for relationships all over the globe and being proactive had failed dismally; in the end, the right guy had been waiting down at her local bank the whole time. Maybe things come when you just give up, or maybe wanting something too much drives it away from you. Maybe it's different for everyone, anyway ...

'Hell-llow!' shouted Frances, and Valda's philosophising was cut short. 'You were miles away there; did I give you decaf by mistake?'

'No, I just have a lot to do before I fly back,' lied Valda.

Valda allowed herself to engage in some neighbourhood gossip, before getting to the crux of her visit. According to Frances, the residents of No. 17 had decided to undertake some garden landscaping and the results had been so outrageous that the rest of the street were up in arms and had formed a committee to present objections to the local council. It was obvious to Valda that some people did not have enough worries in their lives. The conversation about trivial neighbourhood disputes gave Valda an ideal leader though.

'Talking about neighbours, maybe you can help me out on this one ... I have a small patch of garden in Dubai and my neighbour's dogs keep crapping there. It's turning into a four-legged ablution block. What can I do to discourage them?' Valda had no garden and was not even sure if there was such a thing in Dubai; it was not the kind of thing she would usually notice.

'I have some red and yellow "No Fouling" signs,' said Frances with energy.

'I'm not sure if Dubai dogs can read English, Fran!'

Frances laughed, 'Yeah! Yeah! Very funny! I was being serious, they tend to embarrass the owner and they usually get the hint. I do have other methods though. What kind of dogs are they?'

'Small brown ones,' said Valda seriously.

'Right! I was thinking about the breed, maybe.' Frances sounded despairing.

'Does it matter?' asked Valda with concern and then quickly added, 'Could be a Labrador, Alsatian, terriers, there are quite a few, you know.' It was a horrible, muddled description and it was just as well Frances was in a love bubble, or she may have demanded more explanations.

'It doesn't really matter, I was just curious. Anyway, I do have something that will help. It's an aromatherapy dog repellent: totally green and harmless. I developed it myself,' said Frances with pride.

'Really, what do I do with it?' Valda said with excitement for the first time that moring.

'You just sprinkle it every few days around the area you want to deter the dogs from. It's highly concentrated, so it only takes a few drops. I put it around the washing line to keep mine away from my clean washing – works like black magic.'

'Yeah, but does it actually repel them, or does it just mask their old smells?' asked Valda.

'Oh no, it actually repels dogs, even if there are other smells around that may attract them.'

'Sounds tremendous stuff, can humans smell it?'

'No, that's the beauty of it. It's excellent, but I am having trouble marketing it; seems customers still prefer that useless pepper stuff!' sighed Frances.

'So it really will repel dogs, even if there is something else in the area whose smell may attract them?' asked Valda again, just to be sure.

'Yes, absolutely. To a dog's sense of smell, it is so pungent that it will drown out almost anything. Kind of like heavy-metal music,' laughed Frances, not having any clue of the importance her unique potion held for Valda.

Frances disappeared to find a little green bottle of her yet-to-be-named aromatherapy dog repellent. While Valda waited, she looked out of the kitchen window and observed that Frances' dogs were, indeed, giving the washing line a wide berth. Perfect, all bases covered.

Chapter Eight

It was Saturday morning and Valda was packing her suitcase. She had carefully placed her pretty "parcel" and birthday card in one corner of the case, having delicately sprinkled several drops of Frances' potion onto the tissue paper. The potion was, indeed, odourless and also colourless. Just to be safe, Valda sprinkled some of it on her duffel bag as well. She was feeling more and more confident now, which was essential if she was to pull this off. Being nervous and jittery was a sure way to get spotted and pulled aside by a customs official – it seemed they were more likely to pull aside a respectable yet uptight person than someone with the profile of a drug trafficker. Ted worked with a woman called Helen, who was the most upstanding of citizens: attended church regularly; was always immaculately dressed and had never even had a traffic violation, yet since she was terrified of flying, she always looked tense at airports and was inevitably searched every time, much to her humiliation.

Valda was also diligent in ensuring that all her documentation was in perfect order: she had recently heard of a case where a young British mother, travelling home to England after a holiday in Dubai with her family, had failed to fill in one of the relevant forms properly. As a result, she was taken aside and made to do a urine test; codeine (an illegal substance in the Emirates) was found due to the fact that she was on medication which had been prescribed in the UK. She had been promptly thrown in a Dubai prison and after six weeks of intense diplomacy had still not been released. It was a sobering thought and Valda knew that if she was caught, she would never see the light of day again. Dubai had a very strict anti-drugs policy, with the death sentence for traffickers; however, she had a good feeling that it would be OK.

She had a few minutes to go before leaving for the airport, so she quickly sent Brett a text, letting him know that she was heading back to Dubai, but that she hoped to see him sometime soon anyway. It was a bland, open-ended text that gave nothing away. She hoped that there would be a chapter two with Mr Morgan; he had seemed a fascinating guy.

After an emotional goodbye to Ted, Valda headed away to the airport. It had briefly occurred to her that she may never see Ted again, but she had quickly dismissed the thought; she could not afford any negative thoughts and so she focused on an event-free trip back.

She returned her hired car and checked her baggage in. She refrained from eating anything, as the flight to Johannesburg was often turbulent and her stomach felt wobbly as it was. Two o'clock came round quickly and she boarded the plane, taking no notice of the other passengers. The flight was uneventful and the two hours seemed to take forever. Valda tried to eat some of the plasticky food on offer in an effort to keep her mind off anything serious or negative and she listened in to the light-hearted banter of the university students around her, thinking back, with some pleasure, to her own varsity days. She watched the orange sands of the Karoo give way to the farmlands of the Free State – she was nearly there.

She was relieved when they touched down in Johannesburg and wasted no time in getting off the plane and retrieving her duffel bag. By the time she had reached the international departure lounge, it was 4.45 p.m. and boarding for the Emirates EK764 flight to Dubai had already begun. Valda checked in her baggage and went though passport control, looking very much like the seasoned traveller. She was wearing jeans, a white linen blouse and a khaki cord jacket, all chosen for desired effect. Valda casually browsed the duty-free shops, briefly toying with the idea of taking some presents back for her friends at Flanagan's. The idea was soon cast aside; such thoughtful acts were rarely appreciated and she was sure any gifts would quickly find their way to the back of a cupboard or into the dustbin. Valda was determined to buy something though – a friend had once remarked that a woman with an assortment of duty-free shopping bags looked innocent and was rarely checked by airport officials. After some deliberation, she purchased some twisted-brass African bangles, a jasper and silver beaded necklace and an elephant carving made of soapstone from different stores, ensuring that the elephant had its trunk up for good luck. Although she was not a superstitious person by nature, Valda often wondered whether superstitions had evolved from some universal truths – in times of danger, she was not going to arrogantly rule anything out.

She had successfully whiled away the time and at seven thirty, she could hear the first boarding call for her flight to Dubai. Valda wondered who her flying companion would be in cattle class that night. An advert at the CNA caught her eye and she decided that there was just enough time to buy a book for the flight. It was years since she had read a book and she had no idea what to choose, so she grabbed something from the best-seller shelf, paid and made her way to Gate 22.

Sitting next to Valda were two children, who were off on holiday to Dubai with their parents. Jonty and Kim, six and eight. Before take-off, they had already given Valda a synopsis of the latest movies on offer and a full initiation into the joys of Harry Potter. Their parents were blissfully relieved that their energetic offspring had found an in-flight playmate. Within thirty minutes of the flight, Jonty and Kim had mastered the entire in-flight entertainment system and had attempted most of the games on offer as well. Their attention then shifted to Valda's parcels and she was amazed to discover that her soapstone elephant and bangles amused them more than anything else – can't beat the simple things, she thought.

Dinner during that flight was a perfect example of what happens when you try and please all of the people all of the time: by the time the vegans, vegetarians, kosher-eaters, halal-eaters, diabetics and whatever other category there was had been identified and served their special meals, all the remainder were starving and very irritable. Rattled air hostesses were racing up and down with specialised meals, trying to find out who they were for – in desperation, passengers were just taking whatever came their way in the end. By the time Valda was brought her standard, no-nonsense meal, it was cold and in dire need of generous helpings of salt and ketchup.

Valda had some pink pills in her bag and was ready to take as many as she needed just to get some sleep. The last thing she wanted was to lie awake all night and be tense and frayed for her arrival. Jonty and Kim would just have to climb over her if they needed the loo.

Somewhere over Tanzania, she fell asleep.

* * *

'Hey there. Wake up, you! We're nearly there.' Jonty was excitedly tugging at Valda's sleeve.

She stirred and murmured something, just wanting to be left alone. But it was not to be, for the air hostess was anxious to deliver their breakfasts and wanted all passengers awake, so that she could complete her jobs before they landed.

'I think you should take these off and have some coffee, ma'am.' The air hostess spoke with authority as she pulled back Valda's eye mask and gave her a shake.

Valda reluctantly sat up and pushed her blanket aside; she'd had better mornings after the night before. Her head was muzzy and she felt nauseous – air travel never agreed with her. After rubbing her face and taking some deep breaths, she accepted her breakfast, which the air hostess was eager to thrust in front of her. The meal just looked like a yellow and brown blur and Valda replaced the foil lid before the sight and smell of it made her hurl. The coffee was passable, especially after adding the extra sugars, which Jonty and Kim had donated to her. Valda felt too off-colour to entertain any concerns about what lay ahead and so she sat back quietly while the caffeine and some anti-queasiness pills got to work. Fortunately, the plane was cleared to land promptly and the landing and taxiing out to their slot was free from the usual delays.

The more impatient travellers were out of their seats the moment the plane stopped moving, aggressively flinging open the overhead compartments and yanking out their hand luggage and general paraphernalia. Valda was always surprised that serious injuries didn't arise, what with all the Samsonite baggage flying around overhead. Passengers were jostling for positions near the door, despite the captain's pleas for people to remain seated.

Valda remained in her chair, waiting for the majority of the cattle to fight their way through. She was in no mood for push and shove – her head was too fragile at that hour of the morning. Once things had eased off, she reached for her overnight bag and made her way calmly to the doors. The walk to passport control was not a long one and she soon found herself in the large hall filled with passengers waiting in rows of queues to have their passports checked. For some reason, 4.00 a.m. seemed to be a particularly busy time for arrivals and the queues were long and sluggish. On a balcony above the arrival hall, Valda could see two serious-looking armed security guards scrutinising the sea of passengers. She wondered what they were looking out for.

She chose a queue and began to wait semi-patiently, occasionally glancing at her watch with irritation and sighing, while she shifted her weight from foot to foot. Dozens of spontaneous conversations had struck up around her – it appeared that men travelling alone were eager to find someone to chat to, particularly women; perhaps they surmised that it would give them an innocent appearance for the sake of anyone who may be watching. Valda wondered what percentage of people in that arrival hall had something to hide; probably fifty, she thought, smiling!

After a forty-five minute wait, she passed through passport control without further ado and started making her way to collect her duffel bag. As it turned out, she was one of the last passengers from flight EK764 to collect her bag. She retrieved it, flung it on a trolley and made her way to the "Nothing to Declare" exit. Valda had the feeling of almost being high and dry; she was eager to get home for a serious bit of shut-eye, and she was perhaps going just a tad too fast through "Nothing to Declare", when a uniformed officer held up a hand to catch her attention and waved her over. Although Valda's heart skipped a beat, her face demonstrated only minor irritation.

'You have your passport, please?' said the officer in an officious monotone. Valda obliged promptly; under usual circumstances, she would have been tempted to ask him how he thought she'd got that far without one, but this was not the day for insolence.

'Enjoy your flight?' asked the officer automatically as he flicked through the passport, briefly perusing her work permit.

'Not too bad, thanks,' said Valda with a polite smile.

'Please place the keys for your case on the desk,' he instructed Valda.

Things were not going quite as Valda had hoped, yet she was doing a remarkable job of looking unfazed. She reached into her pocket and casually handed him a set of keys. The officer lifted the case onto the large, nondescript table and fidgeted around until he found the correct key; he was then able to open the lock in the most in-adept of fashions she had ever seen.

He looked at the neatly packed contents of Valda's case, not appearing to know quite what to do next. Valda felt momentarily relaxed, guessing that this drone was not the brightest in the hive. He sifted around the edges aimlessly, examined a pair of her trainers and then came across Valda's pretty pink parcel. He paused for a moment and then lifted it out very carefully. Valda's heart was banging against her chest so loudly, she was certain that he would hear it. She prayed that the colour would not drain from her face and give away her inner panic. Her armpits felt moist and it was getting harder and harder for her to conceal her tension.

He peered at the parcel with amusement rather than suspicion and then he read the card with interest and placed the parcel on the counter. Reaching once again for Valda's passport, he looked at her birth date and said, 'A very happy birthday for Thursday!'

'Oh, thank you very much,' said Valda with genuine cheerfulness. She was not arrogant enough to feel out of the woods yet, but was hugely relieved nonetheless.

With that, the officer replaced the trainers and present carefully back in her case, locked it and handed back her keys.

'Thank you for your patience, enjoy your stay!'

Valda nodded, smiled and thanked him. She walked away towards the arrivals lounge and onto the taxi rank, where she hailed one of the many cream taxis. Relief had given way to a wave of excitement and self- congratulations. Valda felt such a rush, a surge of euphoria, as if she had just achieved something of note. She felt elated to have pulled it off.

Within a matter of fifteen minutes, she was in a taxi speeding away towards her flat. Unlike that very first early morning in Dubai when she had travelled to her hotel, this time, she felt confident and optimistic. The dreadful feelings of self-doubt, despair and pessimism had given way to a buoyancy and enthusiasm and she was amazed at how, in the last six weeks, her old self had made a return – with a vengeance.

Sleep was her only priority on reaching her flat; the dog-repelling duffel bag was abandoned somewhere in the middle of the lounge and that was where it stayed for at least the next six hours.

Valda woke up feeling cold and dazed; the powerful air-conditioning had left the air crisp and clear and being the middle of the afternoon, things were deathly quiet outside in the contrasting heat. Sleepiness and hunger battled for control over her and eventually, the hunger won and she wandered into the kitchen to search in vain for some food, which she knew would not be there. A couple of out-of-date yogurts and some stale rice cakes were the extent of the selection on offer, other than the soggy remains of a pear right at the back of the fridge. She decided that a shawarma from the Lebanese takeaway downstairs would do nicely and within ten minutes, she was halfway through one and feeling half-human again.

The Sheikh's package was on her mind once more; she was eager to deliver it, yet there was one final hurdle to overcome. After rummaging through the cupboards, she produced a fine sieve and placed it in a large, glass bowl. It remained to be seen how ingenious her idea of mixing the white powder and sea salts had been. She ripped off the pink tissue paper and the lid and began to pour the concoction into the sieve. Valda was delighted to find that most of the fine powder fell through the sieve with ease. She carefully stirred the remainder to make sure that the balance of the powder fell through as well. No doubt some of the sea salts had become mixed in with the powder, contaminating it somewhat, and whilst she was unsure what effect that would have on the final consumer, she could not have cared less. In her mind, she had done what was expected of her.

She weighed the powder – 289g. Close enough. Valda rewrapped it in plastic and then once again in the remaining pink tissue.

Being back at Flanagan's that night felt like being home. She was excited at the chance to get back on stage and had a slight feeling of anticipation at seeing the Sheikh once more. The pink package stayed in her sight at all times and she was impatient for the opportunity to offload it.

At around ten o'clock, Valda spotted Ahmed lurking in the shadows – that could only mean that the Sheikh had now arrived. Valda wasted no time in making her way up to his lounge.

He was sitting smoking a cigar as usual and although he was obviously aware of her presence, he did not look around to greet her.

'Hello, I'm back. I brought you a present,' Valda's greeting was awkward and sounded shallow and forced.

The Sheikh acknowledged her with a nod and a grunt as she set the parcel down on the table in front of him. If Valda had expected some display of appreciation or congratulation, it was certainly not forthcoming. Quite the opposite; indeed, the Sheikh's response was one of indifference. He stared ahead, caught up in his own world. He treated her like an employee, who had been sufficiently remunerated and to whom no further gratitude was owed. She stared at him for a few moments, angry and deflated, before adopting an arrogant body language as she offered the Sheikh a curt goodbye.

The performance which followed was lacklustre. Something in the Sheikh's manner – his cold, dismissive attitude to her today – reminded her of Richard. Perhaps it was partly the jet lag or emotional exhaustion, but for the first time in many weeks, she felt very alone and in need of reassurance.

Chapter Nine

The weeks that followed were typical of Valda's new routine: nightly performances and lazy days. Her attempts at sightseeing had tailed off, as they inevitable do when routine sets in and the novelty wears off. She avoided the Sheikh where possible and had made up her mind never to stoop so low as to carry out any of his dirty-work again.

She was neither happy nor unhappy; numbness was the best way to describe her emotional outlook. She felt lonely: lonely in a loner's kind of way. Although she craved some quality, one-to-one companionship, she had no appetite for a social life as such. Valda did buy a car as she had promised herself though: a black Mini Cooper, with the traditional white stripes. She had a weakness for sporty cars. The car was her new best pal and they had adventures daily, tackling the Dubai traffic together. Brett no longer managed to break into her thoughts; she had put him down to a brief yet pleasant encounter and did not expect to hear from him again.

About two weeks after her return from Cape Town, Valda read an article about a young Australian woman, who had been arrested in Thailand for smuggling drugs concealed in a surfboard. Compared to the imagination and sophistication behind that attempt, her own endeavour seemed childish and pathetic and yet it had been effective. However, it's often the simple things that work: when one tries to get too technical, there is more chance of a mishap. She put it down to beginner's luck and dismissed the thought; after all, she did not intend to do it again, so it hardly mattered.

It was another sunny, scorching day in Dubai. Valda was driving home after a frustrating attempt at buying her aunt a birthday gift in the Gold Souk. She felt as if every ounce of energy had been drained from her body; fighting off 1,000 salesmen, with 300,000 deals, needed an Olympian fitness level and the patience of Job. She had neither. Although her aunt's birthday was the following week and the present had yet to be purchased and posted in time, her immediate plans involved only a bed and a pillow.

Valda indicated and turned into her apartment block, with only the thought of five hours uninterrupted sleep in a chilly, air-conditioned heaven; however, much to her irritation, there was a car parked in her bay. After spitting out a string of expletives and threats, she looked about to see if there were any clues as to the whereabouts of the owner. She knew none of her neighbours; she came and went anonymously and had made it clear that any approaches would be rebuffed. But while she took scant notice of her fellow residents' appearances, she knew precisely which car belonged to which bay. She was also convinced that she had never seen this gunmetal Carrera GT in the bay before; in fact, it looked like it had been driven right out of the showroom.

'Gorgeous bit of torque,' marvelled Valda, 'but I want it the hell out of my place right now!'

Valda double-parked and reluctantly climbed out of the coolness of her Mini into the blistering afternoon sunshine. She checked out the smooth, elegant lines of the German car with both admiration and a pang of envy, wondering what it would set her back if she was to buy one. The car doors were unlocked, which was not unusual in Dubai, as crime rates were very low. A white envelope tucked under the windscreen wiper caught her attention and so she walked towards the front of the car and snatched at the envelope, sighing to herself. She assumed the owner had left a note, in case she came home and needed her parking space. The envelope, however, appeared quite thick and chunky; there was obviously more than a brief note inside. Without analysing any further, Valda ripped open the envelope irritably.

Inside was some sort of document resembling a car registration form, another envelope in bright red and various other bits of paperwork. Her immediate thought was that she had opened something private; however, she could not help but take a closer look at the documents. She immediately recognised that one of the forms was, indeed, just like the car registration document for her Mini Cooper. Her eyes jumped to the owner's name box and her heart started racing when she saw her own name there. Although the red envelope remained sealed, its contents were no longer a mystery. Valda's heart sank as her intuition was confirmed as correct – in the red envelope was a ticket to South Africa.

Back in her apartment, she laid the envelope's contents out on her coffee table. There was a handwritten note with it:

To my Dear Valda,
In appreciation of all your hard work!
Best wishes,
Sheikh Abdullah
P.S. Keys are in the glove compartment.

She stared at the note, while flicking ash off her fast-diminishing cigarette. If she had felt used before, she now felt like a highly-paid lackey. This time, she was determined not to cave in to the seventh deadly sin – greed – and she made up her mind to tell the Sheikh to stick his Porsche up his anal passage, but in the most diplomatic of terms, of course. It had to be done quickly, as she feared that the longer the car remained in her possession, the harder it would be to relinquish it; morality and common sense may once again succumb to materialism and desire. She wondered how he had known that cars were her weakness, he was either a master judge of character or she was undisguisably shallow. Either way, at that point, Valda could not bear the sight of the car; it sickened her and was a very concrete reminder of her deviation onto the "Low Road".

That night, she took the car keys, tickets and documents to Flanagan's, eager to return them as soon as she could. Her eyes scanned the crowds, waiting for the moment she would spot Ahmed or the Sheikh, when she would seize the opportunity to rid herself of the offending envelope in the knowledge that the sense of relief would be huge.

Valda was not amused though, when by two in the morning, there was still no sign of the Sheikh. He did not have a regular pattern and although she had no reason to expect him to be there that night, she had counted on it. At three, the waiting became too much and she decided to enquire of Jo if he was any more enlightened about the movements of the Sheikh.

Jo did, indeed, have the information she was after and it did not please Valda; the Sheikh was in Kuwait for a conference and would be away for several days.

Valda managed to survive the first two days without caving in to her desire to give the Carrera GT a spin. The keys on her coffee table tormented her constantly and there was little apart from eating and sleeping to distract her during the days.

By the end of the third day, she had managed to convince herself that there was no harm in a short drive. With the keys in her hand, she felt a surge of excitement, like an electric current shooting through her limbs, bringing life to her senses. It was years since she had felt this kind of positive anticipation.

There it was, exactly where she had found it three days ago, shining magnificently. For days now it had beckoned her, as if it was as eager as she was to go for a drive. In Valda's mind, cars assumed personalities and emotions and this particular one appeared to be her perfect match. Wasting no time, she opened the door carefully and eased herself into the low, sleek, lightweight roadster. She sensually ran her hands over the steering wheel, gently toyed with the gear lever, savouring every moment of foreplay with her 605-horsepower friend.

After a few more indulgent minutes, she eased the keys into the ignition, turned it over and – wow – the insanely powerful engine sprang to life. Still not sure what to do next, she sat quietly while the monocoque chassis gently vibrated.

Racing clutches can be testy and this particular one was one of the testiest – Valda stalled three times before successfully pulling off. Her new car was akin to an Olympic sprinter itching to get out of the blocks. With so much grit coming out of the engine, the residential streets of Jumeirah were hardly the right arena for this calibre of vehicle's virgin journey, but Valda was undeterred. Even on the main roads, her GT stayed well within itself, with only the rare opportunity of reaching 30 per cent of its top speed. No matter what, it was an orgasmic experience and she relished each moment.

Tuesday night and the keys and envelope were once again in her jacket pocket. She was certain the Sheikh would be there, although it had dawned on her that he may avoid her, just in case she did return the keys and refuse his new offer. The date on the plane tickets was fast approaching and she wanted things settled before that time.

At around eleven o'clock, the Sheikh and Ahmed did, indeed, arrive. Within twenty minutes, Valda was heading up the stairs to his private lounge area with the envelope. His arrogant confidence that she was now at his beck and call offended her. Valda was not good at saying, "No!" Usually, she felt the need to accompany a no with a heated argument, which would, she felt, be inappropriate this time – even though "inappropriateness" per se had never stopped her before. She had no idea what she was going to say.

'Aah, Valda, it's been so long!' greeted the Sheikh convivially.

Valda replied with an equally insincere smile. She immediately waved the envelope at the Sheikh, before placing it on the table. 'Thank you, but I think this is just too much and the answer is, no!' Her line had not come out as emphatically as she would have liked, but she turned to walk away with no intention of waiting for any response.

'Causing offence was the last thing on my mind, Valda! We have served each other well and for that, I am grateful to you. You, on the other hand, appear somewhat ungracious.' The Sheikh spoke with the calmness of a preacher. As usual, he was able to strike a chord somewhere in Valda's psyche and she immediately felt the urge to explain herself. Again, saying no was no simple task.

'Of course, I appreciate … you know … what happened last time … uhm.' Valda was losing her composure and she was in danger of letting the Sheikh see behind the cool-cat mask. 'But I don't want to take that risk again; I was lucky last time; if I do it again, who knows?' she shrugged and frowned and then stood, staring at the Sheikh. She was disappointed that she had let her guard down and had been honest, possibly not a good tactic, for she was sure that the Sheikh would have the sympathy of a brick wall.

'Please, sit down.' His gentle tone surprised her and she obliged. 'I understand your concerns, but I trust in your ability and intelligence fully. It is both of our risk and I would only ever choose a person of your rare discretion and ingenuity.'

Valda failed to see how he was at risk, but his praise of her had hit its mark once again.

'It is your decision entirely, but please, keep the car as a token of my goodwill,' he smiled warmly and spoke softly.

Valda remained seated, her mind blank. The Sheikh stared at the dance floor while he smoked his usual Cubans and Valda stared at him. She was as confused as the first time. She was also certain that the car would now be in lieu of a future unknown favour. She had informally decided, sitting there in the gloom, that she would rather make the trip to Joanna's one more time, than risk facing any "other" challenges. What the hell, she had pulled it off once. There was no decision really; the time to have said no was the first time, it was too late to turn back now.

The trip was just one day away. The thought of another tedious, uncomfortable night crammed in a plane was more troubling for Valda than anything else. As she locked the door to her apartment on the way to the work, she thought to herself about how doing something the second time never quite involved the same amount of trepidation as the first. It seemed to her as if, when one does something for the first time, one breaks down a barrier, which never rebuilds itself.

On her way to her car, she decided to empty her mailbox. The gold-plated flap of each individual flat's mailbox was shining and the whole reception area smelled of some fragranced aerosol polish or other. It was by no means her routine to collect mail on her way out, as her box was invariably empty: she had not yet been detected by the junk mailer's radar and her bills were few. She slipped in the key, opened the box and was mildly surprised to find three white envelopes inside. It was immediately apparent that the two franked envelopes were bills, but it was the third which captured her attention: a white envelope, address handwritten in Arabic, with her name written in Roman letters, postmarked Dubai. The envelope was thin and flimsy. Valda shoved the two bills back into the box, locked it and walked out to her car, curious to find out what the mystery envelope contained. Sitting in her Mini, she was slightly apprehensive as she ripped open the flap; she was half expecting some new ploy of the Sheikh's.

Inside the envelope was what looked like a newspaper clipping and Valda gently unfolded it. It was an article from a Dubai newspaper, *Gulf News*, which had been carefully cut, so that the date of the paper appeared. The title of the article was, "Sharjah Road Tragedy", from 21 June 2004 edition, and it reported the death of an Argentinian tennis pro Andres Perez, age 32, who had been knocked off his Ducati on the road from Dubai to Abu Dhabi late one night. It was a hit-and-run accident of which there were, at the time of the article, no witnesses.

Valda lit herself a JPS. Of one thing she was certain, the article was not random; it was meant for her and undoubtedly held some significance. Although it left her with an uneasy feeling, she made no other decision but to keep it safely.

Valda's second trip to Cape Town was brief and businesslike. It contained none of the apprehensions of the first occasion and within three days, she was safely back in Dubai. She had kept to her original strategy, minus the birthday card. More relaxed and confident, she had breezed through customs with no hiccups. The Sheikh was pleased, although this time she could not have cared less – the deed was performed out of a sinister obligation, rather than a need for approval.

On her arrival back in the foyer of her Dubai apartment, with her second consignment safely stashed in her duffel bag, she was not at all surprised to find an array of envelopes protruding from her letterbox. She grabbed them with her free hand and yanked them out of the box with a sigh: there were not that many, but the postman had not been diligent enough to shove them right into the box. Upstairs in her flat, she tossed the mail onto the coffee table, with no intention of having anything more to do with it until the weekend at least. Paying bills on time and dealing with paperwork were hardly her forte.

Valda wandered tiredly into the kitchen, debating whether or not she had the energy or the desire to make a cup of tea. Some chocolate biscuits were sitting invitingly on the counter and this swayed her decision; within a matter of minutes, she was lounging on the couch, feet on the table, tea in hand and three biscuits to the good. She switched on *Sky News*, just in time to catch the latest Premiership news, which, of course, was not complete without a rundown of Jose Mourinho's latest burst of sarcastic backchat. She drained her mug and promised herself that number five would be her last biscuit. As she lifted her feet off the coffee table, the bottom of her bootleg jeans caught one of the larger items of mail, causing most of the envelopes to tumble onto the floor. Her attention was immediately drawn to another stamped, handwritten letter. She snatched it off the floor and looked at it with irritation. It had been OK to pass the first such letter off as nothing – but the arrival of a second indicated that there was some definite motive behind them.

Curiosity was her predominant emotion as she carefully tore open the envelope. It was another newspaper article. This time, the cutting was from the *Khaleej Times*, dated December 2004: page seven of the Dubai Daily detailed the death of a 26-year-old waiter from Lebanon, who had fallen over the balcony of his twelfth-floor flat in Bur Dubai, after a night of heavy drinking.

Valda was surprised to receive this second article; she had decided to write the first off as a scare tactic of the Sheikh's – should she be having second thoughts again. However, if this was the case, then why would another article arrive while she was in South Africa performing another "mission" at his request? It made her uncomfortable and left her in no doubt that choosing the "low road" was never free from danger.

Not knowing what to think, she wandered into her bedroom and placed the second article safely with the first. She knelt down and reached into the back of her typically messy bedside-table cupboard and out came a white book, with golden-edged pages, and it fell open where the other article lay tucked away. Valda placed the second clipping there amongst the delicate pages of her Bible, along with the first article.

As she undressed, still troubled and uneasy, she pondered over attempting a prayer; something she had not done for years. Within her heart, there was a hint of desperation and she didn't dare to think how far down the abyss she was falling, or how quickly, for that matter. She decided against the prayer – assuming that God would show no mercy to those like her, who had eaten the apple of greed and stupidity.

You make your choices and then you pay the price – *c'est la vie.*

Chapter Ten

It was three weeks after her third trip to SA. Valda was about to leave Flanagan's, when she heard a voice calling out her name. If the voice was not recognisable, then the 6 foot 7 frame approaching from the shadows certainly was.

Her heart bounced; she blushed uncharacteristically and offered an unoriginal, 'Hi, what a surprise!'

Brett sauntered up in his "Harry Cool" way and said, 'You're not too bad!'

Valda felt like rolling her eyes; in typical South African male fashion, he was unable or unwilling to venture a slight compliment. She smiled at him and laughed, suddenly realising that like her, he probably did not know what to say, either.

'Are you in Dubai for long?'

'No, just for a few days' break. I've done all the regular joints, so I thought I would come and check you out.'

'You feel like a coffee? Not here, maybe Jumeirah, Moscow Beach?' she asked casually.

Brett smiled and nodded, so Valda gestured towards the elevators. There was an awkward silence as they waited for the lift to arrive and Valda leaned back with her weight on one leg, watching the numbers light up as the lift passed through the floors. Valda had initially been excited and very flattered that Brett had sought her out after all those months, but those naive emotions had soon given way to the more cynical feeling that he was after one thing, assuming her to be a sure bet. However, for the moment she was starved of decent conversation and stimulating company and so whatever his motives were, coffee still sounded appealing.

Once in the lift, she enquired if Brett had a car waiting or whether they should use her car. Brett had come by taxi, so Valda offered to drive them to Jumeirah's Beach Road in her Mini, which was parked in the basement. She was struck by a stab of pretentious regret that she had not driven the GT into work that day – that would have been sure to impress Mr Harry Cool, she thought. It would also have given him another wrong reason to like her.

On the way down in the lift, Valda sneaked a discreet peek at herself in the mirror. She felt rather sweaty and dishevelled after the night's performance and was eager to see what, if anything, she could do to enhance her appearance. She had been really surprised by Brett's arrival. She ran her fingers through her hair, which was about all she could do, being minus a comb and a make-up bag. Mr Cool was looking at her with an amused smile.

'Women can't walk past a mirror without checking themselves out!' he laughed and then continued, 'Sorry I missed you in Cape Town. You weren't there for long, were you?'

It sounded like a comment that required an explanation and so Valda answered, 'Well I was only there to sign papers ... the sale of my car and flat had come through and I needed to finalise things! It was not really a holiday.'

'So have you sold up in South Africa altogether?' Brett looked quite shocked.

'Well, yes.' She paused and then added, 'My dad is still there and so I can go back at any time. I am just making a total break with the past.'

'Would you really want to stay here permanently?' Brett asked curiously with one of his dark eyebrows raised, as if to say, surely not!

Valda delayed answering as the lift stopped opportunely to collect some guests and she and Brett were obliged to move towards the back to allow more room. 'I'm just living day-to-day; I haven't even thought that far ahead. Right now, it's a new start and it's working. When I've had enough of it ... well, we'll see.' Valda shrugged and tailed off. She knew in her heart of hearts that her future did not lie in Dubai, even though it was a welcome experience, but what exactly her next step in life was, was vaguer to her than ever. She had never been a planner, she always had faith that when the time came, the map for the next leg of her journey would magically show up. Their conversation was interrupted again as the lift stopped to allow the guests out into the lobby.

'So why the new start?' asked Brett.

'Meaning?' asked Valda flatly. She was realising that Brett had a subtly probing way of teasing information out of her and within a very short time, he had already unearthed a seriously sensitive issue.

'No one makes a new start if things are going well.' Brett's tone was very matter-of-fact.

Valda would not have taken well to that line of questioning from anyone else, but Brett's cheekiness was so sexy and appealing that she waived the urge to snap back. Nonetheless, she was reluctant to encourage any close-to-the-bone conversations at this stage; as far as she was concerned, she hardly knew Brett and they were still in a strictly small-talk zone.

'You don't like talking about the weather, do you?' Valda smiled and looked away.

'It's as hot as hell as usual; so why did you need a new start?'

It was obvious that he wanted an answer; Valda was not sure if it was simply a pointless fascination or whether it was motivated by a real interest in her. She was very relieved when the elevator stopped and the doors opened. As they walked into the car park, she gestured in the direction of her car, taking time to think of how best to respond and at the same time, bring to a close this segment of conversation.

'I got to the stage where everything in my life, relationships, career … everything, had run its course. I was stale and I really needed to find me again, find a way of making life mean something, something more than just a pointless procession. You can't really ever move on until you make that break.' She took a deliberately dramatic breath. 'Satisfied? Are you sure didn't major in psycho at varsity?'

'I'm a geologist, I like digging: maybe one day I'll find something worthwhile.'

For one moment, Valda detected a certain sad and lonely look in his eyes; perhaps there was another side to Mr Harry Cool.

They jumped into her car, where both were highly amused by Brett's long legs, which were almost up to his ears, despite all efforts to adjust the seat. Luckily for him, it was not a long journey to the Jumeirah Beach Corniche. Shortly after, they were cruising along the Sheikh Zayed Road. Even at two in the morning, air conditioning was essential to combat the stickiness of the night air. Brett and Valda were silent for a while, but it felt pleasant rather than awkward and they were both surprised at how relaxed they felt in each other's company. She certainly had no expectations and was prepared to just enjoy the evening for what it was: a distraction from the nagging fears and worries that usually overtook her mind at this time of the night. Although she, too, was very curious about her surprise visitor, Valda was less gung-ho about launching into questions; if she did, it was bound to ring of interrogation. She would have to approach things slowly.

'So where are you working right now?' she asked.

'Off Sumatra.'

'Isn't it kinda boring living on an oil rig?'

Brett smiled. 'For a woman, maybe; there are no shops, no hairdressers and no nail bars!' He laughed and then added, 'You're too busy to be bored. There's lots of people to talk to and good recreational facilities and besides, if the rig is close to land, you don't live on it, you travel in each day.'

'Any women on the rig?'

'A few engineers and some in the canteen – let's put it this way, there is no need for condom dispensers in the gents!'

They laughed and it was clear that they were both beginning to relax and loosen up. Brett continued to chat on about life on the rigs, Indonesia and his job. He was not one to go into morbid details and he flitted from topic to topic, touching lightly on each. His tales never lacked amusing asides; he obviously had an opinion on everything and was not afraid to air it. Valda was quite happy to sit back and play the role of a good listener; it was far more enjoyable, not to mention more light-hearted, than having to wade through any of her traumatic past. Brett was great at extracting details and the last thing Valda wanted was for him to think he'd come across as a woman with "issues". She was relieved that he was not one to talk at length or in depth about his job, for nothing bored her more; if you are not involved in a job, you really cannot relate to stories about it, they mean nothing to you – at least that's what she felt at any rate.

The journey was soon over and Brett was relieved to get out of his cramped position in the Mini. He made some crack about bringing the Jaws of Life next time she offered him a lift. She suggested they go to a cafe and they strolled over, while Brett continued to chat; this time about Dubai and its attractions; he obviously knew the place well. Valda reached into her pocket for her lighter and trusty companion, her JPS. She offered one to Brett.

'You smoke?'

'Gave up two years ago – it was sheer hell!'

'Wouldn't know the feeling, I've never tried.' Valda already had one in her mouth and was lighting up.

This time it was Brett who felt the need to say more. 'All that "Smoking Kills" stuff on the boxes was ruining the experience.'

'What I find a problem is that that's only a warning, not a money-back guarantee!' Valda smiled ruefully; she was only half joking.

They fell silent and she feared that she may be giving Brett an insight into the darker, more self-destructive side of her nature. After a short silence, Valda pepped up the conversation again by explaining why she frequented Izzie's cafe late at night and all the à-la-carte highlights. They concurred that it was cool enough to sit outside and found a fairly secluded table. After ordering, Valda decided that it was her turn to ask some questions about Brett's background and he obliged. He had been brought up in Kloof, Durban and had a sister, who was now married. He had been to a good school and had gone on to study civil engineering at uni. He divulged that a mixture of babes, booze and more time at the bar than in class had left him with two E's and three F's in his second year, which had brought his university experience to an abrupt close.

He continued, 'It was a real shock, I had been so used to just breezing along, thinking that everything would just go to plan, without any major effort on my part. My folks went wild!' Brett widened his eyes and then shook his head; the memory was plainly far from pleasant. 'I really lost it after that – had a string of deadbeat jobs and had to watch all my mates graduate and go on to find top jobs in industry, banking, whatever ... Not a good time!'

'So how did you bail yourself out?' Valda sat forwards, more than a little interested; this was certainly a life story she could relate to.

'I saw an ad in the paper – all about working on oil rigs: the great pay, the travel. It sounded fantastic and what's more, it was offering an escape route from home. I went to night school, got the necessary qualifications and eventually landed the job!'

Valda listened; she had more respect for Brett by the minute and was scaring herself that she was beginning to like him. Could this really be happening? she wondered. As he was talking, she admired his lean, tanned and youthfully rugged face, with his contrasting blue-green eyes. She could easily see that girls must be a major distraction for him – he could have anyone he wanted, at any time. All the more reason to keep very aloof emotionally, she thought.

While they ate, Valda made her contribution to the conversation by telling Brett all about her life in Dubai. She thought it best to focus on her as she was now, which was more relevant and more positive, rather than her past. There was an easy-going atmosphere between them and an obvious rapport and although they shared few interests, they did share a sense of humour and had a similar outlook on life. She was still unsure of Brett's motives though; at this stage, she was wondering if it was the company he sought more than anything else. She always tended to over-analyse emotions, rather than just waiting for them to develop.

It was almost morning and they were both ready for either sleep or another double espresso. Brett suggested they meet up at his beachfront hotel for lunch – a late lunch – the next day. Valda was thrilled at the prospect, even though it would mean a very long and gruelling day for her; she usually slept until five in the afternoon after a night's work.

Brett walked Valda back to her car; he had insisted on taking a taxi home, rather than having her drive him back to his hotel, which was some way away. As she slipped her car key into the lock, Brett leaned back against the car door with his arms folded and grinned as if to say, "Aren't you forgetting something?" They locked eyes and slowly moved towards each other for a brief kiss – it was more electric than passionate, as if they were both unsure and yet curious as to where it may lead.

As Valda drove home, the uppermost question on her mind was: what do I wear? Some seven leather jackets and a burgeoning population of jeans and T-shirts (many of which were dirty) hardly constituted a well-rounded wardrobe. When she had packed and shopped for clothes in the past, dating-clothes had been the last thing on her mind. There was no time to shop between then and lunchtime and so whatever she pulled out would have to suffice!

Valda was always at her lowest when she woke up and the next morning was no different; in fact, if she'd had the energy or willpower to get to the phone, she would have called off her date with Mr Morgan. After much procrastination and a strong tea, she surveyed her wardrobe, which offered no surprises. 'Shit-all to wear,' she muttered.

Her doubts had surfaced once again and a litany of questions and self-recriminations were racing through her head: why am I bothering;

I'll only get hurt; he's only after one thing; he can have anyone, probably has a girl in every city; I promised myself no more relationships; I'm not ready for this; I'm getting too deep too soon; I'm not over Richard!

Despite all the negativity, she did manage to throw herself together and a few hours later, she was looking very appealing in white jeans, with a black-and-white striped halterneck top, and white sandals. As she went down the stairs, she threw a glance at her mailbox; the sight of it sent chills through her, for she was tormented by fears of when the Sheikh would call up his next favour or when she would receive her next "mystery" letter. She had resolved that she was going to enjoy her day and that would certainly not involve opening any mail. She decided to use the Mini again, rather than risk any potentially uncomfortable queries from Brett as to how she had afforded such a rare and expensive car as the GT.

Brett's hotel on Jumeirah Beach was plush and boasted all the mod cons and facilities you didn't need. Brett was sitting on a couch in reception, perusing the sports section of a UK broadsheet. Valda was rather impressed to see him in a pair of khaki cargo trousers and shirt, rather than sporting his lived-in look, with exhausted old jeans and seen-better-days T-shirt. He looked smarter and neater, but had not lost that rugged look which so appealed to her. Despite feeling confident in her own appearance, Valda felt shy and a little awkward. As she approached the seating area, Brett sensed her presence, even though the reception area was filled with the hubbub of holidaymakers excitedly buzzing around, and he looked up from his paper. There was evidence of both shyness and mutual attraction in their smiles.

At first, they both felt stiff and there was little sign of the previous night's free-flowing banter. Without many words, they decided on an immediate lunch at the Al Maridani restaurant. Valda used the menu as a springboard for conversation the meals looked superb and she was keen to find out what Brett recommended. As it happened, Brett had never eaten there before; he was a strict burger and chips man, uninspired by "fancy food" as he called it. Although Brett offered to order a bottle of wine, he was more than happy to have a beer, while Valda stuck to Coke. She loved his lack of pretentiousness and down-to-earth manner. It was clear that he made no attempt to be anything other than himself.

The upbeat holiday ambience helped to relax them both and soon the conversation was once again flowing. Valda was beginning to feel very at ease with Brett and thus more willing to share her experiences.

They were waiting for dessert, when Brett leaned forwards and asked, in a sympathetic way, almost as if he instinctively knew what a painful issue it was for her, 'Why did your last relationship end?'

'He walked out of the door and never came back!' Valda laughed, initially unsure as to whether making light of the event was the best way to deal with it. Brett made no comment, but stared into her eyes as if he needed and wanted to understand more. She continued, half talking to Brett and half to herself, 'When I think back now, I realise that I contributed to the breakdown, but I took it very badly at the time. I was devastated, very let down and I felt betrayed – especially as he had someone else!'

'How do you think you contributed?' asked Brett quietly.

'Ever lived with a manic depressive?' Valda raised her eyebrows, laughed again and then looked down at her napkin. Brett remained expressionless. She then continued after a sip of Coke, 'OK, seriously ... during the last few years of the relationship, I was very depressed, nothing was going right for me and I needed some kind of emotional nourishment – reassurance from Richard. He was so cold. He was fastidious about health and fitness – couldn't tolerate smoking and drinking. But the more depressed I was, the more I did of both and he hated it. I was hard to live with, I admit.' She smiled and looked down at the table, for a moment feeling an unpleasant surge of those old, rancid emotions.

'So that's why you came to Dubai!' He looked satisfied, as if a huge mystery had been solved.

Valda took a deep breath and decided that this was the moment to clear something else up; she looked into Brett's eyes with sincerity. 'I'm not sure if I am over it,' she paused, not taking her eyes off Brett. 'I am getting there though!' Valda almost expected an unpleasant and uneasy moment to follow, but she was overwhelmed with relief when Brett's face broke into a warm and caring smile. No words were needed. Valda was sensing a new dimension to Mr Cool, a sympathetic and understanding nature. There was something else too; something far deeper – an emotional connection, which made sharing her darkest issues seem effortless and natural. The freezing fog that had hung over her life was beginning to be warmed away by Brett's appearance in her life.

Conversation resumed on a more superficial level during dessert, which was a delicious crème brûlée, delicately flavoured with rose water and pistachio. With every passing minute, they were more comfortable in each other's company. Brett shared his feelings of loneliness on the rigs with Valda and his quest for a meaningful challenge in life.

As the last morsels of pudding were scraped out of the bowl, Brett asked, 'So where do you see yourself in five years time?'

Valda smirked, 'That sounds like one of those trite questions they ask you at job interviews!' Valda spoke as if she was a job application veteran, when, in truth, she had only ever been to one interview in her life. She continued sarcastically, 'Let me see. Realistically, I would like to be the managing executive of Anglo American, happily married with four kids and a have a handicap of four!'

Brett leaned back in his chair, laughing and shaking his head. 'Wow, can I be the great man behind this great woman?'

'Why don't you answer your own question first?' suggested Valda.

Brett looked thoughtful as he stroked his chin. 'I would like to be living happily with someone who I care about deeply, but not necessarily in a conventional relationship. I hope that by then, one of the doors I have been knocking on will have opened to reveal my true path in life!' Brett finished and blushed, almost as if he was momentarily embarrassed by his metophoric turn of phrase.

Valda was impressed by the answer. She felt as if they both were allowing fate to take charge of their fledgling relationship, without clipping its wings under the weight of expectation. She replied sincerely, 'I want to be in love again one day and I want to share my life with that special person, but I am not pinning my happiness on the institution of marriage or on having children. I want to find myself, but I think that it could be more fun doing so with someone!'

Time had flown. After their late lunch, it was now evening and the new couple took a walk along the beach. The sea breeze freshened the air and it felt cool compared to the furnace-like temperatures of the daytime. Lights twinkled and were reflected in the softly lapping waters of the Gulf. The humid air had made Valda's dark hair take on a wavy texture and it was sensually dancing on her tanned shoulders in the light breeze. Brett did not take Valda's hand or even link his arm in hers at any stage; yet walking side by side, there was an unmistakable togetherness apparent between them. Valda disliked men who were too tactile – that was something that had appealed to her in Richard; he was a Virgo and was not fond of cuddling or any public displays of slushy affection and emotion. When he did do or say something though, he really meant it and that was what counted!

Brett was a real man and Valda guessed that in his world, an iron (ion) was a positively charged particle and not an item of household equipment for getting rid of creases. This endeared him to her even more. Even though Valda was a twenty-first century independent, working woman, she did not embrace the idea of her man helping around the house like many of her peers. Although the idea of the house-trained, domesticated husband, who happily shared chores, seemed to make sense, Valda knew that finding her man at the sink or watching TV while cheerfully doing the ironing would be an instant turn off.

'Do you have to go to work tonight?' asked Brett suddenly.

She thought briefly before answering, 'Uh, yes, I can't let everyone down, especially not at such short notice.' She continued after glancing at her Gucci watch, 'Speaking of which, I really should be getting back now.'

'Are you going home first?'

'No, there's no time, I'll change when I get there – I've got other clothes in my dressing room.' Valda grinned, 'OK, it's a broom cupboard, with a mirror on the door; but don't tell Madonna, she'll get jealous!'

'I'll come with you!' said Brett eagerly. Valda looked at him for a second with big eyes and Brett immediately sensed that she had reservations. 'Unless, that doesn't suit you ...?'

Valda would have loved to stretch out the magic of the evening long into the night, but the thought of Brett at Flanagan's made her uncomfortable. Flanagan's was synonymous with the Sheikh and Valda wanted to ensure that she kept Brett well away from his seedy influence. Valda was not able to rationally explain why, but intuitively she felt the need to keep her new romance out of the Sheikh's sphere of influence. At the same time, she hardly wanted to give Brett the impression she was keeping secrets or hiding something. Weighing up the two mentally, she found herself saying, 'Sure, of course you can come – but hey, it's your own fault if you're bored shitless by twelve o'clock.'

Ten minutes later, Brett was once again in the confined space of the Mini and they were heading for the Burg Emir. Valda was very quiet on the journey and she explained this to Brett as a need to think about various issues relating to the band, equipment and the evening performance. She was, in fact, playing over how she would handle the possible rendezvous with the Sheikh.

The golden doors of the lift opened and Valda, Brett and several young German tourists filled with anticipation of a hedonistic night out poured out into the elaborate foyer, at the end of which was the entrance to Flanagan's. At one end of the foyer was a large, rectangular window framed in an Ulf Moritz fabric of gunmetal-coloured organza with golden embroidery. Valda pulled aside the silky voile and pointed outside. 'Great views of the city, huh?' Brett leaned forwards, with his hands on the sill, and stared into the night. She followed his gaze, but he appeared to focus on nothing in particular. It had suddenly gone very quiet around them. Valda touched his upper arm lightly and said softly, 'I haven't had a day like this for years. Thank you!'

Brett turned and slipped his arms around her waist; he gently drew their bodies together. Valda reached up and wrapped her arms around his neck. She gave him a big smile, just before their lips met in a passionate kiss. While the kiss was sensual and electric, what Valda enjoyed most was the feeling of closeness and she held him tighter and tighter, revelling in the warmth of their embrace. In that one moment, all the emptiness of her life was a distant memory and time stood still.

Their moment was brought to an end as the lift once again opened to deliver yet more excited clubbers to the floor. Brett took her hand and they walked towards Flanagan's.

They wandered towards the bar area and Valda purchased a beer for Brett, before she made her way to her "dressing" room.

'Wait a moment!' shouted Brett after her.

'What?'

Brett walked up to Valda and once again slipped his arms around her. 'I don't think I thanked you for today yet!' They embraced again, but this time there was no kiss. Valda made no attempt to pull away, her head was on his chest and she could have cried; there were so many emotions shaking the very core of her.

Unexpectedly, Brett's arms slackened around Valda and she looked up to see that he was staring over her shoulder. At the same time, she felt the psychic sensation of cold eyes glaring into her back and she turned to see the Sheikh and Ahmed. The latter looked doleful, as per usual, and the Sheikh had the expression of someone who had just been exposed to the smell of gangrene. Valda pulled away from Brett and immediately launched into an introduction.

'Sheikh Abdullah, hello! This is Brett Morgan a geologist friend of mine; he's on holiday in Dubai.' She gestured towards Brett. Without pausing, she continued, 'Brett, this is Sheikh Abdullah bin Rashid Al Khaimah, owner of Flanagan's and the Burg Emir, and this is Ahmed,' she paused, 'Sheikh Abdullah's PA!' PA was the best way she could think of to describe Ahmed at that particular moment.

Ahmed's face immediately broke into an uncharacteristic yet genuine smile; he was obviously not used to being considered a person worthy of introduction.

The Sheikh remained surly and he did not extend his hand, although he did acknowledge Brett with a nod and a curt, 'Good evening.'

The Sheikh made a polite and cold excuse to Valda and disappeared into the foyer, after exchanging mutually hostile glances with Brett. Ahmed was close on his heels.

The encounter had left Brett and Valda experiencing an unexpectedly awkward moment together. Valda looked into Brett's eyes and detected both disappointment and confusion. Brett's expression suddenly changed to one of anger. 'Is there something I should know about you, Valda?'

'You had better explain yourself; I'm not in the mood for cryptic puzzles!' said Valda tensely.

'The Sheikh is a very wealthy and important man; you have an extremely casual, familiar manner with him.' Brett's face was beginning to redden.

'I've known him for six months, what do you expect me to do, kiss his feet?' retorted Valda sarcastically.

'Six months!' exclaimed Brett. 'I've never seen a Westerner act so offhandedly with someone of his stature, even when they've been acquainted for twenty years!'

Valda decided that the best way to deal with the situation was to go on the offensive, so rather than resorting to a whiny, apologetic tone, she sneered, 'Yeah, I know what you mean, most people are so high up his ass, they have shit round their ankles, but that's not me!'

She turned and marched away. In moments of anger she was impulsive and impetuous and would throw caution to the wind. Despite the pleasures of the day, she stormed away, not caring whether Brett followed, stayed put or walked right out of her life again.

There was no danger of the latter. Brett raced after Valda and with his height, he only took a couple of strides to catch up with her. 'Where are you going?' he demanded.

Valda sensed that his anger was mixed with desperation.

'I am not prepared to continue this conversation and certainly not in public!' she replied forcefully.

Valda turned away from Brett and pointed him in the direction of backstage. Inzie and Jeff looked surprised as Valda and the tall stranger walked into the featureless room, which lay behind the stage area. Valda directed Brett to a more private room off the main backstage area. Then she closed the door and they were alone with the amps, guitars and mike stands, which languished amongst metres of cable and discarded paper cups. Valda folded her arms and looked at Brett. If he had more to say, now was his chance.

Brett ran his fingers through his hair and sighed. 'Sorry!' He was looking at the floor, but then he looked up again and met her gaze. 'Sorry for making something out of nothing!'

Valda sat down on the edge of one of the older amps and smiled at Brett, indicating that his apology was accepted. 'I am sure that the Sheikh has certain things,' and she raised an eyebrow, 'on his mind, but he is barking up the wrong tree with me and he knows it!'

'I've heard a lot of stories ...' Brett sighed, 'and I am sad to say that they are not all urban legends!'

'The Sheikh makes me very uncomfortable; he alludes to many things, but I just keep him at bay. I think my best defence is that he can't figure out how to take me. He's the one reason I know I can't work here indefinitely.' Valda was being as honest as she could, without revealing that she was, indeed, caught up in one of the Sheikh's inescapable webs.

Brett came very close to Valda and looked into her eyes seriously. 'If ever you need me, I'll be on the next plane, wherever I am!'

Tears flooded into Valda's eyes; she laughed and waved her hand in front of her face, trying to make light of this display of emotion. She was unable to speak for a while and when she did, it was to casually say, 'Thanks, mate! I might take you up on that!'

Valda took frequent breaks to make sure that Brett was not bored or agitated – he seemed to have no particular music preference and she was at pains to know what to sing to impress him. He seemed to look very contented just sitting there watching both her and the clubbers. Valda felt energised and threw herself into every song with passion; that night, all the words meant so much more.

They left immediately she was done and after much debate, Brett conceded to allow her to drive him back to the hotel.

The car park of the hotel seemed very quiet and Valda parked and switched off the engine. She looked at Brett, who was staring straight ahead. 'What are you thinking?' she asked.

'Did I tell you I fly back tomorrow afternoon?' he said with great regret.

Valda nodded. 'You said something of the sort, yes!'

Brett suddenly turned, twisting his long body around awkwardly to face her, his left knee becoming wedged between the gear lever and the handbrake, and Valda giggled.

Brett's face was serious. 'Spend the night with me!' he whispered earnestly.

Valda was not caught off guard; she had rehearsed this moment as inevitable. She put her hand on his shoulder and when she spoke, her tone was gentle yet firm. 'There's plenty of time for that down the line; it's not right for me yet. You've hooked me and I am counting on you visiting Dubai regularly,' then she added, 'but next time you can check in at my place!' Brett looked disappointed, but he half smiled and nodded. 'I'll pick you up and take you to the airport,' suggested, or rather ordered, Valda.

They kissed once more; passion overriding the pain and discomfort caused by their awkward, confined location. His arms held her firmly and his hands explored her body with zest and aggression but, in contrast, his kisses were gentle and tender and came in sporadic bursts, which teased her lips. It had been a day of rare passion for both of them.

Valda awoke with her heart pounding; she was drenched in a cold sweat and it felt almost as if it was the morning of an important exam. She had been dreaming strange, muddled, twisted dreams, which had led her to awaken feeling disorientated and stressed. She reached for her cigarettes, doubled up her pillow and lay back, lighting up her first of the day. As she lay watching the smoke swirling up to the bland whiteness of the ceiling, she thought back to her dream. Within the manic montage of images which made up her dream was a recurring theme; she was sitting at a wrought-iron table in a beautiful summer's garden eating raspberries, when a raven had landed on the table, startling her. Valda hated birds. The dream had moved on and she was with Richard; they were on Clifton beach and he was kissing her and caressing her body. It had begun to rain, but they had stayed put, passionately embracing. Suddenly, it was Brett whose arms she was in – they were also on a beach and the tide was coming in quickly. They ran and ran to escape the tide, but the waves were too powerful and they were dragged underneath the foaming water ... She had woken up at that point.

As she flicked some ash into a dirty coffee cup that had been left next to her bed, Valda laughed at herself. She saw no point in analysing dreams, yet it was something she invariably did from time to time, especially when the images were so strong and vivid.

Although she had gone to sleep in a love cloud, Valda had woken with a decidedly cynical slant on Brett. As she took another drag, she scolded herself for allowing herself to become so thoroughly engrossed in the romance of the previous night. What am I doing? It's too soon to feel this way. I hardly know the guy! I promised myself I would keep cold and that I would never allow myself to get so deeply involved again, never mind so quickly! She stubbed out the last of her fag and swung her legs out of bed and walked angrily to the shower, cringing when she remembered that she had asked Brett to actually stay with her next time he was in Dubai! What an idiot, she thought.

After a giving herself a thorough pep talk in the shower, which involved a thousand negatives about Brett and relationships in general, she was ready to ring him and say she was too busy to take him to the airport. But the phone was already ringing as she re-entered the bedroom. Mental telepathy, she thought.

'Hello.'

'Hi, gorgeous!' It was Brett's deep voice.

'Hi.' Valda was unwilling to repay the compliment.

'There's plenty of time until I have to be at the airport, so let's have lunch first?' suggested Brett with enthusiasm.

'I am a bit busy this morning, but I'll try to be there as soon as I can.' Valda's voice was flat and she was purposely non-committal.

Brett was silent for a second as if perplexed by Valda's tone, but he continued cheerfully, 'Are you sure there'll be space in your car for my luggage?'

'What happened to Mr I Travel Light?' she asked sarcastically and without humorous intent.

Brett replied, sounding deflated, 'Just checking. I'll see you later then?'

'Sure.' Valda put down the phone and congratulated herself on her regain of control; she was pleased her emotions were in check again.

It was not surprising that she chose her old faithful leather jacket to wear that day!

Two hours later, Valda and Brett were sitting having lunch together. The restaurant was busy and the general chatter around them seemed to fill in the long, silent intervals between them. Valda had been rather cool and what conversation there had been had revolved around the menu and Brett's impending return to work that Saturday. They were halfway through their meal, when Brett suddenly threw down his knife and fork, leaned back in his chair and after a deep and dramatic breath, demanded, 'Do you mind telling me what the hell it is that I'm supposed to have done wrong?'

'I wouldn't be here if you had done something wrong!' Valda barely looked up and she continued eating.

'Well your attitude today stinks!' growled Brett.

Valda looked up, swallowed and paused thoughtfully, before saying quietly, 'I'm not ready for this yet, things are moving too fast for me!'

'Too fast!' Brett was furious. 'Any slower and we'd be in reverse!' His words had been delivered in increasing decibels, climaxing in a very loud "reverse". There was a noticeable hush in the restaurant as eyes fixed on the young couple. Brett immediately looked around and held up his hand in a half-hearted apology.

Valda looked with scorn at the other patrons; she knew that their superficially concerned faces were designed to conceal their miserable fascination with the argument at table 23. They were gripped! 'Must be starved of their daily dose of soap operas,' she muttered under her breath.

Brett leaned forwards, with his left elbow and arm on the table and his right hand on his hip. He looked into her eyes with compassion. 'I know you've been badly hurt, we all have! You've had the shutters down, but I thought you were beginning to open up – don't turn back now!' He took a deep breath, 'If you can't see that something great is happening here, you may as well check in to a convent and take a vow of celibacy!' With that, he got to his feet and threw his napkin disdainfully onto the chair.

Valda looked at her plate; she was once again moved at Brett's level of understanding and also by his forthrightness. She did not want to let him see the tears in her eyes.

'You look more interested in that piece of boiled cabbage than in me and so I am going to clear out my room. I'll meet you in the foyer!'

With that, he left the restaurant. Half the patrons followed him with their gaze; the rest remained focused on Valda.

A concerned-looking waiter rushed over to the table. 'Should I charge the meal to Mr Morgan's room?'

'No!' said Valda moodily. 'I'll fix it up, thanks!'

In Deira City, another argument was breaking out.

'You led me on!' shouted Justin.

'You led yourself on!' retorted Larissa.

'I was picking up the signals!'

'Then your receiver must be faulty, is that my fault?' Larissa was exasperated.

'You've screwed my life around for the past two years!' Justin was sounding desperate.

'I can't help it if you choose to live in a delusional fool's paradise.'

'You're the problem, you don't know what you want, Larissa!'

'Maybe! But I have a pretty good grasp of what I don't want!' Larissa's voice had an air of finality in it and she motioned towards the door. As Justin left, Larissa wandered back to her bedroom and collapsed onto her soft white bed, relieved. She felt as though it was the last day of school term. 'Loneliness can't possibly be the worst thing,' she muttered. 'It certainly has stiff competition from living with possessiveness, jealousy, control and manipulation! Who needs relationships?'

* * *

Valda didn't see Brett initially; she looked around the reception area and noticed what looked like his duffel bag, so she made her way over to it and bent over to pick it up. As she straightened up, there he was, standing right over her. He had changed into a crisp white shirt and navy sports jacket. She extended her free hand and touched his hand softly, before looking up into his eyes. 'I've never believed in convents!'

Chapter Eleven

Brett and Valda shared a coffee at Dubai International before saying their goodbyes, which, bearing in mind the day's events, they kept brief and light-hearted. Brett was resolved to return to Dubai within the month and despite herself, Valda was already looking forward to it. She waited at the airport until his flight to Singapore had safely departed.

She felt a twinge of emptiness as she returned to her car; it was as if she had been caught up in a pleasurable tornado, yet the tornado was now over and she was again left to dwell on the less savoury aspects of her existence. She felt at a loose end and spent the rest of the day wandering aimlessly around the shops and making the occasional coffee and cigarette pit stop.

She arrived early at Flanagan's that night – no one else was there and she tinkered around with the piano, lost in some emotional limbo-land! She was so caught up in her reverie that she did not notice Ahmed approaching. He spoke softly, so as not to startle her, and she turned to see him standing near the edge of the stage. Although he was technically the Sheikh's bodyguard, he reminded her more of a trusty Labrador than a feisty Rottweiler. She smiled at Ahmed; he looked immaculate yet downcast. Valda surmised that like herself, he was also struggling against the painful shackles of the Sheikh's employ.

'I have something for you,' said Ahmed plainly, while he held out a white envelope.

Valda regarded the envelope with a dubious and unimpressed expression on her face, before she reluctantly raised herself from the piano stool and crouched down on the edge of the stage to take it from Ahmed's outstretched hand. It bore the Royal Stamp of the Sheikh.

Ahmed was watching her closely. 'An invitation to dinner!' he uttered.

Valda nodded, not bothering to ask for more details. She slowly rose and walked over to the piano, where she lay the envelope down, not intending to open it any time soon. She sat down at the piano again, staring at the keys, which soon melted into each other, black and white turning into a grey blur. A few minutes must have passed, before she realised that Ahmed had not moved from his position at the edge of the stage. He was staring at her. Valda turned to regard him. She was puzzled by his expression, which was rather grave, and yet there was a light in his eyes that she had not seen before; it was as if he had briefly come alive.

'The Sheikh is giving you a long rope, Valda!' Ahmed spoke slowly and there was something foreboding in his tone.

Valda was not sure how to reply, so she shrugged her shoulders and adopted a confused look, before looking back at the keys. Long rope? Long rope with which to hang yourself, she wondered. She looked back at Ahmed and their eyes locked once more, before Ahmed nodded, turned and left Flanagan's.

The Sheikh's letter turned out to be nothing more alarming than a simple invitation to dinner at one of his many restaurants, but Ahmed's words played on her mind: was it a warning or another cryptic scare tactic? Ahmed's deadpan face was hard to interpret, but his vibe had been unthreatening and Valda had the feeling that what he had said had been of his own accord.

Later, in her apartment, Valda sat quietly smoking and yearning for someone to talk to. She could always ring Brett and pour her heart out, but she did not want to involve him or to jeopardise their promising relationship. 'If only there was someone I could talk to,' she sighed as she slumped back onto the couch, gazing hopelessly at the ceiling.

Valda began to think of Brett. She wondered if he had arrived at his hotel in Singapore yet and for the twentieth time that night, she flicked open her mobile to check, in vain, whether or not there was a message. Images of Brett with tantalising and exotic Indonesian women flooded and taunted her mind and she scowled, once again regretting having let her emotions off the leash. An array of negative scenes washed over her mind and that dark cloud of depression, which never seemed far away, once again blocked out those sunny rays of the last few days.

On impulse, Valda bounced off the couch, vowing not to succumb to any negativity. She marched determinedly into the kitchen and began to scour the fridge for something easy and filling. Within a few minutes, she had an open cheese sandwich grilling in the oven. While waiting for the cheese to go all crispy, she reached for an old newspaper in which to wrap her empty soda bottle before throwing it away. She was just about to scrunch the paper around the bottle, when something caught her attention:

Taurus: ... a week of mixed messages romantically, so beware of getting your wires crossed. In all aspects of your life, do not act in isolation; remember to seek out good advice.

It was the first time Valda could remember finding her horoscope useful and she continued to scan the text of the scrap of newspaper, until she found what she was looking for.

'Now that's just what I need!' she exclaimed.

Sitting on the couch with her toasted cheese sandwich, Valda was almost smiling. She felt as if some kind of help was on the way and for the first night in ages she had a peaceful, dreamless night's sleep.

Although she would not previously have described herself as a person who suffered from mood swings, Valda was developing the tendency to swing between a state of hopeless despair and worry to one best described as an "ignorance is bliss" complacency. It was the latter attitude which best described her demeanour as she flipped through her wardrobe searching for something to wear for dinner with the Sheikh. A mental cut-out switch had tripped and she was ready to face whatever dinner with Mr Giddy Limit entailed.

It was more than twenty-four hours since Brett had departed for Singapore and he had yet to make contact. Valda could not help but wonder what had transpired, despite herself. She toyed with the option that he had moved on to the next entry in his little black book, but although her head favoured a severe brand of cynicism where men were concerned, in her heart she felt that this was simply the least-likely scenario. She was tempted to send him a text message, worded so as to convey concern; however, she immediately decided that a, "Hope u r OK!" style of text would smack of desperation and neediness. She remained steadfast in her resolve to ensure that he did all the running. She had never been of the brand of woman who wanted a man at heel; she needed to feel loved and wanted to an immeasurable degree, but at the same time, she believed that true love did not grow out of emotional manipulation and control.

Patience was not amongst her top forty qualities and the itch to check her mobile for messages or voicemail was akin to a mental eczema. In a perverse way, she welcomed dinner with the Sheikh – it would be a welcome distraction.

As Valda drove towards the Burg Emir, she smiled at herself, amused at how a trivial matter of the heart had managed to force itself to the forefront of her mind, beating off stiff competition from graver concerns, which should have dominated her thoughts. Ted's sister had always warned Valda not to "cross her bridges before she came to them" – Valda had no idea what the Sheikh wanted to propose this time, but she had her own little plan on how to deal with the uncertainty of her immediate future.

Ahmed was waiting for her at the ornate entrance to The Maghdi, a salubrious and elegant restaurant within the plush surroundings of the Emirates Towers. The entrance was guarded by two life-sized, carved wooden camels, draped in Persian-style rugs threaded with gold. The light beige-and-gold marble floor gleamed, as did the multitude of gold-plated fixtures and fittings, which adorned every inch of the establishment. Waiters, immaculately dressed in claret-and-cream uniforms, hurried efficiently between the tables and the vast array of palms and other potted plants. The restaurant was only a quarter full and the atmosphere was relaxed. Most of the patrons appeared to be Westerners and it occurred to Valda that the Sheikh enjoyed surrounding himself with Western influences. Before she had time to take in the sparkling chandeliers and cut-glass vases, she noticed the Sheikh, who was sitting at a very large yet slightly more secluded table.

As she approached the table she was struck by the fact that he looked more at ease and more refreshed than usual. They exchanged their usual false greetings and Valda chose a seat to his right. She felt more self-assured and relaxed than she usually did; however, as with their previous encounters, the Sheikh was entirely impervious to her mood. He was an immensely experienced and hardened man, unlikely to be fazed or humbled by any experience, and certainly not by Valda's emotional state.

She was no longer enchanted or fascinated by him, but she remained aware of the very powerful and sinister air that he exuded. Perhaps it was the mystique of a culture and religion that she scantly understood, maybe it was intuition or maybe it was purely imagination, but whatever the cause, she had never before felt intimidated by anyone at all and she had to respect the Sheikh for that.

He ordered for them both and politely lit her cigarette and his Cuban cigar with his solid-gold lighter. He then placed the lighter on the table and leaned back, inhaling deeply. Valda picked the lighter up off the table; she had admired it for some time and had decided to grab the opportunity to examine it closely. On one side, baguette diamonds were arranged to form the Sheikh's initials in Roman lettering, while on the other side, smaller, more rounded diamonds spelt out something in Arabic – it may have been "God is Great", "*Allahu Akbar*", a common theme in Arabian jewellery. She placed it carefully back on the table and took a sip of the ice-cold, sparkling mineral water.

The Sheikh reclined back in his chair in a rather nonchalant pose, while Valda observed the growing number of diners occupying the tables and filling the room with laughter and chatter as she slowly smoked her way through another cigarette. The starter was ice-cold balls of galia and honeydew melon, arranged decoratively on a gold-rimmed plate with a mint leaf.

'The food here is much superior to that of the Al Maridani,' uttered the Sheikh as his plate was set before him.

Valda was immediately aware of the reference to her dinner with Brett. Her stomach twisted slightly at the realisation that she was, indeed, being more closely watched than she had first imagined. She gave the Sheikh a sarcastic grin and retorted, 'Well, whoever you have watching me must be having a hard time staying awake, as my lifestyle hardly creates movement on the Richter scale!'

The Sheikh let out a hearty guffaw and then threw back his head, all the while keeping his mocking eyes on Valda. He said nothing.

'You really are a character!' sighed Valda, more to herself than anything else, as she dug her fork into a melon ball.

For the very first time, a look of mild surprise flickered over the Sheikh's face; the mocking smile was gone and there was a thoughtful look in its place. Valda turned her attention back to the plate of orange and green fruit; her offhand comment had somehow found a chink in the immaculate facade of the Sheikh – although the reason for it was inexplicable.

An electronic jingle interrupted the silence and the Sheikh reached into the starched folds of his throbe to retrieve his platinum-encased Vertu mobile phone. He leant back in his chair as he sternly conducted a conversation in Arabic. Valda took the opportunity to sneak a discreet look at her watch; the evening was plodding along: the Sheikh had rambled on about the growth in the construction industry in the Emirates and Valda had found it hard to feign even mild interest. Ostensibly, there was more to dinner than an initiation into Emirates' commerce and Valda was nervously awaiting the crux. She decided to flick open her own mobile to check if Brett had tried to text her, but she sighed with disappointment on finding that once again, there was no flashing-envelope icon. The Sheikh had ordered some kind of chicken for the main course and although the description on the menu had sounded less than appetising, she was so hungry she was eager to give it a try. It was some time before the Sheikh clicked off his state-of-the-art mobile phone, but as soon as he did so, the attentive waiter hurried over with the main course.

As Valda was placing her knife and fork side by side on her empty plate and removing her napkin from her lap, the Sheikh looked up from his plate and smiled. His eyes locked on hers, as he said, 'As I was saying, there is a beautiful, new, luxury apartment block very near the Burg Emir.' He paused to take a sip of water. 'I have purchased ten apartments and had them magnificently decorated.' He paused again, as if he was momentarily unsure of how to continue.

Valda felt obliged to demonstrate some interest and found herself saying, 'On spec?'

'Oh no, no!' The Sheikh shook his head and frowned. 'They are for my business associates to stay at when they are in Dubai for extended periods of time.' He took a another sip of water from his crystal glass and continued, 'One of the apartments would be perfect for you and I would be greatly pleased if you would accept my offer this time.' His dark eyes softened and he looked at Valda. His tiptronic personality had shifted instantaneously to a mode of fatherly concern.

She, however, was not softened this time and was able to utter a firm, 'No!' while holding his gaze.

The Sheikh was undeterred and persisted earnestly, while maintaining a gentle tone of voice. 'But where you are now is too small.' He waved his hand dismissively and added, 'There is no space to entertain and no second room for guests ... surely you have friends and family in Cape Town who are eager to visit you.' His last comment was more of a statement than a question.

Valda smiled; she was not about to reveal that the only person she had any intention of entertaining or inviting to her flat would not require a second bedroom. She was also not about to analyse his intentions any further at this stage and she had realised that no's tended to fall on deaf ears and so her answer was simply, 'I'll think about it!' There was a heavy note of finality in her voice, to discourage any further conversation on the topic, for the time being at least.

Valda politely endured the third course and then made her excuses. It was apparent that the Sheikh's latest apartment offer had been the highlight of the evening's agenda and since that part was out of the way (albeit temporarily), he was willing to let her go without argument.

Valda was past the stage of dwelling on the Sheikh's motives and her mind drifted once again to Brett. She took a peek at her mobile as she sat in her car – it was still as it was before, with no new message, and she frowned and sighed miserably, before turning the wretched thing off and hurling it into the glove compartment.

Back at her apartment, Valda idly looked in the fridge; she felt peckish, despite the three-course meal she had just consumed in a hunger brought on by nervous anticipation of the Sheikh's next move, and so after some deliberation, she grabbed a chunk of Cheddar cheese, cut off a wedge and leant back against the counter, savouring the rich taste. Valda absently began to look at the photographs she had stuck on the fridge with fridge magnets: snapshots of a life of highs and high living. Prompted by a best-selling self-help book, which she had picked up at the supermarket, she had collated some old pictures of her own, which represented the good times and the highlights of her past, and she had plastered them in the most conspicuous place she could think of: the fridge. The idea suggested in the book being to focus attention on positive aspects of one's past, rather than on the negative. Valda was rather proud that she had even managed to pick out one photo of her and Richard for the fridge collection. Despite the bitter ending, she was now able to appreciate that there had been some pretty OK times with the bastard, too. The fridge was invariably the place she came when she was feeling low and so what better place than here to highlight the good moments.

The old photographs inspired many emotions in her, but as she stood there looking at them once more, a totally new sensation gripped her. An odd and uneasy feeling, something akin to a cold draught, began in the small of her back and worked its way up her spine, until it disturbed the hairs on the back of her neck. Valda had been quite specific about the manner in which she had arranged the photos and she was dammed sure that the "Clifton Beach" shot had been above the one of her and a group of Cape Town socialites at a charity golf day and not below it.

Valda continued to stare at the photos. She momentarily doubted her memory, but the more she looked at the collage, the more uneasy she became. It was not possible for her to put her finger on any other changes, but there was something not quite right.

Struck by impulse, Valda grabbed the cheese knife and in fearless anger, she searched through the apartment – almost expecting to find an intruder there. The rooms, however, were quiet and still and everything looked innocent enough. Valda returned to the kitchen and poured herself a beer, berating herself for being so jumpy. She rationalised the movement of the photographs as something of her own doing, which, in her weary and distracted state, she had merely forgotten. Yes, Valda! Too busy daydreaming about that player Brett, that's your problem! she thought to herself.

Valda had underestimated how much the mysterious newspaper clippings had psyched her out and she was concerned that she was beginning to jump at shadows. She flicked on the TV, jabbed at the controls on the remote and slumped down on the couch. The sound of the news anchor's voice drifted into the background and Valda gazed away from the TV, towards her computer table. What she saw sent a shock wave through her and she sat there staring, frozen to the spot!

'Aaah!' she screamed with shock, as the tones of her mobile phone rang out, breaking the silence. Her heart was thudding, her hands shaking and it was some moments before she was composed enough to answer the phone.

'Yes!' she said, sounding quite firm under the circumstances.

'Where the hell have you been?' boomed the voice of an exasperated Brett.

'Where the hell have I been – where the hell have you been?' Valda's adrenalin rush was now releasing itself in anger.

'I tried to ring you when I got to Singapore, but my mobile was out of charge. I had the most ... shit, you just don't want to know trip out to the rig,' he paused, as if not sure how to explain further. 'Power was out on the rig, so no phone lines … it's just been chaos. I've been trying to get you today, but either your phone was off or the network was down. I had kinda hoped there would have been a message from you when I switched my phone on. But I guess you don't care enough!'

'Brett,' said Valda gently, 'I am so damn glad you called! And I was getting worried. How are you?'

Brett detected not only sincerity, but also the vulnerability in her voice and his anger dissipated. 'OK, not as good as last week though!'

For just one moment, Valda almost blurted out her fears about the intruder, she was desperate to share the problem. She knew that Brett would either rationalise it as her overactive imagination or ask some probing questions in his typical manner; it was the latter that deterred her from mentioning anything about it though. The conversation did provide a great deal of comfort though and her anxiety levels began to drop.

Brett sounded lonely and bored, which was in stark contrast to all the scenarios that had run the gamut through Valda's mind. She was very pleased that he had called and was beginning to believe that he was genuinely interested in her, after all. Valda, too, was lonely, but there was no antidote for her loneliness. She had misguidedly chosen a path that had isolated her: there was no person she dared share the truth with and so her only companions day and night were fear and worry. Valda yearned to be with Brett again, in that romantic bubble, where ignorance was bliss, but at the same time, she knew that her secrets would be the snake in the grass in their relationship.

'Are you sure you are OK?' enquired Brett. 'You sound … different.'

'I'm great,' she lied. 'Just tired, that's all.'

'I thought you may be in one of those strange moods again,' sighed Brett.

Usually, a comment like that would have irritated Valda, but she knew that she probably had sounded rather downbeat and so she could hardly blame Brett for inferring she was in a "strange mood", as he so eloquently put it.

'I've been criticised for my temper, but never before have I been accused of being in a strange mood,' she laughed and added, 'I promise no more strange moods when you come and visit me next time.'

'I'm glad you mentioned next time, because I have four days off at the end of the month … is your offer still open?'

'Sorry, what offer was that? The offer to teach you to camel ride?' she joked.

'Well, you know how passionate I am about desert sports!' he joked back. 'It's a date then?'

'Sure! I hope you'll call before then though!'

'Ditto! Now, I'll let you go before I interfere with any more of your beauty sleep.'

They exchanged friendly goodbyes and Valda smiled as she clicked off her mobile phone and placed it on the coffee table. But that creepy feeling was descending on her fast as her gaze once again fixed on the computer table. The mouse had been moved – it was now to the right of the keyboard.

Valda lay awake in the dark, staring at the ceiling, cigarette in hand. She was now convinced that someone had been in her apartment. There was no sign of forced entry and nothing had been taken, so burglary was no motive. Whoever had been there had been interested in her photographs and her PC, which contained nothing at all, except for traces of emails: superfluous drivel to any outsider. She had not yet discovered any other irregularities. She pondered over whether the purpose had been to scare her and that was why the intruder had left certain telltale signs she was sure to notice. Somehow, that theory did not feel quite right.

As she took a deep drag, she wondered if the intruder was also the sender of the clippings. Valda was not even sure when exactly the break-in, for lack of a better term, had happened. It made sense that it had been something to do with the Sheikh – there would have been ample time for the intruder to sneak in and rummage around for what whoever it was wanted, while she was tied up with the long and boring dinner. However, not having used the PC or paid attention to the fridge that morning, Valda could not rule out the possibility that the break-in had been the previous night, while she had been at the club.

Whichever it was, Valda's intuition and logic were on the same page: only the Sheikh could be responsible, but she wondered what he was up to now. A consoling thought was that as far as Valda could see, there was virtually nothing of value to be gleaned from her computer or her belongings. Everything in her apartment fell under the category of personal bric-a-brac. The only items of any interest were those sinister clippings, which were tucked away in her Bible. Stubbing her cigarette out, she threw off the covers and opened her bedside table to retrieve the Bible. The clippings were there, just as before. In the morning, she would have to find a new place for those clippings.

The next morning, Valda placed the clippings in a brown envelope. After thinking of all the obvious places (and she was amazed at how many "obvious places" there were), she made a decision on where to hide them. Out in the car park, she opened her boot ostensibly to retrieve a bottle of water and a jacket. Careful not to be seen, she lifted the carpet lining the boot and slipped the envelope into the crevice that contained the spare wheel. While this was not a foolproof hiding place, someone would have to be on a very specific mission in order to look there and from appearances, the intruder had been on a general rather than a specific search.

It was two weeks later; fortunately, two uneventful weeks. Ahmed was waiting, looking as lugubrious as ever, in the foyer of the Burg Emir as Valda arrived for work. She immediately noticed that he was holding an envelope and her heart sunk.

'I must be an eternal optimist,' Valda said under her breath, 'I just keep thinking that this problem is going to go away.'

'I have something for you from Sheikh Abdullah,' uttered Ahmed.

Valda reached out and took the dreaded envelope; she didn't think a "thank you" was necessary. Bearing in mind their last conversation, Valda looked into Ahmed's eyes, searching for something, perhaps a clue as to his cryptic comment. There was nothing – he met her quizzical gaze with a totally blank look. She realised that his usual brick-wall persona was back.

Valda smiled, not quite sure what to say. 'You keeping well, Ahmed?' she said awkwardly. She was hoping, in vain, to make some connection with him – something was telling her that he was not her enemy.

'Sheikh Abdullah may see you later; if not, he sends his regards and wishes you a safe trip.' Ahmed delivered the message in an almost automated voice and then turned and disappeared towards the conference centre.

'Screw his regards!' she muttered under her breath, grimacing as she stuffed the envelope in her jacket pocket. Blatantly ignoring the "No Smoking" signs in the lift, she lit up. The lift stopped to collect some American guests on their way up to their room and although they were less than impressed at standing there in Valda's swirling cigarette smoke, they didn't dare say anything, owing to the "pissed-off-as-hell" vibe she was so tangibly emitting.

Valda's mood with her colleagues was abrupt and acerbic and while some, including Jo, were clearly wounded, they dared not to press the issue. She was filled with anger and while her anger was in the main for herself, she found it far easier to project it onto all and sundry. She performed with more passion and energy than ever before and during her breaks, she retreated into the dark recesses backstage, avoiding everyone, not least the Sheikh.

That night, she crawled into bed, shattered. She wondered where she would get the strength to conduct another mission for the Sheikh. The ticket was booked for that Saturday.

Valda was beginning to feel as if she spent her life being thoroughly exhausted: ten or even twelve hours of sleep never seemed enough and she would habitually wake-up feeling more drained and depleted than she had when she had fallen asleep. Her explanation was that worry was more mentally and physically sapping than training for a marathon – not that she could vouch for that, having never really been a lover of running. Valda had read how clairvoyants, healers and psychics expended vast amounts of mental energy, which would drain them physically, to the point of collapse. Her own take on this was that emotions and thoughts, especially negative ones, did, indeed, have a profound physical impact.

Chapter Twelve

Riding home in the taxi, Valda felt mildly relieved that another ugly mission was behind her. This was the first time she had travelled business class and besides the obvious benefits, the journey through immigration and customs had been surprisingly smooth and quick. Whether or not there was a conspiracy to grant all business and first-class passengers certain "privileges", she was not sure; perhaps it was the case that the Sheikh, in his eminence, had pulled the required strings to make sure that her arrival was smooth and expeditious.

She gazed out of the window, not really seeing anything. The landmarks of Dubai flashed past, yet while they were now very familiar to her, they did not welcome her and they were no longer symbolic of change and regeneration. The desert skies were clear, blue, vast and open and yet she felt hemmed in and trapped. The heat was oppressive and the burning sun seemed omnipotent and intent on torturing the earth with its deadly rays.

On a lighter note, Valda was counting the days until Brett arrived. With the mission out of the way, she had nothing better to think and dream of than the tall, tanned, rugged geologist and this time, she was determined to enjoy every moment fearlessly.

As the taxi drew up outside her modest apartment building, Valda was devoid of emotion. She carried her suitcase into the foyer, feeling no sensation of "coming home". There was no mail in her box, which was hardly surprising, since she had only been away for three days. Somehow, she had expected there to be some mystery paper cutting again and she was relieved at the sight of the empty box.

She wearily turned the key in the door and pushed it open. She was about to drag her suitcase in, when she looked into the apartment, initially struck with pure astonishment and disbelief at what she was seeing. As the realisation dawned that her eyes were not deceiving her, it was as if thunderbolts of fright and anger were hitting her in the stomach. She threw the suitcase down and raced from room to room. All empty.

All empty; but for a set of keys and an envelope lying on the floor in the middle of the lounge, where the coffee table had been. The realisation of what had happened came not as a result of a logical deduction process, but rather as a flash; an instantaneous falling into place of the pieces. In an irrational and passionate burst of anger, she grabbed the keys and hurled them across the room furiously. They crashed into the wall and then fell into a neat heap on the floor, where they lay, almost mocking her. Still wild, she stormed over to where the keys were and kicked them, sending them clattering against the door. Her attention and anger turned from the keys and letting out a cry of exasperation, Valda pounded the wall with her fists.

Never before had someone so consistently got the better of her. Ignoring her suitcase, which had been abandoned in the entrance hall, she charged down the stairs and along the passageway to Mr Hassam the landlord's flat. There was no answer, even though she angrily banged at his door. She swung her head around, looking out for someone; perhaps one of her fellow residents, whom she had made a point of ignoring, might now have some valuable piece of the puzzle to offer her. However, the whole apartment building seemed deserted that day, only the walls, which were as anonymous as her neighbours, could bear testament to the events that had unfolded. Sighing with resignation, she traipsed back to her apartment, lighting a comforting fag on the way.

Sitting on the floor of her empty apartment, well into her third JPS, Valda thought back to her first meeting with the Sheikh. Ever since then, he had been calling the shots and she felt more and more impotent. More out of lack of anything better to do than curiosity, she reached over for the envelope and began to open it:

1729 Concorde Tower
Jumeirah Lake Towers.

The address was written in gold on a black postcard. She decided that doing anything else would simply be postponing the inevitable and so with less anger, she surrendered. Twenty minutes later, she was driving down Sheikh Zayed Road on the way to her new home.

The Lake Towers complex was easy to find opposite Jumeirah Marina and so was Concorde Tower. Too easy: Valda had no time to think about what had happened or to prepare herself for what seemed like a new level of entrapment in that thickening web. She soon found that there was extensive underground parking and her new apartment keys included what she could only describe as a gold-plated mini screwdriver, which served as an access "key" to the Concorde Tower's "Residents' Parking" section.

She parked and made her way to the elevators: the basement lobby was cold and impersonal; the black marble floor and chrome lift doors gleamed and the smell of fresh paint was strong in the frigid, air-conditioned room. The Sheikh had described the building as being perfect for his business associates and Valda had to agree that it was ideal; the whole establishment had what she would describe as a boardroom aura: everything of the highest quality and craftsmanship, yet no personal touches. There was a large screen in the lift, displaying collages of images depicting what Concorde Towers had to offer; even though the copy waxed on about sparkling swimming pools, state-of-the-art gyms, children's play centres and even boutiques, to Valda, the atmosphere was about as welcoming and inspiring as an academic library.

The lift doors opened on the seventeenth floor and Valda stepped out onto a russet-coloured Persian carpet. Ahead of her, she could see the golden digits of number twenty-nine gleaming as if especially polished for her arrival. With surprisingly little emotion, she slipped the key in the door and sauntered in. She found herself in a large entrance hall, which led into the main living area. She immediately noticed that her meagre tally of furniture had been carefully arranged around the apartment. So large was the lounge, that her modest bits and bobs looked lost and pathetic. A brief wander around revealed that her clothes and bedroom furniture were now arranged in the main bedroom. Valda felt violated; all her personal things had been touched and moved, her home and her life had been invaded and she was powerless to stop the onslaught, but her overriding emotional state was torpid.

The flooring was beautifully and tastefully done in cream Amtico, with a bronze Greek-key effect, and the walls were of pale-peach Vymura. The open-plan kitchen boasted units of solid cherry, slemosa granite worktops, with golden accents, Miele appliances and brushed-bronze faucets. Luxurious cream voile with golden thread running through it framed the huge living-room windows and light filtered gently through the vertical blinds. The bathrooms boasted toilet pedestals of Emporium Maron Marble and direct sunlight, reflective solar loading and shading coefficients were just some of the other unique features of the flat. A theme of opulence ran through the entire decorating concept of the flat, but there was nothing homely or welcoming about it. Standing there in her new "home", Valda had never felt more alone; her heart was as cold as the icy blast from the Carrier A/C.

It was only later that she noticed a large, cut-glass vase full of flowers standing on a glass-topped table in the entrance hall. She was not quite sure how she had missed it. Accompanying the flowers was a card, with a handwritten message:

Welcome! I think that this apartment will be felicitous!
Kind regards,
Sheikh Abdullah.

Valda grunted with bemusement, shook her head and then tossed the note down with disgust.

A week passed very quickly and she slowly became accustomed to her new residence; she was amazed at herself and how quickly she had adjusted to her new circumstances. She only saw the Sheikh briefly to offload his parcel, which was a great relief to her, as she had grown tired of their polite yet loaded conversations.

Disturbingly, on her third day at the Towers, there had been mail: another hand-addressed envelope from within Dubai, complete with a newspaper article. This time, the article was about a chef from Thailand, who had been killed in a freak gas explosion in his luxury flat. The article was a year old. Valda had safely kept the card the Sheikh had sent with the flowers and so she compared the handwriting to that on the envelope. There was little to compare, as the writer of the envelope had only written her name in Roman letters and the address was written in Arabic. However, she could see that the styles were vastly different; the writing on the Sheikh's card (if it was, indeed, his) was bold and sprawling, while that on the envelope was smaller and neater and it sloped downwards. Valda was not able to draw any conclusions from it. The article reminded Valda that the other clippings were still in her boot with the spare wheel; she made a mental note to retrieve them and to find an original new hiding place for them all.

Valda wondered how she was going to explain her grand new home to Brett; he was inclined to ask such probing questions. Valda decided that some lies would be in order; she would tell Brett that she was investing in property.

She had promised to phone Brett as soon as she returned from her trip to Cape Town and she had duly done so, but this time there had been none of her previous fears and doubts creeping in. Valda could feel herself beginning to trust again. She sensed that Brett's macho, cool image was very much like her own tough-girl persona, a facade to keep potential hurt at bay. The more she knew him, the more his tender, emotional side was coming to the fore.

The small ad she had cut out of the newspaper the night Brett had flown back to Singapore had almost been reduced to papier mâché, it had been in her pocket for so long. She reached for it again, read it for the one hundredth time and chastised herself aloud for being such a nerd, 'Just ring, for Christ's sake, what is your problem?'

Being a little reticent about finding out about one's future was not uncommon; in fact, it was normal. Valda picked up the phone and dialled, putting all doubts aside.

'Hello.' The voice the other end seemed friendly.

'Hi, is that Larissa?' Valda launched into an explanation before waiting for a reply. 'I saw your ad in the paper and I wondered how I go about having a reading ... uh ... chart ... Is that what you call it?'

'OK, I'll need your date, place and time of birth, and then I can draw up your chart and we can make an appointment from there.'

'I was born in Cape Town, but I was adopted, so I have no idea of what time I was born. Is that a problem?'

'Check on your birth certificate; sometimes it's written on there. If it is, you can ring me back with the details before our appointment; otherwise, we can try and rectify your chart when we meet. Should I pencil you in for Thursday afternoon?'

'Yeah, that should be fine. What does a reading set you back these days?'

'My rate is 300 dirhams for an hour,' said Larissa emphatically – she was trying to curb her old habit of offering discounts; after all, she had to live. Larissa always felt sorry for her clients and inevitably lowered her price or allowed clients to pay on the never-never; after all, no one consulted an astrologer when times were good. No longer though, she was now employing a tough, money-up-front strategy.

'OK! And the venue?'

'Meet me at three at Khalehla's; it's a coffee shop in Deira on Salahuddin, near the Al Reef Mall. Easy to find! Look at the back; I'll be the one with the laptop.'

'Terrific, I'll see you then. Ciao.' Valda did not know where the "ciao" came from; maybe she was trying too hard to create the impression that she was comfortable with the whole "reading" thing.

'Ciao ni!' replied Larissa.

Larissa had sounded young and cheerful and Valda had detected a hint of a South African accent as well. This helped dilute her fears some – previously, her idea of an astrologer had been based on the Tarot reader in Cher's song, *Dark Lady*. She had images of a darkened room, with heavy red velvet curtains, candles, black cats lurking, pentagrams on the floor and macabre stuff in general. It was quite ridiculous really and she realised that now.

Valda's next priority was to find out her time of birth. She immediately rang Ted her adoptive dad, and asked him to search out her birth certificate, to see whether there was, indeed, a time written on it.

'Astrology now!' Ted was prepared for anything when it came to Valda; she had always had the knack of getting herself into the most unthinkable predicaments. The fact that she was consulting an astrologer was, in Ted's mind, a great thing; maybe the astrologer could talk some sense into her (he had certainly failed) and maybe, just maybe, she would actually listen to what she was being told. Ted was nonetheless very fond of Valda and he respected her resilience and strength.

Ted rang back within an hour with the time: 11.43 a.m. – he wondered whether that was good or bad.

Larissa was engaged when Valda rang her back and so she sent a text message. Valda intended to be very careful not to drop any hints about herself to Larissa, as she did not want Larissa to extrapolate any information she unwittingly divulged about herself into a reading.

Valda was still sceptical. Scepticism was her defence; it would allow her to dismiss what she didn't want to hear!

Although Thursday arrived before Valda knew it, it took forever for the small hand to approach three o'clock. Fear had given way to excitement and anticipation and Valda had the 300 dirhams safely stowed away in a discreet envelope. At two, she decided it was finally time to drive to Deira.

Khalehla's looked like any other side-street cafe anywhere in the world, with its yellow canopies and selection of wooden chairs and tables outside, which were unoccupied that day owing to the heat. Khalehla's was narrow and yet it extended surprisingly far back towards the rear of the building. Inside, against the right-hand wall, was a long, glass display case, with some sumptuous-looking cakes on offer; the counter was decorated with earthenware containers of various interesting shapes with coffee beans inside. There was a rustic feel to the place and terracotta potted plants were dotted amongst the tables. The stucco walls were a mustard colour and on the walls were shelves with a multitude of what Valda could only describe as Aladdin's lamps – the thing Aladdin rubs to conjure up the genie in the story. Valda was not a great reader: Aladdin may have been a character in one of Shakespeare's plays, for all she knew. Larissa must have a sense of humour, she thought! The lighting towards the rear of Khalehla's was dim and what little light there was reflected off the highly polished Aladdin's lamps, creating an atmosphere that was mystical in a way.

Valda could see an isolated table at the rear, partly hidden behind a screen. Larissa was sat at the table with her HP notebook and Valda stayed close to the wall in the shadows, so that she could observe Larissa for as long as possible, unnoticed. Larissa wore a white embroidered halter-neck top, with white pants and red sandals; her hair was swept back into a "Breakfast at Tiffany's" style. As Larissa looked up and their eyes met, both girls were immediately struck by their remarkable resemblance to each other. Apart from Larissa's green eyes, honey blonde highlights and even thinner figure, they could easily have been mistaken for one another.

'Hi, Val! Have a seat. Can I grab you a cake?' Larissa talked with great enthusiasm as she jumped off her chair and pulled up another for her new client.

Valda hated being called Val by strangers, but Larissa had said it so sweetly that she could hardly object. 'Thanks, I'd love a cake. I'll leave the choice to you, Lar,' she said smiling.

Larissa disappeared off and left Valda sitting at the table, pondering over whatever secrets laid waiting inside that little HP notebook of hers. The manager obviously allowed Larissa to conduct her readings at that secluded table. Safe choice, thought Valda; any weirdo could answer her ad in the paper. It was not long before Larissa arrived back with some mouthwatering-looking pastries, filled with the most delicious pistachio-flavoured cream, and some tea. Valda had placed the envelope right next to the laptop; Larissa saw it immediately and was very thankful.

'Are you ready to roll?' asked Larissa, flashing a smile. Valda nodded, still conscious of not revealing anything. Larissa didn't need any help though, and she fired away. 'To start off, I must tell you that I am not a psychic or a clairvoyant and I don't read Tarot, I only do scientific astrology readings. I don't write newspaper horoscopes: as far as I am concerned, they are as much true astrology as Eminem is Mozart!' They both laughed spontaneously. 'There is nothing to fear, as we all have free will at the end of the day and can overcome any negative karma or planetary influences with spiritual determination and faith. One could say that the astrological chart is a symbolic picture of the vibrations we have set up around this life by virtue of our forgotten actions in past lives – which need to be dealt with in this life.' Larissa continued, 'I am going to kick off your reading with a personality analysis and after that, we'll get more specific and you can ask me some questions.'

Larissa spent the first five minutes engaged in a light-hearted discussion of Valda's more superficial characteristic traits, such as her love of music, temper, work ethic, etc. Then, as she went on, she peeled away the layers of Valda's personality like an onion, until she was touching on emotions and hurts that had been buried so deep in Valda's heart that it brought tears to her eyes. Valda was astonished that a stranger was able to understand her better than she understood herself and was able to verbalise and sensitively explain the powerful feelings which had tortured Valda all her life. The fear; guilt; feelings of rejection; fear of not being good enough; the culmination of it all in the form of manic depression – it was all there. Valda would never have imagined that being "revealed" like that could feel so great – she finally felt understood! She would have parted with the 300 dirhams for the first fifteen minutes alone.

Larissa could see that she was striking a chord with her client and this inspired her further. Despite claiming not to be psychic, Larissa often found that during readings, she was able to come up with things that were beyond what she saw in the chart. She put it down to tapping into the psychic ability, which everybody has, yet which remains latent. Astrology had a way of opening up the psychic channels. Readings were never easy though, and Larissa paused for a long sip of tea, before commencing what she had previously called the "specific" section.

'I see that many opportunities in travel and work have opened up for you since February. Financially, things look fabulous! The Neptune square Venus, which has caused you so much heartache and despondency over the past two years, is finally ebbing away for good.'

Larissa paused as Valda nodded and replied flatly, 'Thank God for that!'

Larissa continued in a serious tone, 'Jupiter is on your progressed ascendant, indicating that you have recently become associated with someone of great wealth, influence and prestige. Since Jupiter rules your progressed second house, this association has been very lucrative for you. However, Pluto on your midheaven is squaring Jupiter, indicating a sinister side to this relationship. Many things are hidden from you and you are playing with fire. Pluto on the midheaven can indicate a perilous course of action, so you need to stop and think. 'Transiting Neptune square, your Mercury indicates some ill-advised decisions that are haunting you. I also have a hint of a mysterious communication.'

Valda's heart skipped a beat and despite her calm, nonchalant expression, she was sure her face had gone white! Larissa was dead-on, again.

'Your association with this person, a man, I think, is somewhat fated.'

'What do you mean by that? Fated?' Valda had decided that it was time to get more proactive.

'What I mean is that both of your fates have been sealed from your first meeting! You have an entwined destiny!'

'But you said before that nothing is inevitable, we all have a free will.' Just an ounce of panic crept into Valda's voice.

'Yes, absolutely. However, once we have committed ourselves to a certain path, we are not always able to change it like the flick of a switch. And I feel that you are already some way down this path. A 747 flying north at 500 miles an hour, can't just turn West instantly – it would be ripped apart by the G-force. See what I mean. There are powerful, unseen forces at work here and you must be careful. My best advice would be to slowly but surely reduce your contact with this man, especially financially. You started a chain of events sometime back in April – around the 19th – whatever those events were, they must be put to an end. Then everything will be fine.'

"Reduce your contact with this man, especially financially". The words rang in Valda's head. She was feeling the G-force already: she not only worked for Sheikh, but she lived in a flat he had bought her and drove the flashy car he had presented her with, in lieu of favours past and future. She was thoroughly entwined in his web.

Larissa knew that it was time to inject some positivity now that the difficult bit of the reading had been dealt with. 'Career-wise, things are really motoring. I can see that you are about to relive the success of your early twenties. Opportunities are everywhere and your energy is sky high.'

This was, indeed, music to Valda's ears and she wanted to hear more. 'Really, I'll repeat the success of my early twenties? I thought that lightning never struck the same place twice.'

'Rubbish, just ask Lee Trevino – he's been struck by lightning four times.'

'Occupational hazard, I'd say.' They both laughed and Valda sensed the reading was concluding. She had to find out more about Larissa though. 'So you are also South African?'

'Well, I went to school in Joburg, but my family moved back to the UK eleven years ago. I spent six of those years back in London and now I've been in Dubai for the last five.'

'What brought you here?' Valda quizzed.

'Running away from things – myself, mainly!'

'Did it work?'

'No, I still kept waking up with me! There's no such thing as a spiritual quick fix.' For the first time, Larissa seemed to give over an air of sadness and Valda decided to lay off the deep questions. The sad air left as soon as it had come and Larissa asked, 'Do you like cricket?'

'Why? Can you see that in my chart?'

'Of course, I even know what kind of knickers you wear!' Larissa laughed and added, 'Just pulling your leg. I have tickets for the South Africa–Pakistan match at Sharjah next week, are you interested? It's more fun with company.'

'What a question. I'd love that!'

Valda suddenly sensed someone hovering in the background and assumed correctly that it was Larissa's four o'clock. She thanked Larissa wholeheartedly and they parted like old buddies, agreeing to be in touch before the match.

Larissa was hardly able to concentrate on her next client's reading. He was a typical case: another wealthy, middle-aged man, who had met a tart in a bar three nights before, was convinced it was true love and wanted to know when the best time was to leave his wife. Viagra syndrome, Larissa called it – desperate for sex, but not desperate enough for sex with a wife.

She was preoccupied with Valda, her new client, who was so similar to herself, and not only in looks. What Larissa saw in Valda's chart was direr than she dared to think about. The danger was grave and so complex and advanced in its stages that Larissa was unsure what to advise; although she already felt she would do anything to help.

Larissa momentarily thought that her family may have had a point with their insistence that she pursue a career in accounting. It probably was a simpler and more financially rewarding job. The thought of being an accountant had always appalled Larissa though, and she had chosen to be an astrologer, as she loved people and they always seemed to ask her advice anyway. Even total strangers she sat next to on a train would pour their hearts out to her. A career in counselling had seemed a logical step. She had never realised the huge responsibility that came with being an astrologer though, and clients often came to her with monumental problems, which were quite literally life and death. But the 300 dirham fee never covered the sleepless nights she spent agonising over her clients' problems.

Back to reality: 'So what did you say your new girlfriend's name was?'

Donald's eyes glazed over in wonder as he said, 'Marvellous Mandy, she's a Libran.'

'Are you sure that's her real name?' Larissa was pretty sure that this was not the Mandy that came and gave without taking! On the contrary ...

Valda stepped out onto the baking pavement. She felt exhilarated and was already thinking about what to ask in her next reading. Valda was too busy thinking about her career star, which was about to rise again, to think about the more immediate problem of the Sheikh. She was intrigued by Larissa. Growing up in foster care, she had often wondered about her real parents: what they looked like; what they did; did she have siblings somewhere? But no one seemed to know the answers.

Some of the answers must be on her birth certificate, which Ted kept. She had never seen it herself and it seemed insensitive to ask Ted if she could see it, as he would immediately suspect that she wanted to see the names of her real parents and would be deeply hurt. That was the last thing she wanted to do. Ted and Angela had adopted Valda when she was nine; they had no children of their own. Some six months later, Angela had left Ted for another man. Ted had commendably continued to raise Valda single-handedly and Valda had always felt terribly guilty; she had, in her child's mind, believed that Angela had left because of her.

After the initial euphoria over Larissa's promising predictions on the career front, Valda began to soberly reflect on what she had said about the Sheikh and their "fated" relationship. Valda could easily understand how her fate, especially her immediate fate, was tied in with the Sheikh, but what she did not understand was how his fate was intertwined with hers. The reading had given rise to more questions than answers; perhaps that was the whole point, she mused cynically. Valda was beginning to understand why psychic readings and astrology were so addictive – just like the shrinks, she laughed to herself. Except you don't have to spend the first three months explaining how you feel and why; the astrologer already knows.

Larissa, Valda had to admit, had been very clear that this association with the Sheikh was ominous and that it would take great effort and mental strength to counter the chain of events, which had already been set in motion. It was a relief to have been able to talk to somebody, even if it was not all what she had wanted to hear. After months of fear and self-recrimination, Valda was feeling the impetus to shift into a proactive gear and start swimming against the tide. She sensed that

Larissa could be a valuable ally and she was going to put her powers and skills to the test. Valda was also more than curious to find out some insider information about Brett and their compatibility. She spontaneously leapt from the couch, grabbed her mobile phone and sent Brett a text enquiring about his birthday.

That night, she slept blissfully and was amazed to wake up feeling almost human. It was like a wave of optimism had washed over her and she felt as if she was on the first day of some sort of mission. She may well have set one chain of events in motion when she had accepted the Sheikh's very first invitation, but by seeing Larissa, she had initiated another chain of events, which would lead her out of this quandary. Valda felt more in control of her life and her destiny than ever before.

The envelope icon on her mobile was flashing: "13 Dec – keep it free".

Mmm, Sagittarius? I know nothing about them, thought Valda. She had been so sure that Richard was the one and only one for her, that she was astounded by the fact that she was now sitting there contemplating whether she had struck gold in love for real this time. Realistically, she knew that it was far too soon to tell, but she also knew that the fact that she was ready to take the chance again had to be a positive step forwards.

No sooner had she replaced the mobile phone on the table than it was ringing again: it was Larissa. Larissa sounded warm and cheerful and began the conversation as if she had known her new client for years.

'So, should I pick you up or what? Have you been to Sharjah before?' asked Larissa.

'No, I haven't,' answered Valda.

'Nor me, so why don't you drive and I'll navigate!'

They went on to discuss time and other logistical issues – in fact, discuss may not have been the right word, for Larissa made the decisions and Valda went along with them. Larissa had a particularly emphatic yet gentle attitude and came across as a very capable, confident person. There was something very reassuring in Larissa's bold manner, which made Valda feel secure; perhaps Larissa reminded Valda of the person she had once been: so in control and sure of herself. There was something important on Valda's mind and she was quick to pounce on an opportunity to change the subject from cricket.

'Larissa?' Valda interjected, 'I want another reading … maybe two more, uhm, about different issues, you know?'

'Yeah! Look, don't worry about appointments – the trip to Sharjah will take a half-hour or so, so we can talk then and the rest of day, too, if you want,' said Larissa sympathetically.

'I'll pay,' offered Valda eagerly.

'Forget that, we're friends; consider it pro bono, my pleasure!' Larissa said in all sincerity. Valda was not the only one in Dubai who had woken with a sense of purpose and a mission that day.

Valda gave Larissa Brett's details, so that she could draw up his chart before the match. With all the arrangements taken care of, Valda set off to the shops for a snack and with the intention of doing some serious shopping. Her head felt clear; suddenly, life had taken on a new meaning. She was filled with anticipation for her day out with Larissa and to add to her joy, the day Brett was to return to her was fast approaching.

Chapter Thirteen

The air-con in the GT was outstanding and the engine was growling as if it was hungry for a long journey. The sound system in the car was very impressive, too; in fact, it was the first time Valda had tried the CD: driving such a magnificent machine was such a thrilling experience, it hardly needed augmentation. She had reasoned that the GT would give Larissa concrete evidence of what she was about to explain to her, if, indeed, she needed it. Valda had chosen cropped khaki chinos and a red cotton top to wear, with, of course, aviator-style sunglasses.

Valda was picking Larissa up at the Wafi Centre, as apparently she had some errands to run there first. As she approached the entrance, she immediately recognised Larissa standing there waiting; there was something very distinctive about her, which made her stand out from the crowd – nothing Valda could put her finger on, but she was very aware of it nonetheless. She was wearing white sawn-off jeans, with a jade green jacket. Larissa immediately noticed the sleek, road-hugging roadster approaching and she smiled, at the same time raising an eyebrow as if to say, I'm not one bit surprised! Valda eased to a stop and leaned over to fling open the passenger door.

'A present from Mr Jupiter, I presume?' asked Larissa, with that same expression on her face. 'Does he want a good astrologer, because I don't mind being paid in horsepower!'

'Oh no, I'm saving him for my worst enemy!' said Valda, wincing and shaking her head.

'This is one heck of a car; there must only be about 500 of them worldwide!' remarked Larissa enthusiastically as she settled in and perused the interior.

'Aah, but it comes with a curse!'

'I'll bet, they usually do! You fire away when you're ready!' Larissa touched Valda's shoulder reassuringly as if to emphasise that she would understand.

'I first want to talk about something else,' she paused shyly, 'the new guy I've met and the ex.'

'OK, let's get on the main highway first though, I don't want to have to interrupt any major emotional dredgings with a "take the next right",' joked Larissa.

Larissa appeared to know her way around pretty well and Valda found her company quite refreshing and amusing. She seemed to know something about everything, which made her very easy to converse with and what was even better was her apparent non-judgemental attitude to people and life.

'So how am I doing?'

'You're doing just fine! Hey, you are a great driver an' these cars aren't that easy to handle, either!'

'Thanks!' Valda paused thoughtfully. 'Thanks.' It was rather an alien feeling to her, receiving a compliment, but it felt good. Valda reached into a compartment under the steering wheel and pulled out her JPS. 'You don't mind, do you?' she asked. Larissa shook her head. Within seconds, Valda had a lit cigarette in her mouth. 'Help yourself, if you want one,' she offered, tossing the box onto Larissa's lap.

'Maybe later. I'm ready when you are!'

Valda exhaled dramatically and then began, 'OK, I was in a seven-year relationship, which ended badly two years ago, uhm ...'

'Let me take it from here,' interjected Larissa. 'Over the past two and a half years, you have had a Venus–Neptune square in your solar chart and in transits: what this means is great disappointment, disillusionment and heartbreak in love; often, deception is involved. 'The whole effect of Neptune is to cause great feelings of hopelessness and despair, low self-worth ... feelings of abandonment and even self-destructive tendencies. Your confidence took a real knock and it was a desperate time.' Larissa paused; then added earnestly, 'Thankfully, that is all over now and you will never go through that again.'

Valda was nodding in agreement throughout. 'Richard was so critical, so clinical about everything; he made me feel self-conscious. He would never just hold me and be loving towards me; especially towards the end. I became more moody, lost my temper more often, drank too much – the more I needed comfort, the more distant he became. To exacerbate things, my career was also going down the tubes. Then, one night, he came home ...' she trailed off and held out her hand, 'another fag, I think!'

Larissa was quick to oblige and she allowed Valda to continue without interruption this time. '... anyway, he came home and told me that he'd met someone else – she was successful, capable, smart – like me before I fell apart, I guess. Wow, did that hurt, I felt so utterly useless, rejected and a complete failure. He walked straight back out again after he had told me and that was that.' Valda paused, her lips tightened and she swallowed hard. Difficult as it was to speak those words out loud, she was surprised to find no moisture in her eyes. Larissa was respectfully silent, but offered a warm, supportive smile. 'I just wanted to crawl away and hide, sleep all day and avoid dealing with things. The depression was terrible. At the time, I felt that I would never get over it.'

Valda fell silent for a while and they rode along, allowing the humming of the engine to fill the silence. 'One consolation, I thought, was that when I died, the pain had to end!' sighed Valda painfully. 'So I ... I OD'd, slit my wrists ... thought that was it!'

'But what happened?' asked Larissa intently.

'My dad found me in time ...' she paused, while she lit another JPS, 'I didn't want to know the finer details ... but as you can see, I'm still here!' She continued, 'I am still convinced that I locked my front door, but my dad insists that it was open – that's why he found me!'

'Well, I'm glad he did! 90 per cent of suicides fail, you know.' Larissa paused, 'The subconscious will to live is incredibly strong; survival instinct, you could call it.' Valda was dragging on her JPS and so Larissa took the opportunity to continue, 'What you said about the pain ending when you die, I am not sure that that's true – I believe that we keep coming back and repeating the cycle, until we resolve it, or conquer it in some way. The lesson has to be learned. Maybe you were given a second chance ... a chance to heal that wound and discover that there is life after Richard.' Valda remained silent, she was not sure what to say and since Larissa seemed on a roll, she decided to let her continue. 'You must forgive him though!' said Larissa compellingly.

'What?' Valda reacted to Larissa's instruction with contempt. 'I could never forgive him, never. He does not deserve forgiveness. Forget it!'

'That's the mistake everybody makes! Do you really think that he's suffering, because you are withholding forgiveness? Put another way, do you think Donald Trump gives two hoots whether his first wife forgives him or not? Of course not,' she said with passion. But then she changed her tone to be more firm and gentle and continued, 'Forgiving him doesn't free him, it frees you! Forgiving is like a panacea for your pain. Harbouring bitterness and anger will be your downfall. Just trust me on this!'

'And you know this for sure, of course!' said Valda, struggling to keep a note sarcasm out of her voice.

'You came to me for advice, no? Take it or leave it,' responded Larissa. She then turned to stare out the side window at the dusty, barren landscape flashing by. Valda suddenly realised how tightly she was gripping the wheel and how close her right foot was to the floor – they were speeding along at some pace and she had no idea of the limit. Larissa noticed her checking the speedo and with a dismissive wave of her hand, she said, 'Don't worry about it; I hear there are no cameras till Sharjah.' After a pause, Larissa decided to get the ball rolling again. 'I'm sorry if I sounded dogmatic, but when I believe something strongly I say it.'

'You're just exposing raw nerves, that's all.' Valda forced a laugh; then, in a more upbeat voice, added, 'OK, why don't we talk about Brett, instead! Is there potential there, or am I up the creek with him, too?'

Larissa's face burst into a smile. 'I did a synastry chart, which is like a comparison chart for your two birth charts ... anyway, I was amazed at the aspects it presented. You guys have a real connection: emotional, physical and spiritual. Very, very promising!'

'But are you saying we have a future?' asked Valda seriously.

'Yeah! Oh yeah! There is loads of Saturn, so lots of stability and security.'

Larissa hoped that she was sounding convincing; she was greatly relieved that Valda was driving and that she had not had to look into Valda's eyes while making that statement. It was not that Larissa thought that Brett and Valda had no potential for a future together, on the contrary, but that future was blighted by the spectre of the Sheikh. Valda appeared to be satisfied though.

'I'm just worried that I'm not truly over Richard yet. I feel very strongly about Brett, I think?' There was an element of doubt in her voice. 'But I haven't seen Richard in months, what if old feelings start to stir when I do see him again. Especially if he breaks up with Sonja ... that's the smart, capable one he left me for, by the way.' Valda was sounding far more in control of her emotions all of a sudden.

'No,' Larissa was insistent, 'that part of your life is over. One day, Richard is going to walk back into your life and I tell you, Val, you are going to be amazed: there are going to be no feelings for him at all, neither anger nor love. In fact, you two will be able to be friends, even good friends.'

'On one level, what you say sounds totally unbelievable, but if I'm honest, I have to admit that something in me tells me you're right ... about everything, that is!'

With that, Valda began to turn the tables and to interrogate Larissa. Larissa proved to be most open about her stumbling career, non-existent love life and chaotic existence in general. What interested Valda most though, was what path was it that had led her into astrology.

Larissa explained, 'I always thought life, at least my life, should mean something: I did not see the point of ambling thoughtlessly from school to uni to some pointless job, and then marrying and having kids, who, despite all the promise of youth, would repeat that same mindless cycle. I couldn't bear the thought of waking every day to an alarm clock, braving the human sardine tin (aka the tube), sitting at a desk, staring at a PC screen, 9 till 6, doing some job that neither inspired me nor made any real difference to the world. For a while, I thought I was being punished for not wanting all that; I mean, 99 per cent of people seem to be fine with it, right?'

'Don't count me in with them.' Valda rolled her eyes, 'Go on then.'

'After uni, I did some modelling; you have to be a real hard case to do that. Then I tried radio journalism – no comment – then web design. Then I even had a brief stint in an office compiling accounts and the best thing that came out of that was that afterwards, I had far more sympathy for the plight of battery chickens.' Larissa paused, while Valda laughed out loud, nodding as if she could picture those horrible chipboard sections dividing the desks in some offices. 'Anyway, there was more, but to summarise, it was one failure after another and I was horribly depressed. So, one day, I ordered some books off Amazon. My order got mixed up and I received the wrong books. However, one of those "wrong" books turned out to be the book that changed my life, Linda Goodman's Star Signs. I call it a New Age Bible: it turned me on to astrology and many other amazing avenues of thought. I think that this was a time when fate stepped in and gave me a shove in the right direction.'

'And it all worked out well?'

'I wouldn't say that; it hasn't been easy, but I do feel that I'm making progress in my search to find my place in this world – or whatever.' She sighed and trailed off. Larissa was beginning to feel that she had rambled on too much about herself and was a little embarrassed.

'So it's not just me that screws up!' Valda gloated.

'Succeeding, screwing up ... same difference, it's the experience that counts. Like that game, one minute you're racing up a ladder and the next thing you're sliding down a snake.' She paused thoughtfully and then added, 'Funnily enough, Snakes and Ladders is an ancient Indian game about karma; I guess some of us have heavier karmic debts to pay ...' Suddenly, Larissa stopped and blurted out, 'OK, this next turn off is us!' Then under her breath, she said, 'Whew, that was getting way too deep.'

Crowds were gathering en masse at the cricket stadium: there were only a handful of international fixtures at Sharjah each year and games were always well attended. Valda was relieved to hear that they would be sitting in an air-conditioned hospitality box and not outside in the soaring temperatures. The tickets had been given to Larissa by a client in lieu of payment.

'Oh, in case it comes up, I'm Mr Hague-Holmes' chiropractor,' Larissa winked. 'How can I expect my business to grow by word of mouth, when no one admits to using me!'

Their box was just alongside that of the Sky Sports commentary team and the view was unrivalled. There was great anticipation amongst the crowd. It was years since Valda had been to a cricket match and she was surprised at her excitement, she was definitely coming alive again. Larissa seemed very up on things and was engaged in a debate about the world's finest all-rounder with an Englishman to her left. Valda was glad of a few moments to herself, she wanted to collect her thoughts and to decide how best to broach the issue of the Sheikh.

In the sixteenth over there was a flurry of South African wickets and a disgusted Larissa suggested that then would be a good time to grab some food. As they made their way out of the hospitality box, Larissa stopped suddenly and gasped, 'My God, there's Geoffrey Boycott! Am I too old to ask for an autograph?'

'Larissa, really!' Valda shook her head light-heartedly; she could hardly fault Larissa for her enthusiasm, for it was quirky but endearing.

'Maybe later! If we don't get in a queue now, we won't eat!' decided Larissa, adding, 'And please, Lara in future!'

The queues for food were, indeed, long and the selection was nothing to rave about.

'Val, I have a confession to make!' said Lara suddenly as they waited in line.

'Oh?' Valda was curious.

'After you came for a reading, I got nosy … well, you only gave me your first name, but since music and performing showed up so strongly in your chart, it didn't take me long to find out where you worked. So I went down to see you in action, as it were.' She stopped and waited for a response.

'So is detective on your resume, as well?' remarked Valda rhetorically.

'I was extremely impressed and I don't say that easily. You reminded me a bit of Laura Branigan!'

'Oh, and I thought this was going to be a compliment,' smirked Valda.

'A twenty-first century camper version, of course!'

'Yeah, I know where you're coming from, I'm only teasing. Hey, you really seem to be hitting it off with that guy next to you!' said Valda with a glint in her eye.

Larissa rolled her eyes. 'I'm strictly a flirter. I have no time for relationships; if I wanted a noose around my neck, I'd tie a loop in a rope and slip it over my head.'

Valda laughed, but then turned serious again. 'Don't you get lonely though?'

'My Venus opposite Pluto means that I attract possessive, controlling, domineering types – I welcome loneliness, believe me!' sighed Lara.

Lunch consisted of a humus, pine nut and avocado salad wrap, which turned out to be very tasty, despite the girls' initial reservations. The hospitality box was refreshingly cool and yet Valda was beginning to feel sticky: she was mentally organising all the information and developments into a cohesive story for Lara. She intended to lay it all on the table, the unabridged version. The cricket match was hardly the right place to begin though; there was no privacy and it was very noisy. There was always the drive home, however. Valda resolved to spill the beans on the ride back to Dubai; she always found that she was able to think clearly while driving.

South Africa set Pakistan a target of 248 runs, but despite a flying start, a middle-order collapse resulted in the required run rate escalating and the win for South Africa becoming inevitable. The players were merely going through the motions, so Valda and Lara decided to quit the stadium early and seek out some dinner and evening entertainment. They drove around Sharjah for some time, taking in the fascinating scenery, including the King Faisal Mosque and Al-Ittihad Square, with the Union Monument, which Lara thought looked something like an enormous lamp stand, with a huge bronze ball cradled at the top of it. Starving hungry and in need of stretching their legs – it had to be said, the GT was not the most comfortable ride – they decided to stop at the Blue Souk, which was right near to the King Faisal Mosque and the Monument. Sharjah's Blue Souk was renowned for selling carpets, gold, silver, perfumes, clothes and antiques, but Valda and Larissa were banking on finding some tempting grub as well. They were in luck as far as the quest for food went and had a delicious Lebanese-style meal of chicken, peppers and tahini. Valda was surprised to find that like Brett, Lara was easy to be with – conversation flowed but was never forced, and silences were natural and never awkward. It amazed her to have found two people, with whom she gelled so well, within such a short space of time, after having spent years feeling like a misfit.

After dinner, they strolled through the Souk, surveying the dazzling wares on offer. Valda learnt that Lara was a collector of "Aladdin's" lamps and she was eager to browse the antique stores for additions to her collection. It was in one such antique store called Sutanah that Valda's attention was drawn to a magnificent, bejewelled dagger. The gold-plated blade gleamed menacingly and the jewel-encrusted handle sparkled with all the colours of the rainbow. She picked it up in order to study it more carefully; she was in awe of the dagger – it was a work of art. Lara, who had been engrossed with a lapis lazuli necklace until then, wandered over to see what had so captivated her friend. Lara immediately ran her finger along the blade and then let out a gasp, 'Heck! It's got bite. Not just a pretty face then, huh!'

'It's functional, that's for sure! I wonder who would have owned this,' mused Valda.

'I have heard that Sikh men carry daggers as part of their tradition, maybe that was its *raison d'être*,' pondered Lara.

'Judging by the price tag, these are real rubies, emeralds and sapphires. May even be imperial topaz.' Valda held out the tag, so that Lara could see the price. Lara gasped! There was something about the way Valda held that dagger and the look in her eyes that led Lara to believe that the ornate and ostentatious weapon would soon be hers. She was right, Valda produced her gold card and soon they were leaving with a shiny black-and-gold carrier bag, bearing the name "Sutanah". 'Are you sure there was nothing you wanted?' asked Valda.

'Oh, I wanted alright, but I didn't think my card would oblige,' answered Lara light-heartedly.

Back in the car on the way to Dubai, Valda began to tell the story of events since her arrival in the Emirates. Lara listened intently, saying nothing but nodding periodically to show her interest. Lara did burst into uncontrollable giggles on one occasion though, 'Your anti-dog device is hilarious!' she managed to say. Still laughing, she added, 'I don't think they use dogs that often, only if there is a specific threat: sniffer dogs get tired very quickly and so they are not suitable to be used on a continuous basis. Anyway, I think they are preoccupied with sharp objects and liquids these days; so as long as you don't pack your knitting and a quart of milk, you'll be fine.' Valda was actually pleased for the light relief, but Lara was quick to offer an apology. 'Geez, I'm sorry; I don't mean to trivialise your problems. Hey, do you want another cig'?'

'No thanks, I'm fine!' she said, flashing a big smile.

'Mind if I have one?' asked Lara.

'Why, my story getting too much for you?' Valda asked, sounding a touch concerned.

'No, I'm riveted; I'll take popcorn, instead, if you have it!'

They both shared a laugh and then Valda continued, 'Now have the damn fag and shut up, before I forget where I was!'

The trip back to Dubai was over before Valda's story was, so Lara invited Valda up to her flat, which was on the eighteenth floor of an older building, ancient on Dubai standards, typical of eighties-era Arabian architecture. The flat had two bedrooms and a balcony and was quite spacious. Valda glanced around the living room, while Lara made tea;

there was no particular theme, unless, of course, untidiness could be classed as a theme. The glass-and-chrome coffee table was scattered with papers and diagrams, which appeared to be charts; there was a wicker magazine holder overflowing with unopened mail and magazines, and clothes, rather than cushions, decorated the sofas. Valda was fascinated by Lara's wall units, which boasted carvings and artefacts from Africa and Arabia, as well as, of course, an array of Aladdin's lamps in all shapes and sizes, which took her back to her first reading at Khalehla's. The walls were full of photographs, reminding Valda of her own sentimentality over photos and memorabilia. There was a TV, DVD and hi-fi system, all of which were surrounded by haphazardly packed disks and diskettes, most of which lacked covers. Valda strolled over to the kitchen, to see how Lara was getting on. In contrast to the lounge, the modern kitchen was very neat and organised. Lara noticed Valda watching her. 'I wondered why you were so quiet; I had hoped you were tidying up for me.'

'You wish, Miss Poppins! Actually, I was scared to sit down, in case I squashed something important.'

Lara added some more sugar to her tea. 'Have you seen my study yet? I call it Ground Zero – my own personal disaster area!' With that, she arranged the mugs of sweet, strong black tea, the way they both liked it, on a tray, with some cheese and crackers. After placing the tray on top of everything else on the coffee table, Lara gathered up the "rubble" on her sofas in one fell swoop and relocated it to an empty chair in the corner.

They sat down and Valda continued where she had left off. A pack of cream crackers and half a pack of JPS later, she was finished. 'So what do you think?' was her simple question.

Lara set down her cup of tea and sat forwards on the couch. 'The articles are a warning, that's for sure. All those men died in "supposed" accidents,' she raised an eyebrow, 'and they all worked in careers like catering ... uhm, tennis pro, stuff which may have brought them into contact with the Sheikh via his hotels. They were most probably doing the same as you.'

'Why do you think he killed them or had them killed?' asked Valda frowning.

'All relationships, be it love, business or otherwise, have their rocky times; someone usually becomes unhappy or wants out. When things got rocky, I guess the Sheikh did a wet job on them.'

'I have never heard it called that before. So who is behind these articles, do you think?' Valda was sounding very troubled.

'It doesn't really matter, Val,' Lara spoke intently, staring into Valda's eyes. 'Listen, wearing my Best Mate and Astrologer's hat, I can only say one thing, get out of Dubai as soon as you can! Go back to Cape Town.'

'I can't do that!' snapped Valda belligerently. With that, she rose from the couch and started pacing the room. Cigarette in mouth, she argued, 'He knows people there, doesn't he? Cape Town is exactly where he'll expect me to run to.' Valda was becoming more and more agitated and she continued to rave on, more to herself than to Lara. 'And won't I look the fool to everyone; they'll all think: she failed again, couldn't make it in Dubai, back living with Daddy. Lovely, lovely.' Smoke whirled around the room as Valda paced furiously and gesticulated dramatically as she talked, pausing frequently for puffs. 'What am I going to do for a living? I'm washed up, finished in South Africa! I'll have to go back to school; I'm not even computer literate!' On that note, she turned and stared at Lara, almost challenging her, daring her to suggest a solution.

'I don't have all the answers or a bloody magic wand, OK!' Valda was quite taken aback at Lara's ferocious reaction. 'What I can tell you is that you had better get the hell outta here and the sooner the better.' Lara swallowed hard and took a deep breath; she sat down again and pointed to the other sofa as if to invite Valda to take a seat. Valda stubbed out her cigarette butt and sat down, looking exhausted and defeated. Lara adopted a more positive and reassuring tone when she next spoke. 'Look, we'll work things out together! Your chart shows great opportunities within your career, so there have to be options out there. It'll all work out, trust me! I'll help you get out of Dubai, that's our first priority.'

Valda was looking willing to hang on to any shred of hope at that point. 'How long do I have?' she asked quietly.

'We have time, we have time!' Lara spontaneously slipped her arms around Valda and hugged her tightly. Valda responded, finding Lara's tenderness soothing. 'You can stay over tonight. If I remember rightly, there is a bed in Ground Zero; you can help me find it!'

They spoke no more about the Sheikh or anything else, for that matter. Lara lent Valda some pyjamas and they both prepared the guest bed. At that stage, Valda felt so tired and emotionally drained that she was oblivious to the paperwork Armageddon that was Lara's spare room.

Valda's eyes flickered open as she heard an unfamiliar sound. Lara was placing a mug of steaming-hot tea on a rickety table near the spare bed, where Valda lay.

'I'm sorry,' she whispered. 'Didn't mean to wake you. Thought you'd fancy some tea when you surfaced.'

Valda frowned as if she was nursing a hangover and rubbed her face, asking, 'What time is it?'

'Half past ten!'

'How can you sound so perky in the morning?' moaned Valda grumpily.

Lara laughed softly. 'Don't let that fool you, I find that life usually looks its most dire and depressing in the morning,' pausing briefly, 'hence the saying, "the cold light of day", I guess.' On her way out of the room, she added, 'Come and have some brekkie when you are ready and I'll fix you up with some fresh clothes, we're about the same size.'

Valda pulled the covers over her head; "brekkie" was the furthest thing from her thoughts. She felt as if she needed another eight hours sleep. Fifteen minutes later, enticed out of bed by the appetising aroma of eggs and toast, Valda ambled towards the kitchen. Lara served up the most delicious scrambled eggs Valda had ever tasted, on brown seed bread, dripping with her own freshly made tomato sauce.

'That was fantastic; in fact, it was so good, I think I should propose to you!' she exclaimed. 'This on a daily basis for breakfast would cure my morning blues,' mumbled Valda as she was finishing off her last mouthful.

Lara chuckled before a serious look came over her face. 'What we talked about last night …' she stopped and looked intently at Valda, 'I'll help you get things organised!'

'Yeah, we have to be careful though, because he has me watched,' answered Valda.

Lara became thoughtful and remained silent, while she stirred her tea.

*   *   *

Valda soon discovered that Lara had a beautiful closet of clothes, though perhaps a touch on the girlie side for Valda's taste; however, she had no trouble picking out something to wear. Lara was very obliging with her make-up as well and they sat on her bed amongst her huge range of liners, lipstick and eyeshadows getting "dolled up".

'Feels like a teenage sleepover party,' remarked Valda, grinning happily.

'It's weird how we look so alike,' said Lara in a quizzical tone as she applied lashings of mascara.

'Like sisters,' replied Valda. 'By the way, I never asked, do you have any siblings?'

'No, I'm an only child...' Lara was about to continue, but she was interupted by the ringing of her mobile phone. It appeared to be a client or something of that nature, but Valda did not listen in with any interest.

After Lara had come off the phone, she started rummaging through one of her wardrobe drawers with intent and after some minutes, she appeared to find what she was looking for: it was a mobile phone. She walked over to where Valda was sitting on the edge of the bed and handed her the phone. 'Here, take this. It's a pay-as-you-go mobile registered to a fake name and address. It's topped up.' Valda was looking confused, so Lara explained, 'If ever you need to ring me to chat urgently about something and you want to be sure of privacy and it being untraceable, use this. I came up with this idea for a previous client of mine; let's just say that he had plenty of people on his tail.'

Valda smiled gratefully and slipped the phone into her bag. 'I can't thank you enough for everything, Lara,' she said with great depth and sincerity. 'I'll ring you and we will get together again after Brett's visit to discuss "things"!' she said, raising her eyebrows.

'There is another thing I've been thinking about,' Lara paused, 'not that I'd know what the going rate for dope is, but he seems to be paying you well in excess of it? He must have something else in mind.'

'Well, that's what I thought from my first meeting with him, but I really don't think so, there have been no signs. He probably has a harem anyway!' pondered Valda vaguely, while pulling on her jeans.

'All the articles are about men; it appears you are the first woman he has been using!' Lara stopped and shook her head, 'There must be something else ...' she tailed off.

Somehow, Valda did not seem as concerned as the night before; she looked as if her mind was elsewhere – either that, or she was clamming up. Lara was not sure, but she decided not to press the issue.

Chapter Fourteen

'Flight EK433 from Singapore has now landed,' the voice boomed over the PA system.

Valda looked at her watch, it was three thirty in the morning; the plane had landed on time. She pushed her empty mug into the centre of the table and looked about, trying to attract the attention of a waiter; she made a signing gesture in the air to indicate she was ready for the bill. Although she realised it would take some time for the passengers to disembark and make their way through immigration, she knew that Brett was not one to dawdle and that he would lose no time in making his way from the plane to the arrival hall. She paid her bill and walked towards the arrivals area, where other eager and animated "meeters and greeters" were gathering. There was something about airports that had always thrilled and fascinated Valda; maybe it was the ambience of the comings and goings, the international flavour or perhaps the sense of expectation and excitement. Hearts always tend to be on sleeves at airports: happy hellos, sad goodbyes, adventures beginning or ending, the promise of something new and the reassurance of something old. All those strong feelings and tangible emotions in the air had to have an impact on you. Airports, or so it seemed to Valda, were somewhat of a metaphor for life.

She, of course, was filled with anticipation; there was no hollow, cold feeling in her stomach this time, only butterflies. Valda had secured herself a prominent position in the arrival hall; Brett would be able to see her as soon as he came through the duty-free area. She was feeling so much more confident and was determined to shower him with a warm reception, no mixed messages this time, no dark, fearful feelings would eclipse these next few days together. She looked at her watch for the umpteenth time and sighed. Judging by announcements and the amount of people gathering, several flights had just landed, meaning that long queues must be developing at passport control. Valda had borrowed a very flattering coral-coloured top, with matching linen skirt, from Lara. Brett had always seen her in trousers, so this time she resolved to show off her slim, tanned legs. She had purchased some sexy sandals that dripped with gold, bronze and peach-coloured beads and also a set of gold bangles, which jangled sensually on her wrist.

It was thirty minutes before she glimpsed who she was sure was Brett. He was anxiously trying to hurry past some beleaguered-looking travellers, who were laden with masses of beaten-up bags and carriers bound with masking tape. He looked very smart in new jeans and casual blue striped shirt. She managed to attract his attention and he looked at her quizzically for a moment, almost as if he did not recognise her. After a beat, his face broke into an enormous smile and he marched with determination over to where she was standing.

At this stage, Valda's heart was beating out of control and she could feel her face reddening. Brett let his duffel bag fall to the ground and they embraced over the barrier; it was a moment she would never forget: his embrace felt so passionate and yet so warm and secure as well. She held him so tightly, not wanting the moment to end. Brett buried his face in the waves of her dark, glossy hair and time stood still. They were oblivious to the hubbub going on around them and also to the kind and nostalgic stares of older couples looking on. Eventually, they let each other go, smiling and laughing. Brett grabbed his duffel bag and swung his leg over the barrier – being so tall, it was easily done – then he clasped her hand and they walked happily towards the car park.

The journey in the Mini was as uncomfortable as ever for the lanky geologist, but they were both chatting with such zest that the miles flew by. Brett exchanged his news of the flight and his experiences in rural Indonesia, with her news of the trip to Sharjah and Flanagan's gossip. Valda noted with delight that Brett was impressed with her new look. Not far from their destination, Brett remarked with surprise, 'Didn't you just miss the turning for East Jumeirah?'

'No, I'm heading for the Marina, I moved to a new flat.' Valda tried to sound matter-of-fact, but she knew that there would inevitably be some awkward questions to follow.

'Oh!' Brett sounded baffled. 'But you never mentioned it on the phone.'

'No, that's because I didn't really want to move. It was forced on me. I thought I'd tell you all about it when you came over.' She smiled and patted him on the knee, and then added, with emphasis, 'But not now, let's not destroy the moment!'

Brett looked partly satisfied, but became quiet for an interval. As Valda drove into the Jumeirah Lake Tower complex, she could sense Brett's awe and also his wariness as he regarded the rows of elegant, luxury tower blocks glittering in the early morning darkness. He had a probing mind and she had the distinct feeling it was working overtime.

'Pretentious, don't you think?' she broke the silence.

'I can't wait to hear the story behind this!' Brett's tone was rather sardonic and Valda cringed inside. Suddenly, a feeling of shame overtook all the excitement. Not for the first time, she realised that Brett would most probably take a dim view of her behaviour in Dubai.

Valda drove into the garage and eased the car into a space; then she took a deep breath, before pulling the handbrake on sharply. She turned to look at Brett, 'I know that you won't let this go, so I am going to tell you and then I want to drop it! OK?' She sounded firm. 'The Sheikh offered me this apartment and I refused. Categorically!' she added with emphasis, staring into Brett's eyes to make sure he understood, before continuing, 'Then one day I came home to find all my stuff gone; all that was left in my old pad were the keys: for this place!' Valda waved her hand dismissively to demonstrate her disdain for Concorde Towers. 'He is not a man who takes no for an answer. I don't know what he'll be up to next and I can tell you now that I am weighing up my options!' Valda turned back to look at the steering wheel; what she had told Brett was basically the truth, minus some details.

'I knew it!' Brett exclaimed. 'I had the feeling when we crossed paths with him that night that there was an agenda. I have heard the stories. You are coming back to Singapore with me!'

'No!' she blurted out. 'I'm not being ungrateful; in fact, your offer means a helluva lot to me, but I have things under control. I'm getting myself organised and I have someone to help me!'

'Who?' The sharp tone of Brett's question revealed some jealousy.

'Lara, the friend I went to Sharjah with!' Valda noted that Brett looked sceptical; she surmised he was dubious about what help a woman could offer. 'I promise I can look after myself,' she said emphatically. 'I intend to leave Dubai very soon and that's all I want to say about this. Be careful what you say in the flat, too, the walls tend to have ears!' With that, she flung the car door open and jumped out.

Alone in the lift, Brett slipped his arms around her waist. One hand explored her lower back, while the other gripped her firm, round bottom. She reached up to clasp his head between her hands, drawing his lips closer to hers. His chin felt rough against her skin and it was arousing in a funny sort of way. Her eyes closed, her lips sought out his and they met tenderly, gently at first and then more passionately. An unmusical electronic tinging sound indicated that they had reached floor seventeen and the elevator doors eased silently open. Not wanting the passionate embrace interrupted, they edged out of the lift, Brett dragging his case with one hand, the other arm wrapped around Valda. They giggled as they awkwardly made their way to Valda's front door, clinging to each other ardently, with suitcase still in tow. They soon began to laugh uncontrollably as they became aware of their own ridiculousness and Valda's keys went clattering onto the shiny marble floor.

'Oops, we'd better shush,' Valda managed to utter breathlessly, pointing to the flat opposite hers. 'The cranky old dear Mrs O'Neil will complain that we came home tipsy!'

But Brett could not have cared less as he grabbed Valda's keys, opened the door and without warning, literally swept her off her feet and carried her into the apartment. The door slammed shut behind them. The lights were off and in the moonlight, Brett made his way over to the bulky shape of the couch, where he lay Valda down. She kicked off her shoes and shifted over, so that he could sit alongside her on the couch.

He leaned over and looked into her eyes, 'Are you sure you're ready?' His tone was filled with sincerity and depth.

Valda smiled and nodded. The look of sheer happiness in her eyes touched a very deep place within Brett's heart and he knew that he was about to experience something profoundly beyond the physical. Their lips met at first tenderly and then they kissed with increasing fervour – soulmates caught up in a torrent of passion and emotion.

Suddenly, Valda noticed that they were on the floor – it was as if their clothes had simply melted away – and their limbs were entwined and he was inside her, his tongue easing gently in and out of her mouth. Being with Brett was so natural; he was powerful and yet his touch was so delicate at times and sensual. She caressed the nape of his neck and the base of his spine simultaneously and his hands explored her body in turn, finding all the right places. Every now and again, she would emit a squeal of delight and Brett would chuckle.

The moonlight gave way to the bright rays of the sun rising over the Gulf. Perspiration glistened on Brett's brow and Valda could feel that her hair was moist. Exhausted yet exhilarated, they pushed on, exploring and challenging each other. Eventually, too tired to even make it to the bedroom, they fell asleep amongst the scattered cushions on the lounge floor. Valda felt so protected and so secure in Brett's arms that even the hardness of the Amtico floor could not dilute the sheer pleasure of the moment.

Valda was awakened by a bright shaft of sunlight that had found a gap in the vertical blinds and was falling right on her face. Her mind was immediately flooded with beautiful memories of the previous night. She was still lying in Brett's arms and her body was still tingling. She lay for some time, reliving the moments, minute by minute; she savoured that rare and blissful feeling of awakening in the arms of someone who was so very special to her. He was fast asleep; she kissed him softly and eased herself onto her feet, careful all the while, so as not to disturb him. Feeling incredibly refreshed, she collected a blanket from her room and lovingly covered Brett over with it. She showered quickly and then wrapped herself in a silky cream nightgown. He was still out for the count when she re-entered the room, so she slipped into the kitchen in order to give him the "Lara Treatment".

Fifteen minutes later, Brett was stirring, aroused by the sound and smell of eggs and bacon frying. Valda was watching him from the kitchen and when he saw her, his sun-kissed face broke into a broad grin. He groaned as he began to stretch his legs and ease himself from the hard floor, he stumbled towards the kitchen with the blanket haphazardly wrapped around his waist. He looked very sultry with his sleepy eyes, unshaven chin and thick strands of dark hair straying over his face. He sidled up behind Valda and clasped her around the waist, leaning down to kiss and chew her ear. She suddenly burst into peals of laughter and he stopped to regard her quizzically, 'Do you like that?'

'Yeah, it's OK,' she teased, 'but what cracked me up was that I just remembered something, your suitcase must still be lying in the hall where we left it.' They laughed, both picturing the unimpressed and disapproving stares the case had probably been receiving from the other residents all morning, particularly Mrs O'Neil. Valda continued to prepare breakfast, crisping the bacon and popping the toast, while Brett held on to her waist, playfully refusing to let go – it resembled something akin to a drunken Samba. Very few of Valda's dark fears and insecurities had resurfaced; the negative voices that had plagued her before were now softer, but any lingering doubts about her feelings for Brett and his for her had been assuaged by the fact that in the cold light of day, they were as passionate and romantic as ever about each other. Valda had awaited the arrival of Brett so eagerly, that she had been wary of disappointment; however, her expectations had been exceeded thus far.

Struggling with the impracticalities of his blanket sarong, Brett whisked his case into the flat after a quick look around to check that no neighbours were anywhere in the vicinity. He then disappeared into the bedroom and returned soon after, wearing some Bermuda shorts.

They spoke little over breakfast, merely soaking up the pleasure of the moment, and no words were needed to communicate the harmony and inner peace both were experiencing. After eating, the conversation began to flow and they talked endlessly, neither bothering to remove the greasy, empty plates from the table; such practicalities faded into insignificance. They discovered that they had more in common than they had ever believed possible and it was both a relief and a pleasure for the two to share such deeply held beliefs and emotions.

Valda was surprised when she eventually looked at the kitchen clock to see that it was already three in the afternoon; they had totally lost track of time. She had to admit that she was starting to feel rather stiff, a side-effect of a night's sleep on the floor and all morning being spent sitting in one position. Judging by his appearance, Brett was obviously feeling in a similar state. Valda invited him to make himself at home in the second bathroom, while she took a hot, rejuvenating shower and got dressed. She suggested they then go in search of some good food.

Two hours later, they were polishing off the last of some gorgeous cake at the Mall of the Emirates. Brett leaned forwards, smiling; and she could tell that he was about to say or about to try to say something important. Something inside her flinched briefly, it was that old defence mechanism trying to kick in and remind that this was, after all, treacherous relationship territory. She raised her eyebrows.

'Valda,' he began, not quite sure how to broach the subject, 'if you leave Dubai and I really agree that you soon should, would you go back to South Africa?' He paused, losing direction, but then continued, stumbling shyly over his words, 'If, for example, there was an opportunity to be somewhere else or to travel … umm … if I happened to be living near a place where you could work … you know?' he finally tailed off, unable to find any more words.

'That's a lot of "ifs", Brett. Are we playing emotional Sudoku?' It was apparent that Valda would not respond to anything that was not a definite idea or request.

'OK!' Brett looked very serious indeed, and he earnestly looked her right in the eyes. 'Come and live with me in Indonesia!'

Valda was not sure how to respond; on the one level, what he was offering was the perfect solution: an escape from the Sheikh, from Cape Town and a promising new life with someone she clearly felt so strongly about. However, something inside her was instinctively against the idea and she was unsure as to why. All her doubts about her feelings for Brett had faded and so had her fears about his motivations, but living together was another step entirely, another huge step. Valda found herself looking down into her empty mug and she realised that Brett must be reading the doubts in her mind from the expression her body language undoubtedly conveyed. Anxious not to do anything to destroy the moment, she found herself saying softly, 'OK.' Her acceptance of his offer astounded Brett, who had anticipated more ambivalence and more reticence. She was feeling rather flummoxed by her own reaction and hastened to add, 'Just give me a chance to resolve my "stuff" here; I'm not sure how long that will take though!'

Brett was high on that clichéd old cloud nine, so much so that he hardly noticed that Valda had fallen quiet. Valda's logical mind was attempting to adjudicate an emotional battle raging inside of her. Brett's offer was amazing and filled her with hope, though she was finding it impossible to explain why there was something so strong within her that seemed determined to veto any move to Indonesia with Brett. She found that for the first time since Brett had arrived, she had to force herself to laugh and to be natural. Luckily, she seemed to be pulling it off.

Ever since she had been living in Dubai, Valda had coped with her problems by living strictly in the now; any thoughts of consequences and the future were prohibited and dealt with only when necessary. She was experiencing a great reluctance to make any plans so far into the future. Indeed, the spectre of the Sheikh clouded her immediate horizon and she felt that until such time as that was eradicated, she could not sincerely commit to anything. While Valda felt guilty that she may be leading Brett on, in another way she felt as if she was telling him what he needed to hear.

Feeling as though she needed a few moments to herself in order to collect her thoughts and to drop the act, Valda suggested Brett continue to look around, while she took a pit stop to the ladies' room.

Standing with her back to the mirror against the washbasins, she toyed with her mobile, pondering over whether or not to give Lara a quick call for advice. Her mind was in turmoil, exacerbated by the lack of sleep and excitement, and for the first time in months, she craved a drink. Snapping the phone shut, she took a deep breath and decided that perhaps she was making too much of the situation and that she should resort to her "*manana manana*" mode again. Feeling more composed, she exited the Ladies and went looking for Brett.

She found him peering into the window of an electrical shop and before he had a chance to spot her, she crept up behind him and playfully pounced on him. Brett yelled with surprise and they both roared with laughter at the juvenile prank. Their rowdiness may have drawn some disapproving stares, but it helped Valda to relax and to loosen up. Suddenly, she was allegro again.

'So, I assume you got all measured up for your tux while I was away?' she ragged. He was taken aback for a moment and looked at her quizzically. 'But you did remember to bring your dress suit, didn't you?' she asked, feigning disappointment.

'OK, where is this going?'

'Seriously now! I have a little romantic thing booked for tonight and I think maybe we should make an effort on the clothes front.' Valda was ashamed to admit she was blushing; being romantic was alien to her, but she was prepared to have a stab at it.

Brett was intrigued, but in the spirit of romance, Valda was coy with all the details, other than to emphasise that it was not going to be a jeans and T-shirt-style evening.

It was eight o'clock and several couples, including Valda and Brett, were enjoying a romantic dinner aboard a traditional wooden dhow. The air was filled with the sounds of clinking crockery and sensual conversation as the dhow slipped silently along Dubai Creek, passing the Golf and Yacht Club. The sumptuous Lebanese feast was rounded off with distinctive Arabic coffee and speciality chocolates made locally.

The sparkling lights of modern Dubai bouncing off the waves, the gentle music and the elegance of the dhow made for a magical and ethereal experience. Valda felt a million miles from anywhere; she even felt disconnected from herself in a pleasant sort of way – something akin to being inebriated without the alcohol. She was wearing a lacy, knitted bolero over a strappy dress, all in a very enchanting midnight blue colour. The coolness of the silk bolero on her skin felt comforting in a way: living in Dubai's relentless sunshine had made her crave coolness and she had come to find security in the darkness of the desert nights.

As Brett was sipping the last of his coffee, he reached across the table and clasped Valda's hand; he was beaming. 'We are going to be so happy; I can just feel it!'

Valda squeezed his hand; her loving smile was designed to conceal the fact that she had no words with which to reply, her ambivalent emotions raged on in the back of her mind.

It was ten o'clock and half an hour to drop off – a perfect time for all the couples on the dhow to sit back and soak up the spectacular lights of modern Dubai's twenty-first century architectural landscape. Brett held her tightly from behind, their bodies undulating together with the motion of the dhow. Valda felt very relaxed and extremely contented; indeed, the moment was wonderful and more than she could ever have hoped for during the past few dark years. Thoughts of everything faded as she stared absently into the lights of the glittering Chamber of Commerce.

'No, stop that!' Valda shrieked out.

'So you're ticklish, are you,' grinned Brett with glee.

Valda was lying on the bed and he was kneeling over her, trying to wrestle her dress over her head as she wriggled about giggling. After much hilarity, the dress finally hit the floor and they were both silent as he sat back admiring her svelte figure. The moonlight was illuminating their bodies, highlighting Brett's thin and well-toned torso. Valda suddenly noticed that Brett was staring with surprise at her stomach.

'What is that?' he asked.

Realising that the tattoo encircling her navel was what had captured his attention, she answered, 'It's a compass,' and then added, 'an artistic version of one!' Valda felt quite self-conscious for one moment; it was as if Brett had discovered something about her of which he did not approve.

'Oh, I didn't notice it last night!' he said, in a matter-of-fact tone.

'Well that's because we didn't get far enough apart from each other!' she laughed.

Brett did not comment; instead, he eased himself down and two became one once more. It was a beautiful night of both relaxed togetherness and passion. They slept soundly, satisfied and now exhausted. The bright morning sunshine failed to disrupt their blissful sleep and it was eleven o'clock before they began to stir.

They lay side by side, relaxed and mutually too lazy to summon up the energy to make breakfast. Brett toyed absently with her hair, weaving it between his long fingers, before deciding to search for her hand. He slipped his fingers between hers and drew her hand towards him, placing her hand and his on his chest. Valda gave it a little squeeze, just to let him know that none of the tenderness between them had evaporated. Valda then felt him twist her wrist slightly and she looked around to see him regarding the inside of her arm with some puzzlement. She followed his gaze to the thin, pale scar, which extended from her right wrist halfway to her elbow. She was surprised to see how faint the scar had become, no wonder Brett had only just noticed it. It was only in the harsh morning sunlight that it was apparent. He stared at her arm for a long while, saying nothing, although she could tell that many a thought was streaming through his mind. It was hard for her to gauge his impression, so she remained silent and looked away. After many minutes, he kissed her hand and then released it. Then he swung his body up and out of the bed and announced, 'My turn to look after you, I am going to cook breakfast!'

After a quick and revitalising shower, Valda hurried eagerly to the kitchen; she was starving and would have been impressed with anything from toast and Marmite to cornflakes at that stage. She was, however, ordered out of the kitchen and told to wait another five minutes. Brett was up to his elbows in eggshells and kitchen paraphernalia, but wanted no help. She smiled to herself; he was just her cup of tea, useless enough in a kitchen to retain the macho element, but at least considerate enough to give it a try.

Valda decided that she would while away the next few minutes by checking her email, which was something she had become rather keen on in the past few weeks, especially since Bella had split with her husband and seemed to rely on Valda for advice and observations. It had somehow given Valda a great sense of pride and self-worth to know that her experiences could be put to some use and that they were actually worthwhile in helping someone else through a split. It felt so good to be needed and appreciated.

She sat down and began roving around the screen with the mouse, browsing news items and some showbiz tittle-tattle, before logging on to Yahoo! Mail. Her computer was in the lounge and she could see Brett from where she was sitting – he was very wrapped up in his efforts *à la cuisine* and was taking no notice of her. Valda's mind was focused on a delicious feast of bacon and eggs rather than on her mail, but her attention shifted dramatically as she glanced back at the screen to see the name Richard Sinclair in her in-box. Her heart missed several beats and when she reached for the mouse, she noticed her hand was shaking. Her mind was flooded with questions as she clicked on the "read message" toggle and waited for the screen to refresh.

'Val, your *grand petit dejeuner* awaits,' Brett called out with a flourish as he wafted out of the kitchen, comically wearing a tea towel tucked into his shorts and waving a spatula.

'Coming!' Valda quickly minimised the in-box and flicked the computer off.

She was aware that her face had reddened and that her abrupt actions may have looked odd. She was desperate for a few seconds to compose herself and so she hurriedly made an excuse and returned to the bedroom. Back in the bedroom, she searched for her cigarettes, craving the comfort and release they usually brought. She could not find them anywhere and realised for the first time that she had hardly smoked since Brett's arrival. She cursed herself for being so feeble and for crumbling at the first sight of dear Richard's name. Taking a deep breath, she summoned up some composure and returned to the lounge, determined not to let Brett see that she was stirred up.

'OK,' she smiled enthusiastically, 'I'm ready, lay it on me!'

Brett proudly presented several slices of golden brown French toast and mouth-watering crispy bacon, with fried tomato on the side. It was easy for Valda to put her emotions aside in favour of her appetite and no pretence was needed when complimenting the chef.

'This is fantastic!' she mumbled between mouthfuls. 'I've never thought of adding oregano to French toast, it makes such a difference!'

As her appetite receded, her curiosity about Richard's email surfaced again. Brett was still engrossed in his meal and so she had time to ponder over this bolt from the blue. Larissa had promised that she would never feel the same way about Richard, but at that moment, Valda questioned the accuracy of that statement. She suddenly felt strangely distant from Brett and it was an effort to chat and maintain that effortless togetherness.

After breakfast, Brett went off to shower and a relieved Valda was left alone to look for her cigarettes. After looking for ten minutes, she finally found them in her jacket pocket, the first place she had looked. 'Damn you, Richard! As soon as you pop into my life again I start losing it!' she muttered irritably under her breath.

Halfway though her fag, she contemplated going back online to see what Richard had to say; however, she could hear the Brett turning off the shower and she knew that there would be no time in which to do so. She began mulling over the various scenarios and the sarcastic and facetious replies she would come up with – perhaps she would just "spam" him; after all, did she even want to reply? She was torn over which approach to take and at the same time, she felt guilty about Brett; he was sure to notice that she was detached and disconnected from him.

Brett waltzed out of the shower, towelling off as he shuffled around the room looking for his clothes. 'You've gone very quiet?' he commented without any real concern.

Valda stubbed out her cigarette and moved towards Brett, grabbing him around the waist, 'You're leaving tonight and I am already depressed!'

'Well, I told you that you can come with me?' It was half a question and half a statement.

'I can't this time, but I am counting on you keeping that offer open! We're going to be together very soon.'

Valda was holding on to Brett tightly and she felt a surge of strange emotions. For a few moments, she felt like an actress speaking her lines on a set, nothing felt real and she questioned whether there was any sincerity and depth in her voice. Was it some residual feeling for Richard that was preventing her from taking that next step with Brett? Was her intuition telling her something? Was it that old ogre of fear holding her back? She was tormented by voices in her head arguing and debating but, beyond all the logic and psychology, there was something else: a feeling in her heart that she could not define. Valda suddenly thought back to her conversation with Lara on their trip to Sharjah: 'But do we have a future?' she had asked of her and Brett. Valda could not remember how Lara had responded.

For the rest of the day, Valda tried to maintain an amusing, affectionate and playful manner. Her mind was never far from Richard, no matter how hard she tried to enjoy the trip on the amphibious bus and their lunch out in the desert. Fortunately, Brett was happy to accept an arm around the waist and head on his shoulder as a substitute for conversation. He obviously accepted her explanation that any quietness on her part was due to the anticipatory loneliness after his departure. Valda kept wondering whether Brett really knew her, for she honestly felt that she knew him. She had changed so much since coming to Dubai that she was unsure whether she actually knew herself any more.

At three, they were heading home along Sheikh Zayed Road. Brett's flight was at six o'clock and they wanted some private time alone to say goodbye before the hurly-burly of the airport departure lounge.

'So how much longer do you intend to stay here?' asked Brett; it was a loaded question.

'No longer than six weeks,' she answered with honesty.

'What's going to take so long?' he asked pointedly, adding, 'I really think you need to put some distance between you and that Sheikh character. Sooner the better.'

Where have I hard that before? thought Valda to herself. 'I am trying to save as much money as I can and besides, I can't just walk out and let everyone in the band down!'

'Do you really think the Sheikh is going to let you go that easily? He has shown himself to be pretty obsessed!' argued Brett.

'I am not exactly going to tell him, am I!' snapped Valda. Brett's questioning was making her edgy. Taking a deep breath, she continued in a more controlled tone, 'I know what he's like. That's why I am just taking it one day at a time, feeling out the lay of the land as it were ...' she trailed off, motioning with her hand as if to fill in the rest.

'Don't leave it too long!'

They fell silent for the rest of the journey home.

It was ten minutes before they were supposed to leave for the airport and they were still in the bedroom, wrapped up in each other's arms. For the first time that day, Richard was on the periphery of her mind and she was once again blissfully aware of the strong feelings that Brett had awakened in her. Suddenly remembering something, she eased out of Brett's arms and leant over to her bedside table. Brett watched with interest as she slipped a small black velvet bag out of the drawer. She handed it to him with a smile and raised her eyebrows,.'A present for you!'

Brett's face creased into a smile and she could tell that he was very touched and surprised. He toyed with the velvet ribbon, pensively delaying opening the bag.

'I feel terrible,' he said seriously, 'I never bought you anything!'

'Not all gifts are material!' Valda touched his cheek lovingly; she could feel tears rushing to her eyes and so she suddenly shoved Brett boisterously on the shoulder, adding cheerfully, 'Now, go on and open it!'

Brett loosened the ribbon and slipped the golden paperweight into the palm of his hand, so that he could examine it. It was a golden replica of the headgear that they use in mines.

Valda watched him closely, eager that he should appreciate the symbolism. 'It's to symbolise us: where we come from, like most of the world's gold and where we met, here in Dubai, where most of the world's gold seems to end up!'

Brett continued to regard her gift and as he turned it around with his fingers, he appeared to be deeply lost in thought.

'I think I finally struck gold!' he said simply as he turned to look Valda in the eye.

* * *

'Flight EK 434 to Singapore has now departed.'

Tears were rolling down Valda's cheeks as she heard the announcement. Her final hours with Brett had been the most powerful emotionally of his visit. On the way to the airport they had both cried; then laughed through the tears – two people discovering a new kind of love, a renewed sense of meaning, and riding the emotional breakers together.

Back at her apartment, things felt so quiet and empty. She wandered aimlessly from room to room with her mug in her hand, not knowing quite what to do with herself. Despite being driven to distraction by Richard's email all day, she now had no inclination to log on at all. She missed Brett and she yearned to be with him on that plane, far away from Dubai, from the relentless heat, from the stark, artificial landscape and from the Sheikh. I am running away again, she sighed hopelessly to herself. What am I going to be running away from next?

Fortunately, the ringing of her phone prevented any more dallying with feelings of remorse and moroseness. It was Lara, who, in her usual perky way, was able to encourage Valda to divulge all the gory details about Brett's trip. Valda mentioned the email and was reassured by Larissa that she had nothing to fear from it, that Richard was history.

The chat with Lara left her feeling quite upbeat; narrating the details of the past twenty-four hours to a third person had put them entirely into perspective and she was suddenly mystified at her previously conflicting emotions. Feeling exhausted but happy, she fell into a deep sleep.

It was the ringing of the phone that finally woke her from the deep, restful sleep she was having. It was Brett. Rarely had Valda been so delighted to be woken by the telephone. Keen not to repeat the debacle of the previous occasion, Brett had ensured that he rang as soon as he possibly could. He could not deny that he was eager to hear her voice again: his once care- and commitment-free world of exotic locations and easy women no longer satisfied him. He sensed that Valda was a complicated and somewhat troubled type and yet her disguised vulnerability aroused the protective side of him. He tended to tire of girlfriends fast after he had stripped away the outer layers of their personality; however, he felt that with Valda, he would never stop searching for the core and that was very exciting.

Valda felt elated after his call; there was no longer any room for doubt about Brett's feelings for her. It felt like an appropriate moment to finally check the email from Richard, for she needed to deal with it and consign him to the past once more.

Sitting with a sweet cup of tea and some biscuits, she waited for the message to flash onto the screen. With a small amount of trepidation still fluttering about and wondering what to expect, she read:

> Dear Valda,
> I sincerely regret that we never had a chance to talk about things. I really need to see you again and to say so many things. Sonja and I are over – it was a ridiculous relationship, a non-starter!
> I will be in Dubai on business for three days from the 25th. We are long overdue for a heart-to-heart. I understand things far better now – everything.
> Please seriously consider before you reply.
> Richard.

It was short and to the point in Richard's typically direct, Virgo style. Short it may have been, but the impact was not lessened by its brevity. "Sonja and I are over", "I will be in Dubai", "I really need to see you again", there was so much for her to think about. What is fate up to now, she sighed to herself.

So, Richard is coming to Dubai – the acid test of Larissa's theory, decided Valda. But I never expected it so soon! she thought. Her memories of Richard, both good and bad, were far too emotionally charged for her to be able use logic or philosophy to formulate any theories. While her head toyed with the idea of ignoring the email, her heart knew that they were destined to meet again.

Chapter Fifteen

'Hello!'

'Hi, Lara, are the stars being kind today?'

'Mine are behaving themselves so far, but I hate to speak too soon, and yours?'

Lara sounded as bubbly as ever. Valda was always amazed at how infectious her positivity was. Lara had assured Valda that she, too, could feel very low and desperate, but Valda found that very hard to imagine. Lara had the gift of making everything seem possible and it was very reassuring.

'Ditto! Lara, I was wondering, you said you played tennis, right?' asked Valda.

'Yes,' replied Lara, although the dubiousness in her voice was more for effect than anything else.

'Well, all the staff at the hotel are involved in this sports day thing on Thursday and I have been roped into the tennis and I need a partner,' she explained.

'Did I say I was any good?' asked Lara playfully.

'Not really,' answered Valda.

'Well that's good, because it would have been a terrible lie!' Lara laughed mockingly at herself.

'Stop kidding around and just say Yes,' ordered Valda with impatience.

'Yes, but only because I cannot resist the chance to make a donkey of myself.' Valda was beginning to wish that Lara would be more serious for a moment; after all, the get-together was not merely about a trivial tennis match, but more of a good opportunity to discuss things and to make plans. Lara continued, 'My game is patchy, but since it's doubles and I am a mean volleyer, we'll be OK.'

'And you don't mind if we discuss some things?' She paused and then hastily added, 'About Richard and Brett, you know!' Valda left her words hanging in the air, emphasising that she was alluding to the plans Lara had promised to help her with in relation to her departure from Dubai.

'Naturally, I have lots to tell you myself.'

Lara's allegro tone did not change or give any indication that they were touching on a grave subject. Valda felt reassured, not-withstanding the fact that she instinctively trusted Lara and felt she could rely on her; logically, she had wondered whether Lara would fall by the wayside if the going got tough. Would she give up on her like Richard had? Would she be able to help?

'Good, good and I promise we won't spend the whole day talking about me, me, me!' Valda gave the assurance with a chuckle.

The October evenings were humid and sticky, but playing tennis was just about bearable. The tennis event was a round robin and Valda and Lara were due to play two members of staff from one of the restaurants in the Burg Emir. The whole sports day had been organised by the personnel people, who were ostensibly trying out a new staff motivational and bonding scheme, hatched in some Ivy League think tank. Everyone seemed enthusiastic though, and the atmosphere was congenial. They sat on the sidelines watching the others, drinking Coke and waiting for their match to begin.

'Will His Lordship be here?' asked Lara disdainfully.

'Oh, I doubt it. Sports are not his thing!' replied Valda shaking her head.

'I had this idea he was kinda ubiquitous?'

'No,' she replied thoughtfully, 'just omniscient and that's why I want to be very careful about my plans to leave.'

Lara gave a quick glance around to see if anyone was listening and then said under her breath, 'Talking about his thing, do you think all that stuff is for him personally?'

'By the look of his bloodshot eyes, yes! But who knows, I hardly think he needs to sell it for cash,' she paused thoughtfully while spinning her racket head. 'Maybe he shares it with his mates, perhaps it's some kind of status symbol for him?'

Lara thought for a few moments before asking, 'Have you noticed anything else strange in your apartment, like the time your photos were rearranged, for example?'

'No, nothing,' she answered immediately and with certainty. She suddenly stopped spinning her racket and turned to look at Lara seriously. 'And Richard?' she began. 'How do you think I should handle him?'

'Don't over think it; he said himself in the email that he needs to say so many things, so the pressure is on him!' Lara paused for a quick sip of Coke. 'Just show him the sights, introduce him to your friends, tell him about life here … if he wants to get deeper than that, then it's up to him to bring the subject up. I really think that when the time comes, you'll be easy-going about it.'

'I haven't replied to his email yet, what should I say?' Valda was eager for help.

Lara was beginning to feel that she was once again being asked to cross the fine line between advice-giving and dependency; however, bearing in mind the overall picture, she could not see the point in holding back. 'His was very short and sweet, so why not reply in the same mode: give him your number, ask if he needs picking up from the airport and say that seeing him again will be interesting! Something neutral like that.'

Valda smiled thankfully and made a mental note of Lara's comments; she always seemed to come up with the goods. It was almost time for the pair to take to the court, so Valda suggested they delay any discussion of her flight from Dubai until after dinner.

The pair made a great team with Valda's penetrating ground strokes and Lara's agility at the net. Lara was highly impressed at Valda's very powerful left-handed serves, which won them many free points. The whole experience turned out to be great fun and great therapy for both concerned. Valda was delighted that Lara had embraced the whole thing in such good spirit; she regretted that they had not met in more pleasant circumstances, with more time for fun and less for problems. The match was theirs within 45 minutes.

With three wins under their belt, feeling very sweaty and hungry, they made their way to the buffet.

'Do you work out a lot?' enquired Lara with curiosity. 'Because you can really hit a ball!'

Valda shook her head, 'No, not really; in fact, I hate the gym! I'm just competitive, that's all; the power is my natural aggression coming out. I have to hand it to you though; you're very crafty on court – quite literally thinking on your feet.'

They talked little over food. Lara, however, was rather impatient to get to the business end of the evening; there was a lot on her mind and she was unwittingly bolting her food back. Valda, on the other hand, was more composed; she had subconsciously released her angst onto Lara and had the feeling that things were under control. The sports complex was sprawling and afforded ample private talking space. After dinner they strolled nonchalantly amongst the palms, looking to all the world as if all that concerned them were the trivialities of daily life.

'OK,' Lara began earnestly, 'when you leave Dubai, are you flying straight to Singapore to Brett?'

'No,' Valda was adamant. 'If I go straight there, he'll think "this is it, we're an item" and I'm not ready for that yet, I need some time and space to think about what I really want to do next.' Valda paused and then rambled on, almost as if she was talking things out to herself. 'I like him ... a lot, I may even love him, but what sort of life is living with someone who works on an oil rig? This month in Singapore, next in Nigeria, next ... God knows where?' She paused again, this time to light a cigarette. She continued talking and gesticulating, fag in hand, in her characteristic style, which was rather tomboyish and even quite theatrical, Lara thought. 'Where does that leave my career? I don't want to be the stay-at-home sidekick. I need to live somewhere where I have a chance of continuing my career which, of course, you said would be on the up!' At that point, she turned to stare into Lara's eyes, searching for reassurance that that was, indeed, the case.

'Precisely! You took the words out of my mouth. I think you should go to London or New York, preferably London, because I know for a fact that UK immigration controls are slack and I'll tell you what to say, if you know what I mean.'

'That's why it's so important to me to get as much money as I can out of here, so that I can have a decent start somewhere else!'

Lara reached into the shoulder bag she was carrying and withdrew a white A5 envelope. She handed it to Valda as she explained with great care, 'In here are the bank cards and deposit slips for my old HSBC account in the UK. I haven't used it for a while. I suggest you draw cash from your own account and deposit it in stages into this account. 'Even if the Sheikh finds out that money is disappearing, he won't know where to; he may just think you're living it up or buying furniture, jewellery, whatever. Sell what you can on eBay and have the buyers pay into this account. Everything is done by PIN now, no signatures, so you will be able to use this card anywhere in the world; no one will realise that it's in my name. You can use it to pay for your tickets at the airport.

I suggest you do that rather than buy them in advance. When you get to London, you can open your own account and transfer the funds there.'

'If I could sell the GT I would be set, but I think that selling it unobtrusively could be hard!'

'We could sell it for cash to some wealthy European out here: I have an idea about that, but its not fully formed yet, let me think about it. Whatever you can't fit in a suitcase, you can leave with me; I'll ship it to you when you're ready.'

'Are you sure about letting me have access to your account?' Valda queried politely, even though the envelope was already safely in her tote bag.

'Well, quite frankly, the question really is – do you trust me enough to put all your eggs in my basket?' stated Lara rather bluntly.

Valda had been so eager to jump at any solution offered that it had totally slipped her mind that she was potentially leaving herself open to being swindled by Lara. That possibility, however, felt remote; all her gut instincts told her to trust Lara and to go with whatever she said.

'As soon as you have enough money in the account, you can be out of here and it's all over!' smiled Lara.

Valda felt elated. Suddenly, things seemed so simple. A problem shared is a problem halved, she thought to herself, another cliché that had earned its status.

'Another thing, fly to London via somewhere else, just in case he checks the flights. Best to keep him guessing about where you went, not that I think he is going to hunt you down, right?' Lara looked for Valda's reaction.

'You tell me? You're the astrologer!'

Valda's sarcasm took Lara by surprise, but she managed to keep her tone confident as she replied, 'I am sure it will be fine, but let's not be complacent. Your chart indicates he's of a pernicious character and this thing with you has gotten personal for him!'

'Personal?' Valda raised an eyebrow.

'I don't think you fit quite the same bill as the waiter, the tennis pro and the chef!' she ended with inflection.

Valda nodded in agreement; right from the start, she'd had an inkling that she had made a lasting impression on the man. She rarely thought of him as a man – somehow, his attire and position of royal importance had cloaked him in asceticism which, of course, was a false perception. She immediately remembered what Lara had said about their fates being tied together and made a note to ask for some clarification later.

'Which reminds me,' enquired Lara with grave curiosity, 'you mentioned to me that on your first ever meeting with the Sheikh, he talked about a girl who had worked at Flanagan's, who he had loaned an apartment or something – he wanted you to take the apartment, right?'

Valda nodded vaguely, 'Yes, that's right!'

'Do you remember her name?'

Valda thought for a moment before shaking her head. 'No. Why do you ask?'

Lara took a deep breath and ran her fingers through her hair while looking at the ground, which was something Valda had noticed she did when she was buying time to think. 'Those newspaper clippings reminded me of something; months ago, March, maybe ...' She looked up at Valda, 'Must have been just after you arrived here – a friend of mine was telling me about a young British woman, who was found dead on the beach at Jumeirah. It was presumed she had been struck by a motor boat while swimming, which I found a little odd at the time. I can't remember if the article mentioned her name, but it did say that she worked in a nightclub.' Lara decided not to wait for a response, 'I am sure that I can find out more details, but I'm guessing that she was your predecessor; which would mean that the Sheikh has now turned his attention to women when choosing couriers and that still bugs me!'

Lara may have been engrossed with the mystery, but Valda merely shrugged and answered, 'Sounds like a plausible theory, but no one at Flannagan's has ever mentioned anything about it to me.'

'Why would they? Dubai is a "halfway house", none of us Westerners are here for long enough to get to know each other; we are all on our way somewhere else. When someone disappears, people just assume they went home or moved away.'

'But surely people would have seen the news in the paper,' argued Valda.

'Only if they read articles buried on page 23.' Lara's tone implied that she regarded what she was saying as self-evident. 'None of your clippings were exactly headline news, were they?'

Valda's reply was belligerent, 'So who cares, I'm getting out of here anyway.'

Lara decided to give the subject a rest. Since the social side of the evening was winding down, they were able to slip away. Valda suggested they try a new Afghani restaurant that had recently opened and they were soon burning rubber down Al Wasl Road. Lara could tell by the way Valda was driving that she was deep in thought, for her shoulders were tense and Lara was sure her personal rev counter was in the red. Lara was finding the silence awkward and so she ventured sweetly, 'Can I ask what's on your mind?'

Valda grimaced and remained silent for a few minutes before replying, 'Here I am, running away and having to face the prospect of starting all over again. If I hadn't stuffed up this opportunity ...' Her words were left hanging in the air as she shifted ruthlessly into second and made a sharp turn.

'You didn't stuff up, you had an experience!'

'And you are still sure I'll find success again?'

'You have already!' assured Lara. 'I do get out, you know, and I talk to people. You have made quite an impact out here. You have already found that winning formula again. Which reminds me, I'd like you to give me a demo CD or DVD, if you have one?'

'Why?' Valda was all ears.

'I'm not saying anything yet, weighty expectations can jinx things.' She then went on to add quickly, 'In my experience, that is!' Lara gave her a cheeky smile and a wink. Lara was disappointed to see that Valda was not satisfied with her response; she looked irritable and impatient for definitive answers. For the first time since they had known each other, Lara felt slightly bemused by Valda's attitude; the effect was like an invisible barrier descending between them. 'All you ever think about is success!' It was a statement. Lara felt as if she was throwing down a challenge, a provocation to entice Valda into revealing whether or not this was the case. Lara waited for the response and was surprised when it came.

'What do you think about?' she snarled.

'Everything!' was Lara's reply, although she could not help herself from continuing with, 'I've never been successful and, of course, it used to bother me, but I realised that when you are successful, you define yourself in terms of that success. Success is ephemeral and when it ceases to be, you cease to be with it. We are all more than our DOB, our marital status and our successes and failures. It's all ashes and dust, but the lessons we learn stay within our soul for eternity.' Lara was beginning to feel that she was eulogising and she forced herself to stop.

'But if we stopped aiming for success or whatever it is we aim for, would we ever learn any lessons? Would we even get out of bed?' Valda's answer was profound in its simplicity and Lara had to acknowledge that she had a point.

'OK, I agree with you. Maybe our dreams are devised in order to torment us, drive us, guide us and compel us towards our spiritual destiny?'

'Maybe? I didn't realise that that word was in your vocabulary, Lara, you are always so dogmatic!' Valda shook her head, adding with a smile, 'I don't mean that as a criticism. Now, have you eaten Afghan food before?'

Lara was quite relieved that Valda had shifted the conversation into a lighter and more prosaic gear. 'No, is it spicy? Because although my mouth is adventurous, my stomach is pretty conservative!'

'I have a cupboard full of Gaviscon, so don't worry!' Valda laughed.

Ten minutes later they were sitting cross-legged on the floor on velvet cushions in front of a low table at the Jadi Shahr-i-Nar restaurant. The low table was covered in a dark red linen tablecloth with matching folded linen serviettes and two sets of forks. Lara's eyes roamed the room, sparkling in fascination. The square room was dimly lit with ornate oil lamps made of pewter; on the walls hung richly coloured Persian carpets and the windows were adorned with voluptuous twists and swags of hand-painted silks. She noticed with interest the little bells hanging from some of the light fixtures. Background music sourced from the subcontinent harmonising with the cosmopolitan chatter gave the place a rhythm and a vibe of its own. The atmosphere was quite mesmeric. Valda explained that Afghan food was far blander than the other cuisines of the region and she recommended the boulanee kadu. The service was rather haphazard and disorganised and Lara would have wagered that at any moment, one of the large platters so ineptly handled by the waiters would tip and fall onto some unsuspecting patron. Despite Valda's assurances, Lara secretly anticipated a fiery, hot dish and so she ordered a soda water. Much to Valda's amusement, instead of soda water, the waiter brought *dough,* a yoghurt drink flavoured with coriander. The yoghurt drink was a little challenging for both of their palettes, but they persevered in the name of culinary exploration. They rounded off the meal with pumpkin turnovers, as recommended by Valda, and cardamom tea.

Valda was chuffed to see that Lara had genuinely enjoyed the meal, apart from the yoghurt drink, of course. Valda continued to pick at the remaining morsels of pumpkin, while recounting a story from her more distant past. Lara was only half listening, because she was surprised at the two emotions bubbling within her. She was elated at the buoyant and confident person she now saw in Valda, for it gave her a rare sense of achievement; somehow, she felt as if she was contributing to the rebirth of something. The second emotion was less pleasant though, it was the same feeling Lara used to have in England when she looked up at the pale blue late-August sky and felt the chilly blast that signified that summer was almost over. Although Valda had made no fixed plans, Lara sensed that this was almost a sort of "goodbye meal" and that filled her with sadness – Valda had brought so much into her life in the short space of time they had known each other. But there was more to the sadness than the leaving of a friend: it was a reoccurring theme for Lara, people leaving her life and moving on to something more promising, something better; it made her own monotony seem even more inexorable. Valda was looking forward to the future, whereas Lara was hiding in the present, trapped at the halfway house between a disappointing yesterday and an uncertain future. She wondered when she would finally move on, find a purpose and somehow be released from the intolerable limbo.

It was three in the morning and things were quietening down. Valda and Lara were amongst the last patrons there, but there was no pressure to leave; bottomless cups of coffee and chai would be served until dawn. Valda leaned forward eagerly and began, 'You have talked about fate and free will in the context of your readings – which is it then, which prevails?' She placed her mug down firmly, to indicate that she was listening intently.

'At some level, everything is down to a matter of choice!' said Lara in a matter-of-fact tone.

'At some level?' Valda wanted more.

'When you make a choice, you have to be 100 cent behind it; a minuscule amount of doubt can scupper all your plans, no matter how badly you think you want something!'

'Well, of course, nothing is ever that simple,' she laughed and then became immediately serious again. And where does fate fit in!'

'When we can't decide or fail to choose, or if we believe we have no choice, fate chooses for us! I believe that we fail to decide or commit to something totally due to a battle raging between our conscious will and our spiritual will; this produces a frustrating stalemate of depression and torment. We stumble along until our higher conscious and ego come into alignment, then anything is possible.'

'How do we know what our higher conscious or whatever it is wants?'

'That's a "you'll be the first to know when I find out" answer!' Lara rolled her eyes and sighed.

'I know you well enough to know you must have a theory!'

'Intuition, reading the signs, gut feeling! I've never had much luck with them though.'

'They are not very conclusive; I mean, maybe you just see signs and interpret things according to what your conscious will wants to see.'

'Exactly, which is why those kinds of theories are only relevant to people who have reached a certain level of spiritual evolvement, self-knowledge and total honesty. Maybe when we are old enough and have barked up enough wrong trees, we'll eventually find out what our higher conscious is telling us.'

'And you think what? That this is the truth about life? I'm not being argumentative, I'm genuinely curious!'

'No, I don't think that there is one truth. I think that while this way of thought is true for many, it's not exclusive. I think the problem is that people tend to look for one truth, one ultimate explanation. 'What if there are many truths, which are all equally valid; what if the earth revolves around the sun, but at the same time the sun revolves around the earth.?It sounds odd, but the premise of astrology is that the sun and the planets all orbit around the earth and the fact that this may not be scientifically accurate does not impact at all on the validity of astrology. It all depends on your own perspective.'

'So what does Larissa May actually think then?'

'It shouldn't matter to anyone else but me. I am still working out what exactly my theory really is. In a way, I have stopped making plans, I've stopped dreaming – the page is blank and I've given fate the pen with which to write my script or maybe signpost me to my place in this world.' She stopped abruptly, smiled and remarked, 'Hey, I really get a kick out of these conversations we have, I am going to miss you.'

'I never think of myself as a spiritual person, but I have enjoyed them, too!'

'Spiritual,' scoffed Lara. 'It's such an overused word; everybody seems to call themselves spiritual these days. Human beings always seem so hell-bent on categorising and labelling themselves as something or other.'

Valda remained quiet, she was not sure if she had an answer or not. Perhaps that was the crux: don't nail anything down, don't commit to any one set of beliefs, for as soon as you do that, you become blind. She reached for her car keys and they eased their stiff legs off the floor and made their way to the car.

Conversation on the way back to Valda's flat was more mundane in nature, as the pair of them were weary and the digesting of their carb-packed meal was sucking up the remainder of their energy. The first orangy rays of sunlight were filtering through the mist, the traffic was fairly thin and it felt as if the car was floating along the avenue of Babel-sized towers; both the emotional and the physical atmosphere were surreal. Conversation had tailed off and Valda's mind strayed from subject to subject, not lingering on anything too deep. She felt pleasantly tired and relaxed, almost as if she had finally let-up on the self-criticism and questioning malarkey; she now had solutions rather than confounding obstacles. She was suddenly filled with enthusiasm for the next stage of her adventure; be it London, New York or Indonesia, she was going to write her own script. Soon, she would effectively be able to rub out her less memorable forays within her Dubai experience and begin a new one, with no harm done. All's well that ends well, she thought triumphantly to herself.

Lara was staring ahead – everywhere around her was life: in the huge apartment blocks residents were stirring, about to embark on productive days, taxi drivers were on their way home after a busy night's work and cafes were finally closing their shutters after another lucrative night. Despite being at the heart of a vibrant city, she felt an uncomfortable, cold and damp feeling lurking in her gut – she knew that the feeling resembled the pangs of loneliness and insecurity which so often plagued her, but there was an edge to it that was baffling. She felt very small, very insignificant and very powerless at that moment. She scowled and glanced at the speedometer, wishing that Valda would put her foot down – she was sure that she would feel better once they reached Valda's flat.

After what seemed like a very long time to Lara, they drew into the entrance of the Concorde Tower's underground garage. Valda slipped her flat keys out of a concealed crevice, flicked through them until she found what looked, to Lara, like a fat gold pin and she then inserted the pin swiftly into a hole in a machine alongside the car. The iron gates securing the parking area swung open efficiently and they drove in.

'I had a spare one of these made for you, along with a spare set of keys for my flat,' chirped Valda.

Lara looked at her askance, 'Why?'

Valda shrugged as she manoeuvred the car perfectly into its bay in one elegant swoop, 'No real reason. I was just brushing my teeth the other day, when the idea struck me. You never know.'

Lara nodded quickly, 'Absolutely, good thinking!'

They sipped sweet tea, while lying on adjacent sofas, absently watching Sky News's endless parade of the day's tribulations. It was Valda who broke the relaxed silence.

'Do you consult your own chart often?' she quizzed curiously.

'Sure, usually when I'm depressed,' chuckled Lara dismissively.

'And is it helpful?' she asked with intensity, lifting her head, so that she could see Lara's face.

'Yes, certainly. Problem is: it's like trying to be your own doctor. Or worse, your own hairdresser: you just can't see your head from all the angles, or in my case, inside my head!' answered Lara, puffing on her loaned fag with one hand and massaging her foot with the other while chatting casually.

Valda leant back again, with an amused smile on her face. She lay there for a while, before suddenly rising intently from her relaxed, horizontal position on the couch. She stubbed out her cigarette firmly, almost as if she was making a statement that she was about to say something important. Lara guessed that something had occurred to Valda; Lara remained lying lazily on the couch, although she shifted her position, so that they were face-to-face with each other.

'I keep wondering, Lara,' she paused as she screwed up her face in a gesture of perplexity. 'What was the point of this "thing" with the Sheikh?' She threw up her hands, sighed and continued, 'My aunt always says that everything is "meant", but I can't see why in this case.'

Lara nodded to demonstrate that she knew where Valda was coming from. 'The individual pieces of a puzzle never make sense, you only realise how they fit in when you finish the puzzle.' Lara immediately swung her legs onto the floor and sat up, 'Come to think of it,' she said, excited with the realisation which had now dawned, 'if it hadn't been for this "thing" with the Sheikh, you would have been successful and would have stayed here indefinitely. You may have never been compelled to take that next step, like trying your luck in London or New York!'

Valda's eyes were wide and her voice bullish, 'Of course, and if it hadn't been for Richard breaking it off, I would have never come here to reignite my career!'

'What I have come to see is that the Comfort Zone is the biggest block to potential. When you have nothing to lose, your life is at its most dynamic and you are spurred on to achieve more. However, as soon as you achieve to a certain level, you become semi-satisfied and you stop taking chances, as you are scared to lose what you now have – you begin to stagnate. Astrology often indicates to me that my client is on the brink of something great; however, it can turn out that that client is going through dreadful tribulations – the planets seem to destroy our comfort zones every now and again and although we may see this as the end of the world, it's really just the universe trying to free up our potential again.'

Valda nodded, feeling that she intuitively understood what Lara was getting at.

Lara continued, almost as if she was giving herself a spiritual pep talk at the same time, 'I find it hard to think in these terms all the time; I am also guilty of losing faith and blaming the damned planets or God for not helping me. I always thought that to reach my goals, I had to do A, B, C in that order, but maybe something out there knows that Z, Q, G is the best way. Think about it, did you ever hear a success story, where somebody reached their goals playing strictly by the book – there are always unusual twists and turns of fate and strange, serendipitous events in every life story. The individual pieces of the puzzle never make sense! And here endeth the lesson!' Lara clapped her hands dramatically together and marched off in the direction of the kitchen.

'I like the way you put things,' Valda called after her. 'I am going to write it all down and read it whenever I lose my way. Just one more cup of tea and no more questions, I promise,' assured Valda.

Chapter Sixteen

Valda had wasted no time in putting Lara's plan into action. She had drawn cash every day from different branches and had made sizeable deposits into Lara's account. She had also delivered most of her belongings to Lara's apartment by the boot load; indeed, she was shocked at the amount of stuff she had accumulated in a relatively short space of time. Lara and Valda had agreed to transfer both cars into Lara's name; they filled in and signed all the paperwork, but decided not to file the papers until the eve of Valda's departure, to avoid arousing the suspicions of anyone who may be keeping track of that kind of thing.

'I am not sure whether we are being diligent or paranoid,' Lara commented as she safely stowed the papers at the back of her cupboard.

'I'd rather be paranoid than sorry,' replied Valda. 'This is the era of Big Brother, if you hadn't noticed.'

'I know,' groaned Lara with emphasis. 'The level of surveillance in the UK is second only to North Korea. More often used to tax law-abiding types than to apprehend or deter criminals though.' Lara had buried the folder of papers amongst the some old photo albums and high-school year books and as she closed the cupboard, she paused, doubtful. 'I hope that you're OK with this idea; I promise to sell both cars ASAP and deposit the money in your account!'

'Yes, I don't know why, but I trust you implicitly, Lara!'

'Do you know when you are going yet?' asked Lara, her voice tinged with sadness.

'Not exactly, but I think it'll be fairly soon after Richard leaves.'

'Sometimes, I don't think you take this thing seriously enough,' said Lara, speaking her mind out loud.

'Haven't you noticed I have a high threshold for fear,' she paused, 'or maybe it's stupidity?'

Valda knew that almost everything was in place; however, she still wanted to siphon more money out of her bank account, even though she knew that at some stage, this may arouse suspicion. She had decided to stay until after Richard's visit at the very least; emotionally, she knew that the tide had turned and she was eager to see him again to test the extent of the change within her. As Richard had expressed in his email, there were things that needed to be said and Valda recognised that even though he had instigated the break-up, after living together for so many years, there had to be matters that he needed closure on, too. Valda felt twinges of guilt for keeping Brett in the dark about her plans; she had unintentionally led him to believe that at some not-too-distant point in the future, there was a flat called "Chez Valda et Brett". Valda believed she loved Brett and both her heart and head concurred that what they had was, indeed, worthy of the word love; however, for Valda, the timing felt wrong. She had always sensed a well-disguised ambivalence in Lara whenever she had interrogated her on her future with Brett and that ambivalence was echoed somewhere within Valda, somewhere beyond what her head and her heart told her.

Valda was not sure whether sneaking around had made her uneasy or whether the feeling of unease was rooted in something extrasensory, but it was getting stronger. She suddenly recalled her very first trip to the Burg Emir and the inexplicable sense of foreboding she'd had. Things seemed too quiet; for two weeks now there had been no newspaper clippings and she had neither heard from nor seen the Sheikh. While neither event followed a pattern, their absence continued to disturb her. Richard was arriving that Wednesday and Valda had impulsively mentioned his visit to Brett, who had been unsuccessful in concealing a surge of jealousy. Valda had realised from very early on in her relationship with Richard that his insecurity had both bizarre and far-reaching ramifications and she detected that Brett was grappling with something similar. She had reasoned that a white lie was the best response and so had explained to Brett that she and Lara were merely meeting Richard for lunch, just to show that there were no hard feelings and that was it, nothing more. Brett had appeared satisfied.

That Monday evening before work, Valda was dining at an Italian restaurant on the first floor of the Burg Emir. Unlike the other restaurants in the huge hotel, the Tivoli was casual and relaxed and eating such personal staples as pizza and lasagne made her feel "at home". It was the last place she would have expected to see the Sheikh and she was horrified when she looked up from her "Four Seasons" to see him and Ahmed approaching. Her demeanour was perfectly collected as she casually dabbed her mouth with a napkin and rose to greet the Sheikh. His mode was warm and effusive.

'Aha! Valda, my dear, it has been too long!'

'I know, I was just thinking that myself. Are you well?' asked Valda, faking an enthusiasm she hardly felt. The Sheikh looked surprisingly healthy – his face glowed and he appeared to be rejuvenated.

He ignored her question and Ahmed pulled out a chair for the Sheikh and he sat down. 'How is your friend?'

Valda froze inside, automatically thinking he was talking about Lara. 'Friend?' she shrugged blankly.

'Yes, the geologist.' The Sheikh's large black eyes shone.

She was immediately relieved and hoped that he had not noticed the release of tension in her shoulders. 'He's well,' she smiled. 'Still working in Indonesia!'

'Good! I've been wanting to talk to you about something,' he continued, while warmly looking into her eyes.

Oh God, here we go again, thought Valda as she inwardly rolled her eyes. Valda made a decision that should the Sheikh call up a "favour" she would agree to it, but politely request that the Sheikh wait a week, as she had a friend coming out to see her. She reckoned that would appease him and not arouse any suspicions. Valda pushed aside her plate, for the remaining wedge of pizza was no longer appealing, and she leaned forwards, displaying interest. She watched as the Sheikh elegantly withdrew a cigar and his lighter. Although Valda was very wary of the Sheikh, she did not loathe him; she did not even dislike him. In fact, she quite honestly still found him intriguing; he was an enigma, and although she would be happier when she never had to set eyes on him again, she could not deny that knowing him had been bizarrely indelible.

After a few puffs of his cigar, he enthusiastically continued, 'As you know, Dubai's tourism industry has demonstrated astronomical growth during this last decade. There is huge potential, but the competition is rife and as you can understand, having the right personnel is fundamental to maintaining a competitive advantage. Quality people are increasingly difficult to come by – Jo made a superb find in you!' Valda blushed. 'Since you arrived, Flanagan's has become the place and

I read with interest all the favourable reviews in the papers, but I knew the first time I saw you that you had that certain *je ne sais quoi!*'

Valda could not help but feel a surge of pride, even though she sensed the compliments were a means to a new end. 'Thank you, that means a lot to me, I take a great pride in what I do!'

'You are a perfectionist.' As he said the word "perfectionist", Valda detected a strange look in his eye, which she could not quite define, but she was sure he was alluding to something. 'Now, there is something you can help me with,' he beamed. 'I am looking to recruit attractive, intelligent young women to work in my enterprise, not only in entertainment within the hotels and clubs themselves, but on the PR, promotional and marketing fronts. I suspect that you know many ideal candidates in Cape Town, having worked in the entertainment industry, and I am relying on you to conduct some headhunting on my organisation's behalf. As you can testify, the pay is generous and Dubai has everything to offer.'

Valda nodded in agreement, relieved that this time, the Sheikh was making what she regarded as a normal proposal. She laughed to herself; for once, the Sheikh's judgement of her character was faulty: Valda's circle of female friends and acquaintances was small and select and contained no one who would be interested in what he laid on the table. A wave of relaxation washed over her and she sat back, while finishing off the dregs of her Coke. The Sheikh continued to chat on in general about his business interests; Valda could not fathom any ulterior motive within this branch of the conversation though. She recalled that during their dinner at The Maghdi, he had discussed commerce at length and she wondered if her background in economics had encouraged him in any way.

Despite Lara's warning, the articles, Brett's concerns and her own feelings, Valda doubted for a minute whether the Sheikh would harm her: she was good for his business, she did him "favours" and he seemed to enjoy their strange tête-à-têtes. As her tension abated, she found herself participating more and more in the conversation.

Ahmed had continued to linger in the background unobtrusively, but as the Sheikh paused and turned his attention to refilling his glass with mineral water, he caught Valda's attention by raising his hand, pushing back his sleeve and looking at his wristwatch. Ahmed's actions were so prosaic and yet Valda immediately sensed that they were more pointed and purposeful. She glanced quickly back to the Sheikh, who was still not looking at her. When she looked back at Ahmed, he was staring right into her eyes and his face was deadpan. Valda was not sure whether to describe the look in his eyes as one of menace, but it was certainly intense. His eyes bore into hers for a few moments more and then he glanced at his watch, before locking his eyes on her once more. Everything else in the vicinity blurred and she felt as if her senses had temporarily shut down. She was transfixed on Ahmed and oblivious to anything else. It was the Sheikh's voice that brought reality crashing back, 'Valda, Valda!' he growled.

Valda blinked rapidly and her eyes flicked back to the Sheikh, just in time to see him looking over his shoulder in the direction in which she had been staring. She looked back at Ahmed, to see that he had resumed his obsequious pose. 'I didn't realise how late it was,' she blurted out, 'I haven't held you up, have I?'

'Not in the least,' offered the Sheikh reassuringly, 'but that said I do have other engagements, which I must not neglect! May I thank you; this evening has been most enjoyable!' With that, he rose and headed for the door, without looking back. She looked at Ahmed, but he merely looked at the ground and followed the Sheikh meekly.

Valda thought back to the curious sequence of events and she shook her head with exasperation. That stare. That look he gave me, she thought. She cursed herself for being overtired and edgy, reasoning that Ahmed had merely being trying to convey to her that the Sheikh had more important things to do and she should not be holding him up. Somehow, this explanation would not stick though. The complacency and relaxation of earlier had given way to a dull ache, which crept from her tense shoulders up her neck and settled at the back of her head. She pulled on her denim jacket, hoping that the extra warmth would soothe her. After paying the bill, she made her way to the main entrance and onto the street, where she welcomed the hot night air and the comforting feeling of tobacco in her lungs.

She thought back to how congenial the Sheikh had been. She also realised that she had been more relaxed and pally with him than before – she was usually uptight and cautious when they met – was this due to his mood, or was it due to the fact that she was quite literally all packed and ready to go? She hoped that she had not appeared too nonchalant; such an attitude would create suspicion.

As she stubbed out her fag carelessly on the pavement, she reminded herself that as soon as Richard left, she would make her move and the insidious Sheikh and Ahmed would be nothing more than a distant memory.

Chapter Seventeen

The word "LANDED" was flashing alongside flight EK764 from Johannesburg. Valda scanned the disembarking passengers, hoping that Richard had not come through the gates yet. It was unlike her to be late, but the Mini had been low on petrol and time had marched on quickly while she had refuelled. The majority of passengers in the arrivals hall appeared to have come off flights from the subcontinent and she relaxed, deducing that Richard's flight had only recently landed and he was sure to be held up somewhere in the maze of passages, travelling escalators and security checks. She shoved her keys in her pocket and found a suitable vantage point.

She was surprised that she felt so relaxed. She was eager to see Richard again and felt a similar glow of anticipation as one would expect to feel when arriving home after a long trip away or at the prospect of seeing a close relative after years spent apart.

A wave of fresh passengers flooded into the hall and the gaggle of world-weary taxi drivers pressed forwards, with their array of signs bearing passenger names; some had raggedy scraps of paper, some had fancy electronic boards and one had a banner. Valda's attention was drawn to three young men holding up a St George's flag, with "Phil and Jilly" emblazoned across it. Not far from them was a man with a bunch of yellow flowers. It must be something about Wednesday, thought Valda to herself.

Despite the general chaos as passengers raced across the threshold, she noticed Richard immediately. He was not as tall as Brett, but he was, as always, immaculately dressed and stood out in any crowd. He was wearing a crisp aubergine-and-white striped shirt with navy trousers. He looked straight in Valda's direction and gave her a huge white grin in response to her wave. Valda was initially surprised at receiving such an ardent welcome and then she suddenly realised that she, too, was beaming. Valda waved again and then pointed to her right. She made her way to where the taxi drivers were waiting impatiently and Richard negotiated his trolley through the human traffic. It was too noisy for a hello and too cluttered for an embrace, so Valda gestured to Richard for him to follow her to the car park, where things were less rowdy.

It was already hot in the early morning sunshine, especially standing there on the tarmac. Richard stood holding on to his trolley and Valda stood with her arms folded; neither enjoyed small talk and yet more meaningful words escaped them.

'So how was your flight?' attempted Valda.

'Fine,' he paused. 'Fine! And you? You look really good!'

'It's an inside out thing!' She smiled enigmatically and quickly continued, 'Now, I don't know if you managed to eat any of those synthetic omelettes they serve for airline breakfasts, but I'm starving!' With that, she motioned in the direction of her waiting car and led the way.

They decided to dump Richard's luggage at his hotel, before heading off somewhere to eat. Valda could sense that Richard had been taken aback by her demeanour, she was certain that he had anticipated more tension and rawness. Richard looked just the same as he had when she had last seen him: smart, fit and annoyingly avoiding the sprouting of grey hairs. Richard had thick black hair, hazel eyes, a refined nose and, what appealed to Valda most, his very defined, high cheekbones. He always exuded a distinguished, understated sex appeal. Driving towards Bur Dubai, Valda was still amazed at how relaxed and comfortable she felt in his company. Richard sat quietly, while she waxed on about the various sights and attractions.

'Oh my God, here I am, waffling on about touristy stuff. I sound like a cab driver doing the "get it whether you like it or not" tour of Dubai!' she chuckled.

'Well, at least I'll know all the important place names to rattle off at dinner parties!' he replied with a hint of irony. 'There is an astronomical amount of building going on here!' exclaimed Richard as he observed the skyscrapers mushrooming on every horizon.

'They say a fifth of the world's building cranes are in Dubai. So why are you here, if you don't mind me asking?'

'I'm here to consult with a team of engineers, who are designing the wings for a new fighter jet, which has been commissioned by the UAE government.'

Valda nodded, she knew that Richard often worked on sensitive projects, but he always trusted her discretion. Richard looked out of the window for a long while and Valda could sense that he needed to think and so she allowed the silence to prevail. After some minutes had passed, he turned to Valda, 'You really are making this easy for me!' His voice was quiet and unsure.

Valda did not reply right away, as she was not quite sure what to say. After a pause, she spoke in a puzzled tone, 'But I agreed to see you, didn't I?'

'Of course!' he replied emphatically. 'And even if you hadn't, I would have made dammed sure I saw you regardless!' Valda remained silent. 'I am not sure what I expected,' he continued, 'more tension, more biting sarcasm, confrontation for sure ...' he tailed off.

'I feel very differently about things now!'

Her tone was firm and serious and she chose not to elaborate. She looked over at Richard and saw some confusion and even disappointment in his face. Her reactions had thrown him; he had obviously been geared up for something very different. It seemed opportune that by that stage, they had arrived at the BurJuman Centre and everyday conversation about where to eat and what to eat could resume. In fact, any allusion to the past was avoided for the rest of the day and they enjoyed the time-honoured touristy things, gossiped about mutual friends and updated each other on their "new" lives. The day flowed, as perhaps it should have: Valda and Richard had spent seven years together, they knew each other's habits, likes and dislikes, and they shared interests and values. Valda was not at all surprised that by eight o'clock that evening, she found herself driving Richard back to her place and inviting him in.

Richard failed to remark on the apartment. Although he had become rather distracted, not too distracted that he did not notice the pack of JPS on the coffee table. 'Still haven't kicked that habit, I see.'

'Old ones die hard, don't you know!' An awkward silence fell between them and they both stood in the sparsely furnished lounge looking at one another. Valda drew a deep breath, while looking at the floor and dragging her hand through her hair. 'I am going to get us both a Coke,' she stated. She then looked up across the room into Richard's eyes. 'But before I do, I am not sure exactly when and why things started to go wrong between us, but I can see the part I played – I had a lot to do with pushing us over the edge. I thought that everyone else, you especially, were the problem and I thought there were no solutions. I've come to accept that I was the problem and the solutions were there, but they were the steps I was most afraid of taking. I can understand why you went after someone more stable!' She left her words hanging poignantly, but Richard wasted no time in responding.

'Yes, stable. Cold, hard, unemotional: Sonja was a brick wall. I missed the passion.' He moved closer towards Valda, so that their bodies were almost touching. 'I missed you!' He put his hands gently on her shoulders. 'I always thought that the way to deal with any situation was to be as controlled and detached as possible; I was very misguided! I am so sorry I never came to see you in hospital, I just couldn't face you.' He looked down, avoiding her eyes; he seemed deeply troubled by his thoughts.

'Don't worry about that,' she said emphatically. 'At that stage of my life, I couldn't have faced anyone anyway. I am amazed that I ever even did something like that, but I was not trying to punish you, if that's what you thought! I just could not cope with life any more.'

Richard suddenly smiled with relief; he looked very happy indeed. 'You're just like the Valda I met ten years ago,' he paused. 'Stupid thing to say really – that is who you are, the real you never changed.' He edged even closer and slipped his hands around her neck gently bringing her lips towards his. He kissed her once and then again more ardently.

Valda was slow to react, things had moved so fast and she had not, perhaps naively expected anything like this to happen, but after the second kiss, she turned her head and wedged her hands between them. 'Richard, I'm involved with someone else now,' the words tumbled out.

Richard stiffened and took a step back, although his arms were still around her. 'So it's true then?' He looked deep into her eyes.

'What do you mean?' asked Valda, with a hint of impatience.

'Bella told me you'd met someone, but I thought …'

'… she was bluffing?' finished Valda. Valda pushed Richard away and walked over to the couch, where she flopped down disconsolately, rubbing her face with her hand. 'I'm sorry! It was so stupid of me to invite you up here!'

Richard sighed and went to sit next to her on the couch; he slipped his arm around her warmly, 'No, I'm the one who should be sorry – was I really expecting to just waltz back into your life, just like that? I must be the crazy one!'

At that, Valda burst into spontaneous laughter. 'This must be a first, both of us admitting we may actually be wrong!' Richard joined in her laughter heartily and all the tension of the previous moments dissipated. 'C'mon, let's get that Coke and make something to eat.' Valda stood up and held out her hand.

Richard took it and she led him into the kitchen. What with the general state of emptiness in the fridge, a fry-up seemed the best option. As Valda broke the eggs into the frying pan, she reflected on what had transpired that day, remembering what Lara had said about forgiveness. In a strange way, Valda felt that forgiving Richard had empowered her: she had chosen to forgive and in doing so, she had become more aware that subtle choices like that can be immensely powerful.

There seemed to be no point in Richard going all the way back to his hotel and so Valda suggested he stay over. They drank coffee after coffee and talked late into the night, laughing over and over again as they rehashed the good old, the bad old and the sad old days. Valda had totally forgotten how much she enjoyed Richard's company. They were tuned in to each other on so many levels; perhaps the fact that they were so similar had played a role in the breakdown. Valda was not quite sure how Richard was feeling, but despite all the beautiful emotions she felt inside, she felt no desire to take things any further on a sexual level. She secretly hoped that Richard would some day feel like she did and that they would both be able to reap the benefits of a very unique and spiritual friendship.

They only slept for two hours. Richard had a meeting at ten and so Valda needed to give him a lift back to his hotel, so that he could dress and pick up his laptop and paperwork. Richard headed off for a hot shower in order to surface and Valda sauntered sleepily into the kitchen to make some tea. Before she turned into the kitchen, something caught her attention. Lying in the entrance hall was what appeared to be a small white envelope. Suddenly feeling very awake, she strode towards the front door and snatched up the hand-addressed envelope. Her heart was beating faster. The person behind the mystery newspaper clippings had been in her building, at her front door. Why not just mail it as usual? she wondered.

She could hear Richard in the bedroom. Her hands were shaky from overtiredness and nerves and so she fumbled with the envelope, unsuccessfully trying to slip the article out as fast as she could. By that stage, Richard was heading towards the kitchen and so she quickly shoved the half-open envelope under the keyboard of her computer and swung around, heading back to the kitchen.

'What's wrong?' asked Richard immediately.

'Nothing, why?' she answered very quickly.

'You have that worried look on your face!' observed Richard as he proceeded to reach for the mugs and the tea bags.

'Oh, it's just something unpleasant I have to deal with to do with work! Someone difficult.'

'I'm sure it's nothing you can't handle. I should be finished at six tonight, are we still on for dinner?'

'Yes, of course!' she answered with enthusiasm as she perched on one of the kitchen bar stools. Nothing you can't handle, thought Valda to herself, suddenly feeling a pang of ineptitude and regret at the way she had handled things in Dubai. 'You have my mobile number; you can call me if you are running late!'

Before leaving, Valda slipped the envelope out from its temporary hiding place and shoved it into her pocket. She would deal with it later over a coffee and a cigarette.

Valda was sitting outside at a terrace restaurant in Dubai Marina. It was almost November and things had cooled to the extent that it was only just bearable to be outside. She lit a cigarette and took a drag, whilst simultaneously wrenching the envelope out of her back pocket. Cigarette still in mouth, she ripped the remainder of the envelope open and eased out the familiar newspaper article. It was dated 4 March of that year:

> Jumeirah Beach Tragedy: The body of a young British woman Claire Townsend-Phillips was discovered early today on the beach near Jumeirah Beach Park by two Swedish holidaymakers. The police have conducted enquiries and it is believed that she was the victim of a tragic speedboat accident – there is no suspicion of foul play. Claire was living and working in Dubai as a nightclub hostess. Her family will be flying out from England.

The so-called article was no more than an insert, sidelined in a column for news that was not important enough to warrant more valuable space. An entire life reduced to seventy-three bland words. Valda immediately thought of Lara. She was about to reach for her phone, when she heard its familiar jingle, so she snapped it open and answered.

'I was just about to ring you!' Valda launched straight in.

'Mental telepathy, huh! Listen, I have to speak to you, are you working tonight?'

'No, I'm not working while Richard is here. What about this afternoon; now even?' asked Valda impatiently.

'What about three, at my place!'

'Fine. By the way ... I received another one!' Valda hoped that Lara would catch her drift.

'I thought you may have; anyway, we'll discuss everything later. Ciao.'

Lara barely had a chance to open her front door, when Valda pushed right in. She had a cigarette in her mouth and without any ado, she handed Lara what was now a rather scrunched-up newspaper article.

'Someone slipped this under my front door last night!'

Lara regarded it briefly, before directing Valda to the coffee table, where she had prepared tea and some cheesy snacks.

Lara tossed the piece of paper aside. 'I did some trawling online and I found the same article: it was the only one that appeared in the Dubai press. I did, however, find that the UK papers reported it more extensively. *The Daily Telegraph*, for example. Blonde, very attractive. Apparently, she was an Oxford Uni grad; did a degree in history and was working in Dubai during her gap year, to pay off her student loan. Now here's the crunch: she did work at Flanagan's!'

'No surprise there then,' muttered Valda as she took a sip of tea.

Lara sat down on the couch opposite Valda.

'Her parents were not impressed with the rather non-existent enquiry into her death. The autopsy revealed there had been a head trauma, but concluded that death had occurred as a result of drowning. There were no witnesses and it was surmised that she had been hit by a motor boat, even though there was absolutely no evidence to support this. As for the last person to see her alive,' Lara shrugged, 'some guy she met at a bar two nights before! Her parents were petitioning for an inquiry of sorts, but I doubt anything came of it. The newspapers soon dropped the story.'

'But none of that really tells us anything new, does it?' Valda paused to take a bite of her cheese cracker.

'Sure it does,' Lara sat forwards, concerned. 'The timing! You received the articles in chronological order; Claire is the most recent victim and the first female one. Whoever is sending these things is getting more urgent, plus, he even sticks it under your door to get your attention this time.'

'Are you thinking that whoever is behind this is trying to help me?'

'Could be, but either way, don't piss around any more, OK!'

'I know, alright!' smirked Valda, before continuing, 'By the way, I had an impromptu dinner date with His Lordship the other night!' Lara raised her eyebrows without comment and Valda proceeded to provide a sketchy account of the conversation. She was surprised at the way Lara suddenly sat forwards, her eyes lighting up. 'What is it?' she demanded.

'I have a new theory – it came to me last night and what you are saying confirms it.' If Lara wanted Valda's full attention, she now had it and she eagerly continued, 'What if this whole thing was never about the drugs; what if the whole drugs thing was a charade, a way of getting you into his game?'

'And what is his game?' Valda sounded sceptical.

'White slave trade.'

'You can't be serious,' mocked Valda, 'that's urban legend stuff!'

'I am!' Lara was dogmatic. 'It's well documented that women across South East Asia, especially Indonesia, are lured into the sex trade in Saudi Arabia, with promises of lucrative, reputable employment. Last year, George Bush was considering sanctions against Saudi Arabia as a result of their failure to stop the modern-day slave trade in prostitutes, but that was dropped, because of the whole War on Terror fiasco. What's more, countless Polish and Eastern European women are sold to wealthy Arab businessmen by the mafia each year; this kind of thing is commonplace!'

'Sure, but you are talking about poor countries, where women are desperate!'

Lara held up her hand for Valda to be quiet. 'Why do you think he is now asking you to recruit employees for him, huh? Why did someone break into your flat and look at your photos and your PC?'

'I still think that drugs are his thing. Why does he need me to recruit for him anyway; he could advertise; he could use an employment agency!'

'Too formal, too long-winded!' replied Lara dismissively. 'Whoever saw those photos in your flat – gala events, shows, charity fundraisers etc. – thought the same as I did: you mixed with all the "beautiful people". You know just the sort of people he is after.'

'Why does he need me to recruit, when he could have a steady flow from Poland or Indonesia?' argued Valda.

'Why have a Ferrari, when a Ford does basically the same thing? Maybe he's catering for a market of men who have everything money can buy, who don't want a "desperate woman" – they want the best: intelligent; educated; talented; attractive. You said yourself, he seems to enjoy talking economics to you. Claire was obviously no slouch!' Lara was still selling her theory passionately. 'What young woman in Cape Town would not be lured by the promise of a great tax-free income, exotic foreign travel and the chance of opportunities in the real world? The Sheikh mentions all the buzzwords he knows will get young people going: PR, marketing, entertainment. My gosh, they will be clamouring to sign up!'

'And supposing they do?'

'Some will work in the usual fields, others will disappear! Some may even volunteer, I guess!' mused Lara.

Valda was becoming more reflective. 'Why does he need to do this, do you think?'

'To ingratiate himself to his oil-tycoon peers, perhaps. Or maybe – as you once said yourself – everybody has to want something, else why would they bother to get out of bed!'

Valda may not have bought Lara's story entirely, but she was certainly more pensive. 'I know I asked this before, but why would he harm me, if I am about to deliver what he wants!'

'But you aren't, are you? You want out and you have often told me what a shrewd judge of character he is.' Lara grabbed a crisp and crunched on it while she added, 'I know I have been pretty emphatic today, but it's up to you what you believe. Just ask yourself why you are so anxious not to believe it all.'

Valda had to concede that Lara put forward a convincing argument and she found it hard to answer Lara's last question.

Lara decided not to press further – whether her theory held water or not, the essence of the matter was that Valda should leave Dubai without hesitation. They both turned their attention to the refreshments on the table and Lara decided to steer the conversation round to the other important matter. 'So how's Richard?' she inquired curiously.

Valda's eyes lit up and she was more than happy to provide all the details. '... which reminds me of something else!' Valda finished off, reaching into her denim shoulder bag. She withdrew a flattish, navy velvet box of about 5 inches square and placed it on the coffee table with a flourish. 'A thank you!' she stated simply.

Lara set down her mug and reached slowly for the elegant box. She opened it gently and gasped as she saw the beautiful necklace inside. It was the necklace she had admired in the Blue Souk on their trip to Sharjah: a lapis lazuli heart pendant on a gold snake chain; the wide gold bail was embedded with a one-carat diamond.

'How ... did ... did you know?' she stammered.

'You're not the only one who can play detective!' she said, smiling proudly. 'I knew that something in that Sutanah shop had caught your attention, but I didn't know what; so I went back there and lucky for me, the same woman was serving. She remembered me – no surprise – after all, I did buy that gaudy old dagger and she told me what it was that you were looking at!'

Lara was visibly choked up and all she could manage was, 'I don't know what to say?'

'Well that means a lot in itself, because it's never happened before!' said Valda half-jokingly.

Lara was still staring at the necklace and Valda could not see her reddening eyes and so she was rather startled when she noticed the tears steaming down Lara's cheeks. Valda suddenly began to feel very emotional as well, but her emotions were all trapped on the inside, chaotic and confused. She was relieved when Lara reached over to give her a huge bear hug; indeed, more than relieved, it felt very good, very comforting: it was like experiencing the mothering she'd never had.

'I wanted to say a special thank you for everything you have done for me!'

'I couldn't have done it alone, it was all fifty-fifty. I try to help many people, but most of them just want easy answers: you really listened, took things on board; you changed your way of thinking. You are one of the few clients I've had, who sincerely wanted help – most are just into gratuitous moaning!' she chuckled as she finished her sentence.

Lara lifted the necklace carefully out of the box and tried it on – it was the most beautiful and unusual piece of jewellery she had ever seen.

'Why don't you join Richard and me for dinner tonight!' suggested Valda.

'You sure?' asked Lara sincerely.

'Absolutely, we've discussed all the sensitive stuff. We won't have a showdown in public, so don't you worry about that!' she laughed out loud.

'OK, I never say no to a meal out!' Her eyes twinkled before becoming serious again, 'But promise me you won't leave it any longer before you leave Dubai: even if we don't know why those other men died, we know for sure that Claire was closely acquainted with the Sheikh and for whatever reason, she is now dead.'

Valda was pleased to have Lara there with her and Richard: she was the type of person who knew something about everything from politics to sport and she found it easy keep the conversation flowing. Although she felt neither anxious nor downcast, she was not in the mood for chat: she needed to think, although she was not sure about what. Her face displayed an interest and yet mentally, she was tuned out of the light-hearted banter of her companions. She thought back to her first few days in Dubai: they now seemed so far away and yet conversely, she felt that her time in Dubai had flown by. Her previous life in Cape Town felt like just that – a previous life! Valda noticed with an amused detachment the glint in Richard's eye as he focused on Lara and she smiled inwardly.

She continued to sit there, surrounded by the general restaurant buzz, yet strangely disconnected in her own bubble. She was deep in thought about nothing and she was surprised to note that she felt more relaxed than she had ever remembered being. She thought back to what Lara had said about leaving the page blank and she understood; she, too, now felt as if she had a blank page in front of her. Dubai had not been a new start, but a halfway house, and now she was really ready to start a new journey and she felt wonderfully contented at the thought.

She wondered about Lara and whether she would continue living in Dubai. Initially, the thought of Lara carrying on as usual – as she had before they'd met – had seemed preposterous to Valda and she questioned why on earth Lara would want to stay on. Slowly, Valda began to recognise that perhaps she was projecting her own restlessness and maybe even overestimating her own importance in Lara's life. Valda pondered over Lara's comment about her fate being intertwined with that of the Sheikh; she wondered if hers and Lara's fates were also woven together in some way. Lara had remained an enigma, despite her openness.

Richard would be leaving the following evening after a full day of meetings and so Valda would have the day to finalise her arrangements. She would see Richard off and the night after that, she, too, would be on the plane, jetting away from Dubai. Valda was suddenly impatient to leave; she felt no sentimentality or nostalgia. The time had come and she was totally ready.

'Flight EK 763 is now boarding at Gate 56.'

'That's you!' Valda flung her arms around Richard and gave him a big kiss.

Richard immediately responded by warmly embracing her and he held on to her for some time, his face buried in her hair and his arms wrapped tightly around her. It was some time before they slowly separated and when they did, there were tears in both sets of eyes.

'I wish I had done that years ago!' said Richard poignantly.

'It still means as much as it would have then!' Valda was sincere and reflective. The moment was interrupted by another boarding call for his flight. 'C'mon, you'd better get going, you still have to do the passport control thing!' urged Valda.

Richard grabbed her arm and after another short kiss, added, 'I'll never forget these last few days. You know that I am simply crap at talking about emotions, but I realise that I was very lucky to have spent seven years with such an exceptional woman. A woman who I'll always love.' He paused and blushed, 'I may be back in Dubai in a few months time.'

'Oh, Richard, I haven't told anyone yet, but I have something in the pipeline and I may be moving away soon,' she stopped momentarily to give his arm a squeeze, 'but wherever I am … you're invited!' Richard's eyes opened wide.

'Where to?'

'London,' she stated, as if there was no doubt at all about her future.

She could tell Richard was slightly envious, but he concealed it behind a magnanimous smile.

'Well, keep a room for me, because I go there on business, too!'

They embraced once more, before Richard headed towards the first series of security checks. He looked back frequently and Valda stayed where she was until he was out of sight.

Chapter Eighteen

It was eleven o'clock and Valda was on her way back to her apartment. Her journey across Dubai that day had been motivated out of a desire to give the GT a run out for the last time.

Driving across Dubai Creek, she had little time to notice the landmarks she now knew so well; her mind was totally focused on the last-minute details. She was fully satisfied that she had transferred the bulk of her money into Lara's account and in addition, since it was the end of the month, she had been able to draw her salary. On Lara's advice, she would be heading for London – via some city or other in Europe – and Lara had provided her with details of all the "ropes"! Valda's confidence had grown in Dubai and with the substantial wad of cash and practical advice from Lara, she was damned sure she could make a go of it. She felt incredibly excited about the future and at the same time, relieved that the Sheikh would soon be only a distant memory.

Valda was astonished at how much she had collected over her eight months in Dubai. Most of her favourite clothes and valuables had been stored at Lara's and the only things remaining at her flat were towels, bed linen, crockery, toiletries and unwanted clothes. She had packed a small overnight bag to take on the plane and some last bits and bobs for Lara to look after. Lara was due to pick her up at four that afternoon to take her to the airport.

She was running ahead of time and so she decided to stop off at her favourite haunt in Jumeirah – Izzie's – for some lunch. Waqar the owner was thrilled to see his favourite customer and was quick to share his good news. Apparently, Waqar was opening a new branch of his restaurant in Deira City and he hoped that Valda would be a regular and moreover, that she would sing at the grand opening. Waqar was a real character and his banter had lightened her mood many a time while she had lived in Dubai. She was sincerely pleased for him, because she knew that the past few months had not always been the smoothest business-wise. His enthusiasm for his new venture mirrored that of her own and so she was not inclined to quash his enthusiasms by revealing that she would be leaving Dubai for good. One of the waitresses, Chanaudi, also had good news: she was to be married in December. Valda sat back enjoying a drag; it seemed that that day, everyone had good news to tell: it felt like graduation day, with everyone excitedly talking about their plans for the future.

It was one thirty when she arrived back at Concorde Towers. A large, four-wheel drive was about to drive through the gates and she lazily squeezed in behind him before the gates closed, to avoid having the schlep of finding her own keys and poking her electronic key into the machine. After she had parked, she walked around the Mini and the GT as if to say a final farewell and for the first time that day, she was struck by a pang of sadness: there were things about Dubai she would miss. After one last look, she turned and headed with determination towards the lifts, not looking back.

Five minutes later, she arrived at her floor; the building seemed very quiet, although Valda was not sure why she had even noticed that fact: it was always fairly quiet; she hardly ever saw any of her fellow residents, apart from nosy old Mrs O'Neil opposite, of course. She glanced at Mrs O'Neil's flat as she slipped her key into her door. Suddenly, her attention was drawn to her door; she had heard no click as she had turned the key, although, of course, she may have just missed it. She pushed the door open and walked into her entrance hall, heading towards the table where she always dumped her keys. As she placed the car keys on the table she was suddenly struck by the most eerie sensation and an icy feeling of dread began to develop in the base of her chest. Her back stiffened with fear as she turned slowly towards the lounge. She couldn't help but gasp as she saw the familiar yet menacing figure of the Sheikh standing there in the centre of her lounge. He looked so big standing there, yet so serene, so relaxed even.

While Valda stood riveted to the spot in horror, he smiled and emitted what Valda thought was a grotesquely polite greeting, 'Why, Valda, at last, I have been waiting for you! I am sorry if I shocked you.'

Valda closed her mouth into a hardened grin; she knew that her body language had revealed more than simple shock. Her heart was pounding and she found it impossible to move from where she stood. She swallowed hard, while cursing her lack of composure, fiercely determined to get a grip of herself and to play out the situation to her advantage. 'Well, at least you made yourself at home,' she said sarcastically, at the same time finding the nerve to saunter towards where the Sheikh was standing. She looked him straight in the eye, almost throwing down the gauntlet. He met her stare with his usual self-controlled confidence.

'And you were so agreeable the other night at dinner.' His tone was mocking and Valda felt he was chiding her. He had seen through her phoney chatter at the Tivoli.

She had the overwhelming urge to tell him he was a patronising fuckhouse, but she gritted her teeth. Fear was fast turning into anger.

'So what are you doing here?' she directed her question with defiance.

'I've always admired your passion and your mendacity!' he smirked, obviously getting a kick out of toying with her emotions.

'And likewise, on the mendacity count, that is,' she retorted, almost immediately regretting what she had said. Her temper always used to get the better of her and this was no time for that old habit to jeopardise things. What she really wanted was to be cool, but the red mist tended to linger with Valda.

Something was changing in his eyes and Valda could tell that the game was over.

'I have found you to be a fascinating woman, a woman who makes wise choices!' He stopped, but Valda remained silent, as she wanted him to do the talking, while she decided on her next move. 'We've shared a secret and now I want to share something else with you!' Valda's face initially registered disgust as a series of sordid images flashed through her mind, but she quickly reinstated a bewildered look. 'I was born in Jeddah!' he stated. Valda's confusion was now quite genuine. 'It's a magnificent, ancient and holy city.' His eyes were suddenly filled with wonder. 'I want to share it with you,' he continued. 'My private jet is waiting, let us go now!'

As she thought of being whisked off to Saudi Arabia, Lara's theories came flooding back and that icy feeling of dread began to rupture into panic.

'Now? Right now?' she blurted out. The Sheikh nodded. 'But, I'm busy ... you should have let me know!'

'But your overnight bag is already packed,' he sounded triumphant; he knew he had Valda in a corner.

Oh, shit, shit, shit, thought Valda to herself as all her anger and defiance left her. He had obviously been in her bedroom and seen the near-empty cupboards, boxes and packed overnight bag on her bed.

'I was going to surprise Brett by visiting him in Singapore!' she explained hurriedly, desperate not to allow him through her defences.

'Well, if he is not expecting you, then he won't be disappointed!' he uttered in a low tone.

Valda was wondering if Ahmed was lurking somewhere in her flat. Thoughts of them strong-arming her into a waiting limousine and then onto a jet and into some Arabian Alcatraz flashed though her mind. She thought of Lara; Lara had suspected this might happen. If she disappeared, Lara would at least know or have some idea of her whereabouts. Valda tried to comfort herself, but she knew Lara did not have a modicum of a chance of finding her and no chance at all of finding her alive. She thought of the newspaper articles and wondered if her existence would soon be reduced to a 4 by 1 inch slot in a newspaper column. She glanced at her watch; it was two o'clock, still two hours before Lara was due to pick her up. Valda could tell that the Sheikh was feeling in total control of the situation – he was arrogantly relaxed and she watched as he withdrew his platinum cigar case and distinctive lighter.

'Should I get my overnight bag then?' she enquired, wondering whether an escape to the bedroom would help her chances. She thought hopelessly of her bedroom and her bathroom – there was nowhere to run, unless she wanted to jump seventeen stories.

'No!' he commanded. 'I will buy you whatever you need!'

'But I will need my passport,' tried Valda in desperation.

'No you won't!' he said, looking at her pityingly, before he turned around to look for an ashtray.

Valda was thinking fast, she considered making a dash for the door; however, she reckoned that even if she made it to the door, either the Sheikh or Ahmed – who she was sure was not far away – were bound to catch up with her on the way down the seventeen flights of stairs. She decided that even if she escaped from the building, he was bound to have her picked up by the authorities on some trumped-up charge at the airport. She silently cursed herself for not leaving the previous night with Richard: if only she had not delayed that extra day in order to get her last salary cheque and to take the GT for that last spin. If only. Despondency was all over her.

She watched the Sheikh as he made his way over to her ashtray, which was on a side table. His back was to her and she took the chance to look about the lounge and her gaze ventured towards the kitchen, vainly searching for an answer. She looked over to him again. He was flicking ash from his cigar in such a prissy manner; his cool, controlled attitude riled her: he seemed so dammed sure he had her where he wanted her. Valda hated losing, she hated it when someone got the better of her, and the Sheikh was one person who had consistently done so. She looked about the room again; she could suddenly feel a surge of something, something powerful, something she could only describe as Survival. She thought back to that fateful night in Clifton – she was a survivor. Despondency gave way to a rush of adrenalin; every nerve fibre was on fire. She looked over to the side table and there, sparkling under her Tiffany lamp, lay the dagger. In a flash, it was in her hand. The second hand of her clock seemed to jam and the Sheikh appeared to be motionless on the other side of the room. Stealthily, she stole up behind him, raised her arm and, gripping the dagger as hard as she could, in one almighty motion she sliced it ruthlessly into the side of his neck.

He let out a pathetic and hopeless cry as his head rocked back and his heavy body dropped slowly to the floor with a thud. Crimson blood gushed from the wound. Valda looked at her hand to note that it was covered with his blood, to the extent that the blood was now dripping off her elbow. She straightened her arm and threw the dagger onto the floor alongside the body of the Sheikh. She quickly stepped out of the way, so that the growing lake of blood around the Sheikh would not make contact with her shoes. Her mind felt crystal clear. Careful not to drip blood, she hurried to the guest toilet and thoroughly washed her hands. She was soon free of his blood.

As she walked back into the lounge and looked at his body, Valda thought with amazement how easy it had been; it had only taken that one thrust of the dagger to kill him. In that one split second, he had gone from smug and self-satisfied to stone-cold dead. He never even saw it coming. Valda thought about how just eighteen months previously, also with a knife in her hand, she had tried to end her own life and had failed; now, with a knife in hand again, she had saved her own life. She thoughtfully reflected on how much easier it had been to end someone else's life rather than her own.

Without wasting any more time, she turned and made her way towards her bedroom. In her overnight bag was Lara's "secret" phone, so she unzipped the navy canvas bag's side compartment and slipped out the phone. She immediately dialled the only number in the memory.

'What's wrong? Are you OK?' asked Lara immediately on answering.

'I'm OK! Can you get here now ... and I mean now!' Valda's tone was urgent.

'Be there in fifteen!' Lara snapped off her phone, before Valda had the chance to explain further.

It was the longest fifteen minutes of Valda's life. She did not ponder over the sagacity of her actions in terms of the Sheikh, but she did question her wisdom in dragging Lara into the scene. Valda's adrenalin high had not quite abated and whilst she was feeling a sense of relief, she was still relying on Lara to somehow pull her out of this mess. Why did she have this blind faith that Lara would have all the answers?

Lara opened the door using her own set of keys and walked right in, to find Valda standing, smoking at her kitchen counter. She immediately noticed that Valda was extremely pale.

On seeing Lara, Valda sighed and managed a smile, 'I'm so glad you're here!' Suddenly, Valda was lost for words; how do you explain that you have just murdered someone, she thought. Without saying anything, Valda moved towards the lounge and merely stared at where the body of the Sheikh now lay. His long white garments had soaked up a large amount of the blood and the scene was very gruesome.

Lara followed. She took a step back as she first beheld the grim scene, but she stayed quiet. After a few moments, she moved closer, curiously looking at the dagger and the frozen, open eyes of the Sheikh. Lara looked at the walls and the settee, which Valda noticed for the first time were stained with a splattering of blood. The metallic stench of blood hung in the air, merging with the pungent smell of the Sheikh's smouldering cigar butt.

'So this is him,' she said after some time. Valda had anticipated many different reactions from Lara, but she was perplexed by her seeming indifference. 'Pre-emptive strike, huh?' suggested Lara with a raised eyebrow.

'I can't believe I did it!' said Valda emotionlessly.

'Well, it's not like the alternative was going to be much fun.'

'I can't believe how lightly you are taking this, Lara!'

'He had it coming,' shrugged Lara, before adding emphatically, 'besides, it's done now! And now we're going to deal with it!' Lara walked over to the zombified Valda. 'Now, tell me as quickly as you can everything that happened. In detail!' she demanded urgently.

Within two minutes, Valda had laid out all the important details.

'Have you touched anything?' asked Lara with urgency.

Valda paused to think. 'Uhm, no! Just the taps, soap and the secret phone to ring you!'

'OK, good!' Lara stopped to take a deep breath and then she reached into her handbag and withdrew her British passport and her VISA card. Lara looked intently at Valda, to make sure she was concentrating; and then she explained her plan. 'This is what I want you to do. Take my VISA card, I left it on the window sill one day and my signature on the strip faded, so you can sign my name over it in your own handwriting. The PIN is the same as my debit card. You can use the VISA whenever a signature is needed or where they don't take debit cards. Use my passport and get the first flight out of here! Now, show me where your passport is!'

Valda was looking confused and butted in with, 'Why, what are you going to do with my passport?'

'From now on, I am you!' stated Lara.

Valda shook her head dismissively, 'Lara, I know we look alike, but anyone who knows me will know that you are not me!'

'Sure, but I am not going to see anybody you know,' countered Lara; then she continued, 'Now, just listen! You are going to fly out of here, I am going to stay back here, pretend I am you and sort out this mess.'

'But, but Lara, I can't let you ... I mean ... why don't we both just get the next flight out!' stammered Valda.

'That's a bad idea, just think about it! Now please concentrate. Don't touch anything; just show me where your passport is.' Valda led Lara to her bedroom and with instructions from Valda, Lara unzipped the side compartment of Valda's overnight bag and slipped out her passport, driver's licence and bank cards, which Lara placed in a drawer. Lara removed Valda's mobile phone and put it on the dressing table, but she made sure that their "secret" phone was in Valda's overnight bag. 'I want to make sure that you take everything with you that could possibly have the Sheikh's blood on it.'

Valda just listened, her head was spinning and she felt like she needed to lie down.

'I just remembered,' said Valda weakly, 'I had a fag while I was waiting for you!' They walked back into the kitchen and Lara made sure that Valda put the lighter, cigarette pack and butt in her bag.

'Do you have a spare pack of cigs?' asked Lara.

'Of course I do! Why?'

'I'm you. I'm supposed to smoke – it'll look odd if there are no cigarette packs lying around, especially as you can smell fresh cigarette smoke in here. Besides, I think I need one!' Lara ended with a smile.

Valda gave a half-hearted smile and showed Lara where her spare fags and lighters were. Valda noticed that Lara was on a roll. She seemed to have a plan, but Valda felt too drained and too stressed to even begin to unravel what the plan was, so she followed obediently. Lara was silent for some minutes, as if going through a mental checklist.

'Alright, I have everything of yours and you have everything of mine. I see you have a couple of boxes in your bedroom, which I was meant to keep for you, I am going to take the stuff out and throw it back in the cupboards – fill them up a bit.'

'Lara, how can I let you do this ...' Valda's eyes were full of anguish and she reached out to grab Lara's arm.

Lara quickly pulled away before there was any contact.

'Don't touch me!'

'What?' Valda looked taken aback.

'You may still have traces of blood on your hands – it's not an easy thing to get rid of! Now, just trust me, I know what I'm doing!' Lara reached into her handbag once again; then stopped as a thought suddenly struck her. 'Where are the clippings?'

'Oh, right, I'd better take them with me. The last thing we want is for them to be found.'

Valda directed Lara to their hiding place, which was now behind a picture frame, and Lara adeptly loosened the brackets that held the back of the frame in place and slid the articles out. She gave them to Valda, who stuffed them unceremoniously in the side of her overnight bag.

'Almost done,' sighed Lara. 'Here are the keys to my Golf, drive it to the airport. Get the first flight to Europe and when you get there, buy a ticket to New York!'

'New York?' Valda was puzzled.

Lara's face broke into a big smile as she thrust a piece of paper into Valda's hand. 'I was going to tell you this when we said goodbye at the airport,' she paused and laughed, 'but I guess good news is still good news! I sent your demos to an old client of mine from London, who works in the music biz; he now lives in New York. Anyway, he was bowled over and he wants to meet you. His details are all there.' Lara was delighted to see the look of joy and thanks in Valda's eyes. Valda was too overcome to speak; thoughts of terror, excitement, anticipation, gratitude and happiness were all mingling together. She could feel tears welling in her eyes and she had to fight the urge to throw her arms around Lara. Lara continued, 'I've never been to America and so they don't have any biometric information of mine; they'll only have the passport photo to go on!' Lara paused to catch her breath, she was eager to finalise things. 'So, when you get to New York, stay at the Plaza, that way, I will know where I can get in touch with you, when I get things organised!'

'Why the Plaza?'

'Because that's the only hotel in New York I can think of off the top of my head, OK!' shouted Lara. 'I don't think this is the time to have a debate about the merits of various hotels, when we have a dead fucking body lying around!'

Valda was suddenly shaken back to reality. 'Lara what the hell are –' she was unable to finish.

'We've wasted enough time,' interrupted Lara. 'Take my keys and go. I'm giving you five minutes to get as far away from here as you can, so hurry. And don't worry, I have a plan!'

'I don't know what the hell you are up to, Lara, but thank God for you!'

'You can thank me when I've pulled it off. By the way, does this building have CCTV?' asked Lara as the thought suddenly occurred to her.

'No, definitely not. I know there's going to be a committee meeting to discuss installing it though. It's not as if the crime rate is high enough to warrant it!'

'Excellent!' Lara nodded as she ushered Valda out of the bedroom.

Valda grabbed the overnight bag and headed for the door, realising that she was clutching Lara's car keys so tightly that the VW on the key ring had become embossed onto her palm. Before she opened the door, she looked back at Lara one more time. 'I can't believe you are doing this for me, Lara! Why?'

'Because I can! Now go, we will meet again soon,' Lara smiled reassuringly.

'I owe you one,' chirped Valda. She was finding it impossible to leave; she was racked with guilt at leaving Lara in the mire which she had created.

'No. we're all square!'

As soon as Lara heard the lift doors close, she sprang into action. She hurried into the bedroom and repacked the contents of the boxes into Valda's cupboards. She flattened the empty boxes and stored them at the bottom of the wardrobe, underneath some shoes. She then placed Valda's bank cards and driver's licence in her handbag and made sure that she had no trace of her true identity on her.

Five minutes soon passed. Lara headed back to the lounge and with some trepidation, she picked up the landline phone. She was about to dial 999, when she stopped, realising that she had no idea of what the emergency number actually was in Dubai. She went into the kitchen and yanked open several drawers, before finding a tatty telephone directory. Lara could not help but notice the name "Jo Keane, Flanagan's" scrawled across the front in red marker. She flipped through a few pages and found what she was looking for. Before dialling, Lara swallowed hard and then squeezed her throat with her fingers, so that her voice would sound tight and strained. The phone rang three times.

'Dubai Emergency Services, can I help you!' was the robotic answer.

'Pl ... please help me,' gasped Lara, continuing shakily, 'I'mmm at seventeen ... twenty-nine Concorde To ... wers.'

'What is the problem, do you require an ambulance?' continued the voice in an unconcerned monotone.

'No,' whispered Lara, 'I think he is ... dead! Murdered.' There was silence on the other end of the phone and Lara guessed that the priority of her call had just rocketed.

'Who is dead? What happened?' demanded a new voice urgently.

'I don't know,' cried Lara with anguish, 'I'm so scared, please help me!'

'What is your name?'

'Valda. Valda Kramer.'

'Is anyone with you?'

'No,' whimpered Lara convincingly.

'Don't move; the police are on their way.'

Lara guessed that this would be a good time to put the phone down, she did not want to be drawn into a question and answer session and she needed to prepare for the arrival of the police. She rushed into the kitchen and grabbed Valda's spare pack of cigarettes, slipped one out and lit up. She dragged heavily on the fag, knowing that being unused to cigarettes, it would make her very shaky – all the better for the performance she was about to deliver. Lara toyed with Valda's flat keys, she wanted to make sure that her fingerprints were everywhere – as they should be; after all, she lived there.

Eight minutes had passed and Lara had just finished her second cigarette, she was sure that the police would be there very soon. She sank down onto the floor in the entrance hall and with her back against the wall, she drew her knees up to her chest and wrapped her arms around her knees. Lara always wore eye make-up and her eyes happened to be especially sensitive to the mascara, just a fleck of mascara in her eyes and they would swell up and be flooded with tears for at least half an hour. Knowing this, she rubbed both of her eyes, wanting to set off a reaction. Soon, her eyes were stinging and watering uncontrollably, as brown and black eye make-up streamed down her cheeks. She heard noises outside the door, so she wrapped her arms around her knees once more and rocked back and forth as if trying to comfort herself.

The next moment, three men in police uniform barged into the flat. The first, a tall, thin man with Middle Eastern looks and a black moustache, saw Lara and approached her immediately; the other two, who were both shorter and less refined, started looking around the flat. It was not long before they saw the Sheikh and they immediately burst into frenzied, almost hysterical conversation in Arabic. Lara was not sure if they knew exactly who the Sheikh was, or if they were merely deducing by his dress that he was a man of importance in Dubai society. They were all clearly shocked. The taller one, who appeared to be the superior, maintained more composure as he walked over to regard the Sheikh's body briefly, before barking a long set of instructions to one of the shorter ones, who immediately pulled out his mobile and began to make a call. He then approached Lara and knelt down beside her. Lara no longer had to fake the shaking: a combination of cigarettes, no breakfast that morning and the monumental events of the past hour had left her shaking violently. Her eyes were still filled with tears.

'My name is Officer Faroukh Mohammed,' he said. 'Are you hurt?' Lara shook her head. 'Do you know who this man is?' Lara nodded. 'Were you here when it happened?' Lara shook her head, while wiping her weeping eyes with a trembling hand. Faroukh offered her his hand and helped her to her feet. After giving the other two some more orders, he led Lara to the bedroom and asked her to sit on the bed. In the meantime, he went into the en-suite bathroom, gathered a wad of toilet paper and gave it to her for her eyes. 'I'd like to ask you a few questions when you are ready,' he said gently.

'OK,' said Lara weakly.

Lara had thought about this moment. She knew that to be a good liar, you had to have a good memory. She would concentrate on saying as little as possible, to avoid any danger of contradiction later on. One of the shorter cops appeared in the doorway with a mug of coffee in one hand and a clipboard in the other. He handed her the coffee and she carefully held it in her unsteady hands, before taking a sip. It was very strong and sweet. Lara was glad of the sugar and the caffeine would heighten her shaky state even more so. Faroukh remained standing, but the other cop pulled up a chair and sat down, arranging the clipboard on his knee and getting his pen ready.

'We are going to ask you some questions and then we want you to please tell us what happened as best as you can,' instructed Faroukh. Lara nodded her understanding. 'What is your name?'

'Valda Kramer.'

'Is this where you live?'

'Yes.'

'What is your nationality?'

'South African.'

'Did you know the victim?'

'Yes.'

'Can you tell us his name?'

'Sheikh Abdullah bin Rashid Al Khaimah.'

'What was the nature of your relationship?' asked Faroukh with more than routine interest.

Lara's eyes came alive ever so slightly as she answered disjointedly, 'I've known him ever since I came to Dubai ... I work in one of his hotels, uhm, the Burg Emir.' Lara swallowed hard and blinked the tears from her eyes. 'He's been like a father to me since I came here: he's always been there for me. He is a wonderful man.' Lara's voice broke up as she finished and she reached for the toilet paper and another sip of coffee.

'Does he often visit you?' enquired Faroukh with a raised eyebrow.

'No,' answered Lara calmly. 'We usually meet for a meal or I see him at Flanagan's ... that's where I work.'

'But he does visit you?' insisted Faroukh.

'Yes,' said Lara, as if it was quite normal for the Sheikh to pay her visits. 'His company owns this flat and he has been kind enough to let me stay here.'

Faroukh looked sceptical, but his tone remained balanced and not in the least intimidating. The second cop was taking notes down rapidly.

'Would you please tell us what happened today, if you can.'

Lara took a deep breath before she started. She was sure to hold eye contact with Faroukh at all times and she spoke slowly. 'I arrived home at about twenty past two. I walked in and I was sure that something was different ... it was a weird feeling. I walked into my lounge and that was when I saw him, lying there ...' Lara tailed off, putting her head in her hands, as if the thought was too horrendous to imagine.

'You say you arrived home at two twenty and yet you only rang the emergency services at five to three?'

Lara eyes were filled with angst as she explained, 'First, I was shocked ... awfully shocked ... my mind went numb and I could hardly think. The horror ... it was too much for me to take in. Then, as my mind cleared, I wondered if the murderer was still in the flat. I was paralysed with fear. I was too scared to even look behind me. I kept imagining that the killer was there, right there behind me, waiting to kill me, too. I just stood there, not moving, too scared, I have no idea how much time passed. I was just petrified.' Lara paused. 'Eventually, I summoned up the courage to move. I was shaking uncontrollably and I kept dropping the phone. My mind went blank and I couldn't even remember the number to dial for help. I was fumbling with the numbers, my fingers were so weak. I was so relieved when someone answered.'

Faroukh waited for Lara to compose herself before he continued, 'Did the Sheikh often let himself into your flat, when you weren't here?'

'No.'

'Please forgive me for asking this, madam, but did you and the Sheikh ever have a sexual relationship?'

Lara shook her head vehemently. 'No, as I said, he was like a father figure to me: protective and caring. He was never like that!'

Faroukh paused ostensibly to let the note-taker catch up and, Lara was sure, to collect his own thoughts. Lara could hear sounds coming from the lounge and she guessed that forensics and more back-up had arrived. A man in a white boiler suit popped his head round the door and some terse words were uttered with Faroukh in Arabic. Faroukh then turned his attention back to Lara. 'The murder weapon, the dagger. Was that yours?'

'Yes, I bought it at an antique shop in the Blue Souk,' answered Lara as she took a sip of coffee.

'Officer Latif is going to finish writing this conversation up and then I would like you to read through it and sign it,' instructed Faroukh.

Lara nodded absently. It was a few moments before she was struck by a troubling thought – she had no idea what Valda's signature looked like. Ideas flashed through her mind, she knew that Valda's credit cards were in her handbag, if only she could get a quick look at the signature strip.

'Officer Mohammed,' said Lara respectfully, 'I have some paracetamol in my handbag, may I take one?'

'Where is your handbag?'

'On the entrance-hall table.' Lara was relieved when Faroukh nodded and headed out of the bedroom. He returned a few seconds later with the bag, which he had a brief look in before, much to Lara's relief, handing it over. Lara rummaged through the compartments. She knew where the headache pills were, but she went straight for the cards. She only had a few seconds to take in the nuances of Valda's signature: the V and K were quiet distinctive and Lara figured that if she could pull them off, the signature would pass a superficial examination. She then took out the tablets and Faroukh watched carefully as she popped a couple out of the foil wrapper.

By this stage, Officer Latif had finished with his forms. He raised his portly body off the chair with much effort and headed over to where Lara was sat on the bed. He handed her the set of forms, which were attached to the clipboard, and extended his chubby hand to offer her a pen. 'Please, you initial all pages and sign last page,' he instructed in broken English.

Lara took the pen in her right hand and initialled and signed Valda's name as convincingly as she could, with Faroukh and Officer Latif looking on. She had just finished with the papers, when the man in the white forensics' outfit reappeared. He gave Faroukh some instructions and handed him a strange-looking pair of grey socks. Faroukh turned to Lara. 'Please remove your shoes.'

Lara obediently slipped off her green thong sandals and dropped them into a plastic bag, which the forensics officer was holding out. Faroukh gave her the ugly pair of socks and asked her to put them on. She pulled on the socks, which were somewhat like airline socks with a rubber sole; they were much too big for her and very floppy. Lara recoiled at the thought of who may have worn them before her.

'Now, would you please come with us,' ordered Faroukh as he gestured towards the door. 'You may not take anything with you.'

Lara nodded her understanding and followed Faroukh out of the door. She wondered if she would be handcuffed as she left the flat, but she suspected not. Faroukh had been formal but very respectful of her and she doubted he would find handcuffs necessary. As she walked past the lounge, Lara was torn whether to look once again at the Sheikh's body or not. She debated as to what an innocent person would do? She decided to look towards where he had lain, but all she saw was a room full of policemen and forensic detectives. She looked away, gritted her teeth and followed Faroukh out of the door.

Lara was taken down to the lobby and shown to a waiting police car. She sat in the back with Faroukh and Latif drove. She felt remarkably calm, yet very alert. Her senses seemed alive and it was almost as if she was seeing the world in HD; the sky was a deeper blue, the magnificent skyscrapers of Dubai sparkled, the colours of the buildings were more vibrant. Lara was seeing everything with fresh eyes; it reminded her of the feeling she used to have after a massive reef thunderstorm in Johannesburg. There, in that police car, Lara felt totally at peace. For the first time in her life, she was not worried about the past or the future. Her past suddenly felt irrelevant and her future was in the lap of the Gods. She was living minute to minute and it was the most liberating experience she had ever felt. She observed an aeroplane flying overhead and wondered how far Valda had progressed on her journey. Lara glanced at Faroukh several times. He looked troubled and frequently tugged at the skin on his jawbone; he seemed to have aged that afternoon and even the grey hair at his temples looked more plentiful.

Lara's heart quickened as Latif indicated to turn into the police station. She knew that from then on, everything was out of her hands, but she was not fearful, this was a huge adventure, a gamble with the higher dimension and she felt vitalised. Something ethereal in Lara was alive once again and it was now irrepressible.

Latif drove towards an entrance at the rear of the police station, where several police cars were parked along the side of the building, to the left of the small, unpretentious entrance. Three uniformed police officers walked towards the car as Latif drew slowly to a halt. The car door was opened for Lara and she was immediately shepherded into the building. She looked around and was reassured to note that Faroukh was not far behind her; for some reason, she trusted him and felt that he would be fair. There were some short conversations in Arabic, but in the main, the police officers remained solemn and silent as they walked Lara towards a set of oak doors.

Beyond the oak doors lay a labyrinth of anonymous passages, with vinyl floors, fluorescent lighting and off-white walls, dotted with the occasional wooden door and informative poster. They seemed to walk for a great length of time, turning from one passage into another and another and another. There were no windows and even though Lara had a good sense of direction, it was not long before she felt totally disorientated and she wondered how long it took the people who worked there to figure out where everything was. Eventually, their group came to a standstill outside a large security door. One of the policemen rang the intercom buzzer on the wall. It was soon answered and after a brief exchange, the security door clicked open. Lara was led into a large, bleak-looking reception area. She could smell disinfectant and detected a decidedly medical ambience. Faroukh stepped forwards to speak to a receptionist, who then hurried into one of the many rooms leading off the reception area. A few silent minutes later, a female doctor appeared, wearing standard medical scrubs and a stethoscope.

'This is Dr Khan,' said Faroukh. 'She is going to examine you.'

Dr Khan was an attractive Asian woman in her forties; she had a large, round face and big brown eyes, but she looked very grave. Dr Khan was given, what seemed from the tone of voice to be some instructions by one of the other policemen. She then turned to Lara and said firmly, 'Please come with me!'

Lara followed her into an examination room, where she was instructed to remove all her clothes. Lara was then asked to stand in the middle of the room, naked, while Dr Khan passed a strange instrument with a blue light over Lara's body. Dr Khan then requested that Lara place both of her hands under a device with a similar blue light, after which she took skin samples from underneath Lara's fingernails. Lara followed all the instructions with no comment. Dr Khan was courteous but extremely formal at all times and she only spoke when she had to. Lara was surprised at the extent of the examination, which included her giving a blood sample. Lara was hoping that the examination was almost over, when, to her horror, she was asked to lie on the examination table in order for a vaginal inspection to take place. Lara cringed and squeezed her eyes shut in an ostrich-like attempt to block out the reality. Although Dr Khan was gentle, Lara detested every second of the ordeal and was extremely grateful when it was all over. Dr Khan requested that Lara remain on the bed while she labelled all her samples and placed them in brown envelopes. She then placed Lara's clothes into a plastic bag and sealed that, too. At that stage, she went over to a cupboard and removed a light-blue top and pair of pants, which she gave Lara to put on. The clothes reminded Lara of hospital pyjamas, crossed with an old-fashioned tracksuit and, like the shoes, they were far too big for her.

Wearing her new uniform, she was escorted back to the reception area. Faroukh and two other policemen were waiting there for her to return; Latif and the rest had disappeared. Once again, Lara found herself walking down a dreary corridor; this time, the destination was a large, high-ceilinged room, which was subdivided into cubicles, where she was systematically photographed and fingerprinted.

After another twisting and turning journey through the concrete and plaster maze, Lara found herself entering a rather more austere and frightening part of the establishment. Faroukh led her and the other two through three high-security iron gates, until they found themselves in a narrow corridor, with several steel doors leading off it. Faroukh used a combination of key and code to open one of the doors and then he gestured for Lara to go in. Lara was not quite sure what she was thinking at that precise moment, but Faroukh must have seen the fear and alarm in her face as he was quick to reassure her.

'I will be back with more information for you within an hour.'

Lara looked into his eyes and he appeared to be more at sea than she was, so, with no other option, she walked meekly into her cell. Thoughts of asking for a lawyer flashed through her mind and were quickly dismissed; she wanted to portray herself as weak and defenceless, not as some Western wise guy.

Before Faroukh could shut the door, Lara spun around and pleaded, 'Do you promise?'

'I promise,' he said sincerely, pausing only briefly before firmly shutting and locking the door.

Chapter Nineteen

Lara looked about the cell. There was no window and no carpet. The floor was concrete painted green and the walls were white. There was a basic bed against the one wall and a desk and chair against the other. To Lara's relief and amazement, there was an en-suite bathroom with a basin and a toilet; what's more, everything was clean.

Lara sat down on the bed, feeling exhausted. The coffee and cigarettes had worn off and the events of the day had caught up with her. She had once heard that, "When you place an innocent man in jail, he bounces off the walls; when you place a guilty man in jail, he lays down and goes to sleep". She was not about to do either, she was too physically drained to kick and scream and too overwoundto sleep.

Since she had received that call from Valda, she had been propelled by adrenalin, things had fallen into place and there had been no time to think. Suddenly, all alone in the featureless cell, there was time to think, too much time to think. Lara thought about the strange blue light and wondered if its purpose was to detect traces of blood.

Lara suddenly realised how little she knew about the legal system in Dubai. She thought about the Sheikh's body and the looks on the faces of Latif, Faroukh and the other cop when they had seen him. It was not long before Lara made a determined decision to restrain all negative thoughts. She knew that there was nothing she could do and she simply did not have enough information or knowledge to make hypothesising worthwhile. She decided to mentally rehearse her story and to prepare for any questions that might be thrown at her.

Lara had no idea whether one or two hours had passed, but she was relieved to hear the key in the door. She was even more relieved when she saw Faroukh. Faroukh was holding a paper carrier bag and he walked over to the table, reached into the bag and placed the contents on the table. There was a cheese sandwich wrapped in plastic, a takeaway-style coffee, a bar of soap and some toilet paper. Faroukh fiddled in his pocket and produced two cigarettes and placed them on the table as well. 'Call me if you need a light,' he said, pointing to a bell on the wall. Lara nodded, guessing that he was not allowed to leave her with matches, but even though she was not technically a smoker, she appreciated the gesture of the cigarettes.

'Thank you very much,' said Lara gratefully as she looked over at the meagre sandwich and bare necessities. He did not reply, but he lingered for a moment, giving Lara the opportunity to ask, 'So what happens now?'

'Tomorrow, you will speak with the Detective Superintendent! The Chief of Police has contacted your consulate general; they may send a representative tomorrow.'

Lara thanked Faroukh again; she was greatly relieved to know that some help was on the way, even though she would have preferred to have had the backing of Her Majesty's government.

The tall, thin policeman reached into his pocket once more; he looked pensive as if debating something with himself. At last, he withdrew a small, clear, plastic bottle and handed it to Lara, 'Dr Khan asked me to give you this. To help you sleep.'

As Lara accepted the bottle, she observed that there were two blue pills in the bottle. Faroukh was gone before she could thank him again.

She examined the tablets closely, suspecting they may be some kind of truth pill. The only markings on the tablets were "1mg". They looked to Lara like harmless diazepam or lorazepam, but she could not be sure. She soon decided to take the leap of faith and swallowed one of the pills – she needed to be at her best in the morning and she knew she would never sleep without help. She ate the bland sandwich gratefully and by the time she had finished the coffee, the pills had taken effect and even the bed was feeling more inviting. At some indeterminate time, she fell asleep.

Lara woke to the sound of the key in the door. She had no idea of the time and neither did she know how long she had been asleep, but she could smell coffee. A uniformed officer came into the holding cell with a tray, set it down on the table and left without speaking. On the tray were a croissant and a cup of coffee. Lara was so hungry that even the stale and flaky croissant tasted good and the sweet coffee was like an expensive dessert.

She had no sooner finished her coffee than the door opened once more. This time it was Faroukh, to inform her that she must be ready for her interview with the DS in half an hour's time. Lara smirked inwardly: what am I supposed to do to get ready – style my hair and pop on my best business suit? Lara suddenly realised that she must still have make-up all over her face from the day before, so she took the bar of soap and did her best to have a wash in the tiny basin. She used the sheet on the bed in the absence of a towel and as she got ready, Lara thought about her strategy; she wanted to appear shocked and saddened, perhaps even scared, but always open and ready to cooperate. It was all about an act and she had to pull it off.

It seemed like less than half an hour had passed when Faroukh reappeared, but Lara was ready. He escorted her through a series of security doors to an interview room, where she was instructed to wait. The interview room was stark, containing nothing but a standard-issue wooden table and four chairs, and on one of the walls was a panel of one-way glass. After only a short wait, Faroukh and two other men entered the room. Faroukh and a burly, moustached man in an ill-fitting brown suit, who was introduced as the DS, sat opposite Lara, while the third man, who was in uniform, stood by the door.

'Do you understand that this is a formal interview and it will be recorded?'

'Yes,' nodded Lara.

'You are not under arrest, but we are holding you in custody pending further inquiries.' Lara nodded again, she had developed an immediate dislike for the DS; he had cold, compassionless eyes. She wondered how long they were entitled to hold her without charge: she hoped that the consular official was still coming. 'I would now like to ask you some questions,' continued the DS, who was eager to get down to business.

The DS started off by asking virtually the same questions that Faroukh had asked. He then proceeded to ask essentially the same questions again, but phrased slightly differently. Lara answered calmly and firmly, looking into his eyes and pausing every so often for an emotional gasp or feigned tear. Lara had repeatedly visualised her concocted version of events in such detail that it actually felt like a memory and not a lie. She found it easy to answer the questions and she saw through his feeble attempts to trick her. Lara could see the DS's wristwatch and half an hour had passed, when he decided that Lara should have a break. The DS left the room and Lara guessed he had gone to consult with another detective. Faroukh also left the room, but he returned almost immediately, with four coffees in paper cups. Lara was halfway through her coffee, when the stocky DS shuffled back into the room. He swigged back some coffee and flicked through a wad of paperwork, before continuing with his line of questioning.

'How many times did the Sheikh visit you at your apartment?'

'About twice.'

'About twice? Was it more than two occasions?' pressed the DS.

'I only remember two,' said Lara firmly.

'And when were those two occasions?'

'I don't remember the exact dates, but I know that the first was shortly after I moved in.'

Lara was feeling on shaky territory for the first time. Valda had never mentioned the Sheikh visiting her, so what she was saying was not even based on reality.

'Why did he visit you on those two occasions?'

'The first time was to check how I was settling in and the second time, he was in the building to see a work associate, who was staying in one of his other flats, I think,' she stated in a matter-of-fact tone.

Lara was hoping that he would move on to some other line of questioning, but in the meantime, she was not going to let him see any flicker of indecision or concern in her eyes.

'How long did he stay?'

'Between ten and twenty minutes each time.'

'Did he come alone?' asked the DS.

Lara was about to mention that Ahmed was usually around, but in a split second, she decided to answer, 'Yes.'

'Did you ever engage in any form of sexual activity with Sheikh Abdullah bin Rashid Al Khaimah?'

'No!' answered Lara indignantly. The way he asked the question, one would have thought sex in itself was the crime.

The DS continued to question Lara about her relationship with the Sheikh: what they talked about, how often they met and where they met. Lara found these questions easy to deal with.

'Did you often have other visitors at your flat?'

'Oh, yes!' she answered more cheerfully. 'Friends I'd met here, friends from home.'

'The cupboards at your flat were rather empty, were you planning to move?'

Lara shook her head as if puzzled at the suggestion, 'I only arrived here with a suitcase and quite frankly, I have been too busy working to find time to buy new things or to furnish ... you know?'

The DS looked momentarily impressed, he obviously approved of a woman who could not find the time to shop in a shopper's paradise.

'Tell me about the dagger you bought from the Blue Souk.'

The DS had adopted a more relaxed, laid-back attitude and Lara was wary not to be lulled into complacency. She reminded herself that this was a game; she had to keep the act up at all times. Lara briefly explained how she had come to buy the dagger, but the DS was still curious.

'But what made you buy it?'

'It was so unusual, something you would never see in the West.' Lara's heart jumped; she had almost slipped up and said, "Something you would never see in England". She had been so careful not to allow her true identity to shine through, but she feared her concentration may be slipping.

'We see that you have been back to South Africa a number of times over the course of the last eight months, each time for only a few days.'

'Yes, I wanted to see my family and I needed to go back to sign papers for the sale of my flat and my car.'

'You stayed such a short time though?'

Lara smiled, 'Getting time off is hard in my job, it's not like it's easy to get a stand-in: you ask Jo at Flanagan's, he goes crazy when I want time off.'

'We did actually speak to Mr Keane last night; he was telling me that the Sheikh seemed to take a special interest in you!' Lara expected more questions to follow, but to her surprise, the DS began collecting his papers together and said, 'Anyway, I think we are finished for now. Officer Mohammed will show you back to your cell.'

Lara was disappointed that nothing more had been said about the consular official. She decided that she would ask Faroukh about it. Faroukh led Lara back to the cell and informed her that he would be back within a few minutes with some food. Lunch turned out to be another sweet, strong coffee with a cheese sandwich, but since she was very hungry and it was a "beggars-can't-be-choosers" situation, Lara was looking forward to it. Faroukh was about to turn and leave, when Lara grabbed her chance. 'Faroukh?' she addressed him by his first name for the first time and he looked at her with surprise. 'You said that the consular official may be coming today?'

'I'm not sure, Valda. I will have to find out,' he said sympathetically.

'Can you find out?' implored Lara. 'Please!'

'I will do my best,' said Faroukh with a half-smile as he left.

The afternoon dragged by painfully slowly. Lara had heard marathon runners talk about hitting "The Wall" and she was sure that she had hit the Wall in her own way; the waiting was unbearable and every second, she wondered how much more she could take. The time itself remained a mystery in that windowless room. Lara was saving her second blue pill for the night time, which she presumed would be when they brought her dinner.

At some point during that hideously boring afternoon, Lara decided that she had paced and lain waiting long enough and that it was time for her to take more control. She marched over to the buzzer on the wall and held it down for a good few seconds. It was not long before a hatch within her cell door opened and a moustached policeman peered in anxiously.

'Where is Officer Mohammed?' demanded Lara forcefully. The policeman looked taken aback and somewhat confused and so Lara continued angrily, 'I have answered all your questions; I have done nothing wrong; how long are you going to keep me like this?'

The policeman took a step back, still looking so baffled that Lara wondered if he understood English. He then nodded nervously and held up his hand saying, 'I find him, OK!'

It seemed like four hours, but Lara guessed it was only about ten minutes, before she heard Faroukh turning the key in her door. He said nothing, but gestured for Lara to follow him. She was led though the set of security doors and then down a narrow passage. She was hopeful that the person from the embassy was somewhere in the concrete labyrinth waiting for her. Faroukh unlocked another heavy steel door and Lara followed him through it, to find herself suddenly in daylight. Painful needles shot through her eyes as they adjusted to the bright, natural light. It was dusky, but the light was still intense compared to the fluorescent lighting in the holding area. Lara realised that they were standing in a paved courtyard. It felt quite unreal to be outside again and she had to remind herself that she had only been in the cell for just over a day.

She looked over to Faroukh questioningly and he answered her stare with, 'You have one hour outside for fresh air and exercise. You may smoke a cigarette if you wish.' With that, he reached into his pocket, withdrew a pack of Marlboro and handed her a cigarette. Lara took it, placed it between her lips and accepted his offer to light it for her. It felt so wonderful to be outside that even the heat and humidity escaped her notice. Lara was still wearing the blue outfit Dr Khan had issued her with and it hung off her thin body; her brown, unbrushed hair dangled around her shoulders. Faroukh did not speak for some time and it was only when he had finished his own cigarette that he offered Lara the information she really wanted, 'Jodie van der Velde from your embassy will be here to speak with you tomorrow morning.'

Lara exhaled a plume of smoke, somewhat relieved. 'Thanks, Faroukh!'

Thanks to the second blue pill, Lara slept well that night and she awoke to the now familiar sound of the key in the door. She ate the croissant and coffee, the normal morning offerings, it seemed, and readied herself for the visit from Ms van der Velde. Lara was not sure what to expect or how hopeful to be, but she was buoyed up at the prospect of some more information and even more so by the prospect of help. She did not have to wait long before Faroukh summoned her. She recognised the route to the interview room; however, this time, she was shown into a different room, opposite the interview room, which had four walls and no one-way glass.

Lara waited patiently in the windowless room with Faroukh, who informed her that Ms van de Velde was running late. Late was not as much of a concern to Lara as whether she was still coming. Some twenty minutes later, Jodie van der Velde bustled into the room, laden with an armload of paperwork. She was an athletic-looking brunette, with short, bobbed hair and a youthful face; Lara guessed she was a thirty-something.

'Hello, I am Jodie van der Velde!' she said, extending her hand after dumping the paperwork on the table.

Lara rose and shook her hand, 'I'm Valda, but I guess you already know that!'

Faroukh left the room as Jodie pulled up a chair. Lara noticed that Jodie took some time to neaten her papers and straighten her jacket and her hair several times before speaking and she could only infer from that that Jodie was uncomfortable with either the situation or the information which she was about to deliver. Lara began to feel her blood chilling.

Jodie took a deep breath before she began. 'Now,' she paused agonisingly, 'I am not here in a legal capacity. I am not a lawyer. I am basically here to ensure that you are aware of your rights and that you have been treated appropriately. Neither the embassy itself nor any consular official will become personally involved in your case or any subsequent trial, and nor will financial assistance be offered. Our duty is to ...'

Lara nodded vaguely as she began to tune out. She recognised that Jodie was merely trotting out the standard policy in parrot-fashion. Lara found it intensely irritating when people insisted on starting a conversation by listing everything they could not do, or even worse, had to issue a caveat before every sentence. She was beginning to wonder whether Jodie or the embassy were of any use after all.

'Are you happy with your treatment?' she heard Jodie ask.

'Yes, it's OK under the circumstances,' answered Lara, immediately adding, 'but I am more concerned about how long I can be held.'

Jodie evaded the question. 'If you feel that you have been mistreated or if your human rights have been denied, we can contact the Ombudsman from the Human Rights Department of the Dubai Police Headquarters on your behalf.'

Lara reacted with impatience, 'Look, Jodie, are we actually going to have a two-way conversation or are you just going to quote me chapter and verse.'

'I have a duty to make you aware of what we can or cannot do,' answered Jodie defensively, while adjusting her jacket once more.

'Well can we skip the "what you can't do" part, because I feel that may take all day!' retorted Lara, surprised at her own audacity.

Lara was sensing an impertinent side of her character revealing itself for the first time – it was as if pretending to be Valda had freed the restrained elements of her own predominantly easy-going nature. Jodie flicked through her paperwork, trying to regroup. Lara wondered what the mass of paperwork pertained to, before she sighed, acknowledging that they were living in an age where everything from buying a loaf of bread to tying a shoelace seemed to generate paperwork.

Jodie took another deep breath and started again, 'Sheikh Abdullah was a maverick, a controversial character within his circles; some of his business affairs were dubious; he was not always popular. However, he was nonetheless a member of the Royal Family. His death and the surfacing of stories about his life have been a matter of great embarrassment as well as difficulty for the government and they are very eager to see this matter resolved. I think it safe to say that they will throw every resource available at this in order to charge and prosecute a suspect quickly.'

'I thought as much myself,' sighed Lara. 'I had nothing whatsoever to do with it and I have told the police all I can.'

'Yes, they told me you had been very cooperative. There are no plans to charge you at present and nothing has been submitted to the prosecutor's office.'

'Will I be tried under Shariah Law?' asked Lara apprehensively.

'No, Valda. Shariah Law is only for Muslims. As a non-Muslim, you will be not be tried before a Shariah Court on any matter. You would, should it come to it be tried under Dubai Law, which is a combination of Roman, Egyptian, French and Islamic law. However, there is still the death penalty.'

'So, basically, they are going to hold on to me in lieu of finding the real killer or another suspect.' Lara leant back in her chair hopelessly.

'Honestly, yes! That's the worst-case scenario, but you really need a lawyer,' said Jodie leaning forwards. Lara sensed that Jodie was beginning to relax and to loosen up slightly.

'Can you get me a lawyer, or was that under the list of can'ts I didn't want to hear,' smiled Lara ironically.

'I'll see you get a good lawyer. Unofficially!' ended Jodie with emphasis.

'Thanks, Jodie, the waiting and the not knowing is the hardest part, as you can imagine,' confided Lara.

Jodie suddenly pushed the pile of folders and paperwork aside and leaned forwards, with her folded arms on the table. Lara took the cue and moved closer to Jodie.

'Look, Valda, this is strictly off the record, understand! I am not even sure I should be telling you this at this stage, it's probably best left to your lawyer,' she paused.

'Go on, please,' implored Lara.

'Trade and diplomatic relations between South Africa and the UAE are extremely good; nobody wants anything to jeopardise that. The Chief of Police had a lengthy discussion with the high commissioner and he divulged some details about the ongoing inquiry into the Sheikh's death.' Lara nodded, eager for Jodie to continue. 'At the moment, there is not a scrap of evidence to implicate you in any way: there was no trace of blood or DNA from the Sheikh found on your body, the clothes you were wearing or any of the clothes in your flat. He was struck from behind by someone who was ostensibly left-handed and you are right-handed. The strength and angle with which he was struck indicates someone taller and better built than yourself. Your prints were on the murder weapon, but since you acquired it recently from a shop, there were dozens of prints on it. It seems that your evidence so far has been deemed consistent and plausible. What's more, you appear to have had no motive. They interviewed Jo Keane and he confirmed that you and the Sheikh did, indeed, have a friendly relationship and that you met regularly for dinner. According to Mr Keane, the Sheikh regarded you as an asset of his business. And another thing, no trace of sexual intercourse between you and Sheikh Abdullah was found on the day he died. Given all this, it seems highly unlikely any prosecutor would proceed with a trial; however, you just never know, if you know what I mean.'

Lara could not keep the smile off her face, 'Jodie, my God, thank you! I really needed to hear that, at least I know there is evidence to back my story up.'

'I wanted to tell you, but you know how it is, protocol, etc.!' Jodie rolled her eyes.

'Of course, I know that, and I won't say anything. Anyway, it would be sad if protocol prevailed over compassion.'

'It's a waiting game now!'

Chapter Twenty

There were no more visitors or interviews for Lara over the next three days. Jodie's information had made the waiting easier and furthermore, conditions had improved: Lara was allowed into the courtyard for half an hour twice a day, she had been provided with reading material, albeit out-of-date newspapers and magazines, and was given fresh clothes and towels each day. Meals were uninteresting, but they arrived regularly and either Faroukh or one of the other policemen brought her sweet coffees at intervals throughout the day. Faroukh was generally her companion during her trips to the courtyard and he was free to offer cigarettes, although, to his surprise, Lara usually rejected them. Lara enjoyed their time outside in the courtyard, as what she missed most whilst in prison was being able to talk to people and although Faroukh was a rather reluctant companion, she had discovered that they had a common interest in cricket and she was at least able to draw him into conversation on that topic.

Lara wondered what she should infer from the failure of a lawyer to appear. Jodie had promised she would arrange one and Lara had believed her to be genuine. She doubted she would be seeing a lawyer in the next two days; however, as it was Thursday the next day, the start of the Dubai weekend, her patience and self-belief were really being tested.

It was easy to lose track of the days and each morning, Lara's mental exercise was to work out what day it was; she would try to imagine what Valda was doing, she would try to figure out what Jodie was doing and she tried, in vain, to read in Faroukh's eyes what the police were uncovering.

On the fourth day after Jodie's visit, Lara was reading a back issue of Reader's Digest for the third time, when she heard the key in the door. She was surprised, as it was too soon after breakfast for Faroukh to be bringing coffee, but in he came with the usual paper cup from the coffee machine. As he placed the cup on the table, he turned to Lara, who was sitting on the edge of her bed, and whispered, 'Good news, Valda. A witness has come forward!'

'A witness?' Lara asked with surprise.

Lara was confused. She knew what had happened and that there could have been no witnesses to the actual murder, so she wondered what exactly this witness had seen. Despite the fact that this was a worrying development, which had the potential to cast doubt on her whole story, Lara decided that she had better display some excitement.

'Yes, the DS is interviewing her right now!'

Her! thought Lara in alarm. 'That's great news, Faroukh, thank goodness some information has finally come to light!' she uttered with feigned enthusiasm and relief.

Faroukh immediately made his excuses and left. Lara sank back onto the bed, puzzled and concerned; she was unable to fathom out who this mystery female witness was. She wondered briefly if Valda had returned and was making up some story; she wondered if someone who knew Valda had spotted her at the airport leaving Dubai; theories abounded in her head and she craved another blue pill to make her racing mind stop. She did not see Faroukh again that day and it was some of the other policemen who brought her food and accompanied her to the courtyard. She read nothing in their deadpan faces.

Lara's sleep was troubled and restless and she was still trying to sleep, when Faroukh arrived with her breakfast and to tell her that she was going to be interviewed by the DS in the next half-hour.

Lara sat at the interview table, her head pounding. She had a splitting headache, she was pale and she had dark circles under her eyes. She had not seen a mirror since that fateful day itself and she had no idea how gaunt and depleted she looked.

The DS sat opposite her, sorting his papers and notepad; he had informed her that this session would be brief.

'Now, Miss Kramer, what do you know about Ahmed Atwan?' he asked, leaning forwards.

Lara paused momentarily before answering; she tried to recall everything that Valda had told her about Ahmed. 'He was the Sheikh's … uhm … minder,' she answered quietly.

'Did you know him well?'

'Not really.' Lara shook her head, adding, 'He was always with the Sheikh or hovering in the background.'

'Did you ever have a conversation with him?'

'No, not really. Nothing more than "hello", "how are you", that type of thing.'

'Did you ever see him on any occasion other than when he was with Sheikh Abdullah?'

Lara did not answer immediately, she needed to think, to scan every bit of her memory. 'Yes, there were one or two occasions when he delivered an invitation for me for dinner with the Sheikh.' Lara refrained from elaborating; her tactic, as usual, was to keep all her answers short and to the point.

'You mentioned that Sheikh Abdullah visited you on two occasions in your apartment.' He sat forwards earnestly.

'Yes, that's right.'

'Where was Ahmed on those occasions?'

'I didn't actually see him, but I assumed he was somewhere nearby.'

'Did the Sheikh ever mention Ahmed to you in conversation?'

'No.'

'Thank you very much, Miss Kramer, that will be all for today.'

The rest of that day and the day that followed were routine, but for the absence of Faroukh, who Lara assumed was having some time off. The hours crept tediously by and Lara had given up on her hypothesising. She was neither optimistic nor pessimistic and she held no regrets, she only maintained her belief that there must be a reason behind it all and that somehow, those mysterious puzzle pieces were fitting together.

It was two days since her interview with the DS, when she heard the key in the door. It was morning and she assumed that her breakfast was arriving. She was lying in bed and did not make the effort to sit up or even to look around.

'Valda?' called Faroukh, who, to Lara's surprise, was standing in the doorway, empty-handed, but wearing a huge smile. He motioned for her to get up, 'Come with me!' Lara was quickly on her feet and she followed Faroukh into the passageway.

'Where are we going?' she asked eagerly.

Faroukh, still smiling, held his finger to his lips.

Lara's heart was now beating faster and faster, but she dared not to raise her expectations. She was led through the familiar security doors, but instead of walking in the direction of the interview room, they walked down a long hallway and then climbed some stairs and entered a part of the building Lara had not seen before. The change in decor was dramatic; there were pot plants, carpets, concealed lighting, vending machines and art on the walls – it was like another planet. Faroukh was tall and athletic and he walked very quickly and Lara was out of breath, trying to keep up with his pace. As they passed through a set of wooden doors, Lara immediately noticed the DS, who was standing with a tall, blond man.

He greeted her with a smile and an outstretched hand. 'Aah, Miss Kramer, I would like you to meet Mr Robert Stelling!' said the DS.

Lara held out her hand out to shake both Mr Stelling and the DS's hand.

'Please come into my office,' invited the DS as he shepherded Lara and Mr Stelling into a spacious, modern room. Lara noticed nothing about the office, all her attention was focused on a beaming Jodie, who was standing in the centre of the room.

'You are being released, they've made an arrest,' she squealed with delight as she threw her arms around Lara. Lara embraced Jodie enthusiastically, but looked around for confirmation from the DS.

'Yes, indeed, you are now free to go. In fact, Mr Stelling and Ms van der Velde will fill you in on all the details, while I go and sign the release papers,' announced the DS as he closed the door and left Lara, Jodie and Robert alone in his office.

Lara was overwhelmed with excitement and also questions. She wanted to know who had been arrested; she needed to understand all the details, before she could allow the relief and joy to permeate her body. She looked around for a chair to collapse into, while Jodie and Robert looked on with concern. She put her hands over her eyes, composing herself for a few seconds, before looking up at Jodie and gasping, 'Oh, my God, this is so wonderful! Thank you, thank you!'

'You look terrible, but don't worry, we're going to take you for a big, fat meal and a shopping spree as soon as we leave here,' reassured Jodie cheerfully.

'Who did they arrest?' enquired Lara.

Jodie could not contain her own excitement and began to rattle off the details with enthusiasm. 'Well, lucky for you, you have a very nosy neighbour – Mrs O'Neil?' She paused for a second and Lara acknowledged that she knew who Jodie was referring to. 'Anyway, she came forward a few days after the murder as a crucial witness. On the day of the murder, she was waiting for a phone call from her son in Boston, when she heard noises in the hallway and decided to investigate by looking out of her peephole. This was at about one o'clock. She saw two men matching the descriptions of Ahmed Atwan and Sheikh Abdullah entering your apartment. She claims that about fifteen minutes later, she heard your door slam; she looked out again and saw Ahmed leaving. Incidentally, she said that she had seen Ahmed "lurking" outside your apartment on another occasion as well. She said that she was suspicious. The next thing she saw was you arriving home at about two twenty, a time which was backed up by the garage security system, which logged your key code. She left shortly after that in order to do some shopping.' Jodie stopped to catch her breath and Lara silently reflected on her good fortune; nosy Mrs O' Neil had missed Valda arriving home at one thirty. Jodie continued, 'The police had been suspicious of Ahmed in any case, but after Mrs O' Neil's evidence, they decided to search his flat. Robert will have to tell you the rest, as it gets quite complicated.'

Lara looked towards Robert; she was enthralled by the way things had fitted together. Robert had waited patiently for his turn, but he was equally raring to tell his story. He pulled up a chair and sat forwards, facing Lara. 'When they searched Ahmed's flat, they found an archive of old newspaper articles dating back fifteen years. Bear in mind that Ahmed had worked for the Sheikh for seventeen years. All the articles pertained to seemingly accidental deaths, which had occurred in Dubai at various intervals over those past fifteen years. Taken together, it was easy to see the similarities: all the deceased were men, all were immigrants, all had worked for the Sheikh in some capacity and all were fairly well off prior to their deaths. None of the deaths were considered suspicious at the time. The post-mortem showed that Sheikh Abdullah was a cocaine addict. The police deduced that in view of the strict drug laws in Dubai, it was hard for him to feed his habit and so over the years, he had enlisted the help of various employees to smuggle coke into Dubai for him. He offered handsome rewards. In order to cover his tracks, however, he would have his couriers wiped out after a few months. The police are convinced that Ahmed carried out all the murders and they believe that further investigations and forensic evidence will prove this beyond a doubt, especially as far as the more recent deaths go.' As Robert took a breath, Lara once again marvelled at her luck; the police had ostensibly overlooked the fact that, apart from being a woman, she – or Valda, rather – fitted into exactly the same category as all the deceased couriers.

'So why do they think Ahmed killed Sheikh Abdullah?' asked Lara, perplexed.

'Well,' answered Robert with big eyes, 'ten years ago, a concierge at one of the Sheikh's hotels by the name of Yousef Atwan was found hanged in his apartment. The verdict was suicide. He was Ahmed's brother. It's hard to say whether Ahmed or someone else killed Yousef, but there is no doubt the Sheikh was behind it. It must have been very difficult for Ahmed to accept: Yousef was his younger brother and they were apparently very close. By that stage, it would have been impossible for Ahmed to go to the police – he had so much blood on his own hands and who would have believed his story? The police believe that Ahmed never forgave the Sheikh and he had waited patiently all these years for the opportunity to wreak his revenge. He must have thought that by killing the Sheikh in your apartment, with your knife, you would be arrested and tried and he could walk free. Anyway, the bottom line is that Ahmed has been arrested and the DS has submitted papers to the prosecutor, who will, in time, charge Ahmed with the murder. Most importantly though, you are free to go – I have your passport and apartment keys in my pocket.'

Robert had just finished, when the DS re-entered his office with wads full of paperwork and some papers for Lara to sign. Lara was sure that any decent lawyer would be able to flag up all the gaps and flaws in the "Ahmed did it" theory, but she intended to be very far away from Dubai by that stage. She also thought back to what Jodie had said about the necessity to have this messy saga off the front pages, superseding a quest for truth and justice. She had never seen Ahmed, but she pitied him, especially now that she knew he had been trying to warn Valda all along. Lara wondered why Robert had not mentioned anything about Claire's death; surely Ahmed had retained articles about that, too.

Jodie and Robert drove Lara to the South African Embassy and she was able to shower, wash her hair and change her clothes there. Every small detail of life from brushing her teeth to blow-drying her hair was a revelation, a luxury, something to be very much appreciated. Lara had never been a person to take things for granted, but even for her, there was a renewed pleasure in every aspect of life.

Robert, Jodie and the other staff at the embassy who joined Lara for a slap-up meal at the Burg Al Arab were ravenous for details of her ordeal, from the discovery of the body to prison life. Apparently, her story had made headline news in the papers and her news was even featured on *Al Jazeera*. Lara was happy to oblige with all the details; however, her mind was constantly on the flight she would be taking to JFK the next night and what she needed to do before then.

It was a struggle to satisfy Jodie that she would be OK by herself that night, but after some persuading, Lara managed to get away by herself. She posted off the car documents and removed the final things from Valda's flat, before returning to her own flat in Deira. She was thoroughly relieved to be back in her own flat and yet it no longer felt like home. She was also relieved to be herself again and yet the Lara she was now, felt very different to the Lara she had been when she had received that call on the "secret phone" two weeks before. After another bath and wearing a wonderfully fresh and soft pair of PJ's, she collapsed into bed, blissfully relieved and relaxed and, moreover, feeling more resolved than she had ever felt in her life.

The next morning, Lara began packing her things. She was passing through the lounge, when she saw the large paper bag Robert had given her; apparently, it contained various belongings of Valda's, which the police had confiscated. She curiously peeled back the masking tape and looked inside. She found her own handbag, with Valda's bank cards inside, along with Valda's driving licence, cigarettes and lighter. She found a group of envelopes all tied together and right at the bottom was, to her surprise, the dagger. It was wrapped in plastic, but even through the plastic it sparkled with splendour. It had been beautifully cleaned and polished and looked better than ever. Lara stared at it for some time; it sent a shiver down her spine, but not for the obvious reason, there was something else, which she could not define.

Lara flicked through the envelopes: some were bills, but, more interestingly, some were letters of support from Valda's colleagues at Flanagan's – she saw the names of Jo, Inzie and other people, whom Valda had never mentioned. Lara smiled, knowing how happy Valda would be that people had been worried about her.

Lara knew she would have to return at some stage to sell the cars and her own flat, but she also knew that any return would be brief. She felt as if she had been reinvented as a person – she was on the first leg of a journey, destination unknown, the past unimportant.

That night as she flew over Dubai, she did not look back, not even to see the glittering lights of the magnificent desert city.

Lara marched up to the reception desk of the Plaza Hotel confidently.

'I believe you have someone staying here by the name of Larissa May,' she enquired with confidence. 'Please would you tell her that a very, very old acquaintance of hers in waiting in the lobby!'

Five minutes later, Valda burst through the elevator doors with an ecstatic whoop and the two embraced, overjoyed – their delight was plain for everybody to see. Tears were in their eyes and words failed them both. It was Valda who managed to speak first.

'God, am I pleased to see you. I've been so worried! I can't believe I just left you out there to deal with all that.' Valda found that her glib words were totally inadequate in explaining the horrendous guilt and regret she had felt; she hoped that somehow Lara would understand.

'Well, I told you to go!'

'I know, and I always listen to you for some reason. Let's not talk here, come up to my room.'

Valda helped Lara carry her luggage towards the elevator and soon, they were on the way to her room. Valda shut the door and immediately fired the questions.

'I want to hear everything! By the way, you made the news, or was it me that made the news? Anyway, the story about the Sheikh's death was on CNN. Did I have a job explaining that to my dad, I'll tell you about that later though. You go first.'

Lara explained every second of her ordeal from the time Valda had left the flat to the minute Lara boarded the plane and Valda listened in awe, without a single interruption.

'So it was Ahmed who was sending me those clippings,' mused Valda as Lara finished her story.

'I think he felt protective towards you, perhaps he wanted to save you, where he had failed to save his brother.'

'Shame, poor guy, and now he has to take the rap,' said Valda with regret.

'Should we be that sorry for him? He may have killed all those other people, after all,' countered Lara.

'That may be so, but speaking as someone who was also caught in the Sheikh's clutches, what chance did Ahmed have of escaping: it was a case of do or die! I think it's strange that they never found any articles about Claire or made the connection. It was Ahmed that sent me the clipping about Claire, so he must have had copies.'

'Perhaps he realised that he may be arrested and so he destroyed the information on Claire. He might have wanted to protect other people; I always said that Claire was part of a different strategy. Keeping Claire out of the picture also helped protect you! On the other hand, whoever is in charge of the investigation may not have wanted to open any more cans of worms, especially if other officials or members of the establishment were involved. Bearing in mind Claire was from the UK, it may have become internationally embarrassing, especially if my theory was at all correct,' Lara shrugged.

'Well, I guess mine and Claire's involvement in this whole thing will remain a mystery.' Valda got up and opened the minibar to retrieve a canister of crisps, peanuts and some Coke for them to share. She then sat down on the bed facing Lara and looked directly into her eyes. 'It's amazing that you did this for me. I have to tell you that if I had heard you had been charged with murder, I would have flown back to tell everyone the truth.'

Lara shook her head, 'I never thought it would come to that.'

'You really are incredibly brave!' sighed Valda.

'It was all a calculated risk,' said Lara sincerely.

'How so?' Valda was curious.

'The danger was in your chart, not mine. In fact, my chart showed good fortune and divine protection. But I didn't only take the chart's word for it, I combined some common sense and logic and I concluded I'd get away with it.'

'Talking about charts, Brett is coming out to see me for New Year.'

'I am really looking forward to seeing the outcome of this romance,' winked Lara.

'Lara, I have some more fabulous news!' exclaimed Valda. 'I went to see that record producer you gave me the name of; I did an audition and a screen-test and he signed me up. I am booked to do a show in Vegas next year and I am going to be collaborating on an album with some high-profile up-and-coming song writers. Everything is so amazing.'

'What can I say? I love it when my readings are so accurate!' laughed Lara, mocking herself.

Valda held up her hand. 'I haven't forgotten what you told me about success not being just about career and money. I am still proud of my other success; that is, pulling myself together and coming to terms with myself and my past. But it's all down to you, how can I ever repay you, Lara?'

'Remember what I said before you left Dubai: we're all square!' Valda looked confused and so Lara continued, 'I had a lot of time to think when I was locked up; I mean, it's not like there's a helluva lot to do in there!' She raised her eyebrows sarcastically, before continuing seriously, 'I thought about the synastry between our charts: your sun is on my Fourth House cusp, your Midheaven squares Pluto on my ascendant, and is opposite my Saturn, my sun is conjunct with your Saturn, also square of your Pluto. What I am trying to say is that there is a very strong past life or karmic link between us. I have told you before – how I was always searching for a reason. Up until now, I have always felt my life was in limbo, but suddenly, I feel that that has all changed; it's as if things are going to fall into place for me now. I am sure that I have settled my karmic debt to you.'

'Maybe, maybe, but it still does not diminish how grateful I am to you right now, in this room, in this lifetime. You have given me life, even more so than the mother I never knew.'

'OK, enough of the philosophical stuff, it's getting too heavy! I have some things for you.' With that, Lara bounced off the bed, unzipped her case and pulled out the brown paper envelope. She handed Valda the letters and the dagger, which was still in its plastic bag.

'I'm not sure I want to see that thing again,' groaned Valda disdainfully.

'I think that one of us should keep it. Just in case one day we look back and wonder if all this really happened,' chuckled Lara. 'It kinda symbolises the life–death cycle.'

'Whatever,' Valda waved her hand dismissively. 'You can keep it then. Now, there is the most delish restaurant ten minutes from here, I can't wait to take you there. Get something warm on though, we're not in Dubai any more. This is New York and boy do they have a cold winter here!'

After living in Dubai for so long, Lara had no warm clothes with her and so Valda lent her a warm, stylish duffel coat with a furry hood, which she had purchased from Bloomingdale's.

The freezing and foggy December evening was brightened by the Christmas lights and the buzz of the five o'clock traffic. It was Lara's first trip to New York and she dallied in front of the beautifully decorated shop windows. Valda was eager to eat and literally had to drag Lara along behind her. The bustling shoppers, wrapped up in their colourful scarves and laden with arrays of smartly packaged parcels and designer bags, intermingling with the carol singers and sidewalk bands; the Christmas trees on every building; the festive music drifting out from inside the stores; the party-goers assembling excitedly inside restaurants and pubs, all reminded Lara of London and she realised how much she missed home. She had been away for too long.

Lara was not even looking at the traffic, she was standing on the pavement, staring all around her, caught up in the wonderful atmosphere and waiting for the stream of traffic to come to a halt. The lights eventually changed and the cars were coming to a stop. Lara was still gazing up at the Christmas decorations and she did not immediately notice that an impatient Valda had stepped out into the street and was now crossing the road. She also did not notice the speeding cab, which was careering around the bend, until she heard the screech of brakes. She cried out desperately, but all she could do was to look on with horror, frozen to the spot.

In times of sheer terror, the intensity of our emotional state elevates us into another vibrational frequency, a dimension, where time does not exist and where time can, indeed, stand still. Time appeared to stand still: all the shoppers and cars, like Lara, were silent, frozen in time; the only thing moving was the screeching car, which crashed into Valda, sending her body hurtling across the street. The bone-shattering crunch was so loud that it reverberated in Lara ears, penetrating her mind and her soul – it would haunt and horrify her for the rest of her life. Lara wanted to rush over to Valda, but she, like everything else in that moment, was silently stationary; all she could do was to helplessly watch her friend rolling over and over in the middle of the street.

Then, almost as if a switch had been flicked, the noise began again: there was screaming, hooting, shouting and frenzied movement all around her. Lara was instantly at Valda's side, kneeling next to her in the middle of the street. Lara knew. Valda looked very beautiful; her face framed by her dark wavy hair was perfect and unscarred and she looked peaceful and contented.

Lara looked up into the dark sky, knowing that destiny could not be escaped.

When something terrible happens, we always look back and wonder if there was anything we could have done differently to have prevented the final outcome.

Lara wondered at what stage was it that this all became inevitable: was it when Valda came for her first reading; was it when she first accepted the Sheikh's offer or when she first met the Sheikh; was it when Bella gave her the advert for the job at Flanagan's? Lara pondered over what would have happened if Valda had never come to Dubai: would she have ended up succeeding in taking her own life in Cape Town? Would she still be alive, but maybe living alone in Camps Bay, bitter and depressed? Maybe that was the crux, thought Lara: is the point of life really to be alive as long as possible, to cling desperately to our earthly bodies; is our body not the least of what we are?

Through her deep sorrow, suddenly, a realisation dawned. It was one of those rare moments, when the veneer of conditioned reality slips for just a second and we see the truth. Valda had learned the lessons of this incarnation; she had resolved her issues with her past and made peace with herself; in killing the Sheikh, she had possibly settled a karmic score for Yousef, Claire and all the others and she had put an end to the Sheikh's evil activities. Most importantly, Valda had given Lara the opportunity to repay her age-old karmic debt. Lara was free.

At that moment, Lara was not sure what exactly the future would hold: but she trusted that her path would be revealed. She was now sure that there was a reason; there is always a reason, for everything.

The End, and The Beginning!